moments
like
this

~From Kona with Love ~

From Kona With Love

BOOK ONE:
OAHU

I love the Pacific Ocean precisely for its wildness and unpredictability—it's surrounded by a ring of fire, and the faces on the other side of the sea are different and offer a totally distinct view of life than the old European ways. Two cultures crashing like those waves on the rocks, creating a new life. A new way. Before the first European sailed these seas, the men and women of the islands were sailing all over the map, hopping from one to the other, establishing different tribes, languages, and cultures, and yet they were all family! This ocean is a rolling contradiction and I love it for that.

ANNA GOMEZ

KRISTOFFER POLAHA

moments like this

~ From Kona with Love ~

Moments Like This

Cover design Hang Le
www.ByHangLe.com

ISBN: 978-1-64548-045-7

ROSEWIND

Published by Rosewind Books
An imprint of Vesuvian Books
www.RosewindBooks.com

Printed in the United States

10 9 8 7 6 5 4 3 2 1

This book is dedicated to finding love and cherishing every moment along the way.

Table of Contents

PART ONE:
ANDIE

An unwatched fire
Will burn beyond your control
Be careful with it.

Heartless

My breath caught in my throat. The ceiling, a mere four inches from my nose, suffocated me. My heart raced so fast my ears rang with the rush of blood. I closed my eyes tight, like a child, in an attempt to block out my confined quarters.

Click. Click. Whurrrr. Click.

The technician's voice boomed through the speakers.

"Please don't move, Andie. Not even your eyes."

I whimpered. Ragged breath followed ragged breath until I couldn't take it anymore.

"Get me out of this."

Not waiting for the technician to respond, I wriggled my way toward the foot of the table. Freedom lay beyond the tiny gap of light between me and the round edge of the hellhole.

After a couple of clicks, the table smoothly glided away from the ceiling, then out of the CT scan machine, and into a glaringly bright room. I gulped the air and tried to calm my shaking.

The technician, dressed in a white lab coat, strode into the room.

"I can't do it. I can't go back into that tube." My voice cracked into a high, tight whine. "I'm claustrophobic. I can't even get on the Chunnel without—"

"What's a Chunnel?"

"It's the train that goes from London to—"

The technician sighed loudly. She had probably heard it all before. "Why don't we give you something to calm your anxiety?"

It would take an elephant tranquilizer to get me back in that machine.

After the nurse administered the medication and my pulse slowed to a normal rate, the technician coaxed me back onto the table.

I can do this. Just one more embarrassing memory from this worst day ever to torture me. I took a few deep breaths as they slid me back under the CT scan machine, my head in what resembled a football helmet, loud music blaring in both ears to help keep me calm.

Click.

Click.

Click, click. Whurr. Buzz. Bang. Screech-ch-ch. Click, click.

"Hold still, almost there," the technician's singsong voice interrupted my head trip.

The table jerked this way and that, inching forward and then thrusting back. The music did nothing to mask the loud banging against the machine walls, nor the tremors that followed with every click of the technician's switch.

All I wanted was NSYNC to drown everything out—the noise, her voice, my thoughts. What I remembered was bad enough and I'd rather walk across glass barefoot than go through it again. But what I couldn't remember sent my stress levels back into the stratosphere.

Click, click. Whurr.

My thoughts turned into NSYNC's words and NSYNC's words became a muffled mess.

Bang. Bang. Bang.

Why am I here? Honestly, the club owner should stop the construction work going on outside. It messed with the beat of the band. But before I could complain, I floated into Justin's arms, then on a cloud, and then on a Christmas tree wishing everyone a happy holiday.

"Merry ..."

When I opened my eyes, the holiday cheer and the Christmas tree drifted away, and a huge weight settled on my chest. I must have done something I would regret forever.

Something utterly stupid and embarrassing.

Because the last thing I remembered before landing in the hospital, I had been standing in front of a whole group of people with a drink in my hand. *Except that toast, that celebration—it wasn't for me.*

Heat flooded my cheeks and I lifted my right hand to touch my face. Bad idea when you have an IV stuck in the crease of your arm. The same arm that had been poked more than once, as evidenced by the bruises around the needle still stuck under my skin.

I should have warned them I had no veins. Heartless was what I had been called. *Who needed veins when you didn't have a heart?*

I thought back to that night when Nick, my ex, said I was devoid of a heart. Not ambitious or hard working or motivated, which I would have preferred. *Heartless* because I had stuck to my guns on many occasions, made decisions that would benefit the company and not those who brought their dreams to us. I exemplified the nature of our business—venture capitalists—bent on financing the next big idea, the sexiest startup. How the applicants and businesses got there wasn't my concern. Their lives were retold on a single piece of paper, and no amount of pity or drama would sway our decision to invest. We were in it to make a profit. And profit doesn't have a heart.

Anyway, why was I thinking about this now? I'm in a hospital bed, for heaven's sake, and there's someone snoring quietly behind the curtain next to me.

I peered past the bed rails and surveyed my surroundings. From the IV post to the heart rate machine sidled by me, it was a normal hospital room—and I didn't look like I was dying or anything. Nurses strolled leisurely past the open door, and whoever was next to me didn't seem to be in distress. The TV was on, some anchor on CNN murmuring words I couldn't make out.

Can someone turn the volume up, please? I need to see how the stocks are doing.

Speaking of ... where was my phone? I reached out my left hand and began patting the table next to the side rail, knocking the telephone receiver off and wincing as it landed on the floor with a soft thud.

"Oh good, you're awake." A blurry, elderly gentleman stooped down very slowly and proceeded to arch his back like a cat as he handed me the phone.

I blinked a few times and he came into focus as he leaned over to kiss my forehead.

"Hi, sweetheart."

"Uncle Don," I whispered, relieved. He was my father's brother and the head of Neurology at Northwestern. *Okay, so I'm at his hospital. Still in my city. That's good, I guess.* "What happened?"

I pressed the remote underneath my pillow to prop myself up. My head felt like it was about to fall off, but only right after expelling the contents of my entire body.

"Easy, easy," Uncle Don said, firmly cradling my shoulders.

"What happened?" I asked again.

He pulled out his penlight and shined it into my eyes. First the left one, motioning me to follow the light in tiny circular movements, and then the right. "You passed out at your company meeting. Don't you remember? You've got a slight concussion and a nasty bump on the back of your head."

"But I'm okay, right? I'll be okay. When can I go home?" I asked while he grabbed the tablet at the end of the bed.

"Well," he muttered, swiping his fingers left, then right, then up and down. "Your mom and dad are on their way here now."

"From Florida?" I lurched forward, causing the sharp pain in my head to return. "Why?"

"You're concussed but only slightly. Your dad wanted to make sure we run other tests on you, and I'm glad we did. Everything looks low—blood count, iron. And your cortisol is up, indicating extreme exhaustion, fatigue, and stress."

I shook my head, confused.

"You've lost fifteen pounds in the last year, you—"

"You wouldn't have known that," I cut him short, arms tucked tight and tone terse, grimacing as the needle sank deeper into my skin.

"Your dad told me. They're concerned."

"It was that acquisition and all the traveling I had to do, but nothing out of the ordinary. Things should calm down soon and maybe I'll even get to take a vacation."

Uncle Don gently pushed down on the rail and sat on the side of the bed. I moved my legs over to give him room. He took my hand. "Andrea, listen to me. I've seen these symptoms in my patients all too often. You need more than a one-week vacation. The fact you collapsed means your body is slowly giving out. We ran the blood work, I authorized it. You're malnourished, tired, and emotionally spent. I'm sorry, but I'm going to have to ask your parents to support me on this. You need to take a break. A sabbatical, perhaps. Don't they give that nowadays, especially to executives like you?"

I shrugged. Never thought of it. Never cared to ask. Never dreamed I'd have to even think about taking a break. I had nothing to say, no argument to make. I was on a plane three hundred days out of this year; I'd stayed in over seventy hotels, traveled around the world five times. And for what?

He took my silence as acquiescence and handed me a tiny paper cup with two white pills. "You need to catch up on your sleep. Take these. Get some rest."

Flowers in Every Corner

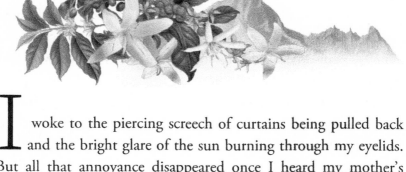

I woke to the piercing screech of curtains being pulled back and the bright glare of the sun burning through my eyelids. But all that annoyance disappeared once I heard my mother's voice. She was humming a song from church, one I knew by heart. Through half closed eyes, I made out her figure vigorously fussing with the curtains and laying flowers in every corner of the room. It dawned on me that I had switched rooms. I shared the room with no one now, a move orchestrated by my parents, no doubt.

My mother was dressed to the nines, as she always was—Gucci, I think, that day, with bright bold prints on a silk blouse and skirt set. We always wore the same size and shared outfits whenever we were together. Obviously less often now, since my parents had moved to Florida. My father had retired two years ago and with work as hectic as it was, I hadn't really had the chance to go and visit them.

"Mom?" I groaned, my vision still foggy from the medication. I pushed up on my elbows, half seated, knees raised.

"Oh, baby," my mother exclaimed, setting her designer purse down and rushing to my side.

She had been an Asian beauty queen, Miss Philippines and then Miss International in the 80s. Met and married my dad who had been in Asia for a urology conference. He was a brilliant man, having pioneered one of the first technologically innovative techniques in laser surgery. But he was also kind and generous. My father flew to Manila twice a year, held free clinics and performed surgery on the poor who couldn't afford healthcare. He called my mom his mail-order bride in jest, when in reality; he knew he had married into one of the most prominent families in the country.

Half of me took after my mother—my eyes and skin—but the other half was so much like my dad. I'd gotten the brown hair and the tiny build while my brother, Steven, had inherited my father's Nordic traits.

My mother slid next to me on the bed, holding my face close. "How are you? Are you feeling better?"

Still a little hazy, actually. But I didn't want to tell her that. "Where's Dad?"

"He's having coffee with Uncle Don. He'll be here soon." For a few seconds, there was nothing to say. "What happened, Andie?"

The floodgates had opened. Everything came rushing back. "I didn't make partner, Mom," I cried. She inched her finger across my cheek, as if trying to catch every falling tear. "All that hard work and I got passed over."

She wrapped her arms around me, resting her chin on my head. "It's okay, baby," she cooed, encouraging me to pour my heart out. My mother was like that. A listener first before giving me her own two cents. We complemented each other. When she had words, I didn't, and when I did, she was all ears. I think my mother recognized that the outspoken, driven young woman in front of her was a direct product of the home she'd been raised in.

"But I worked so hard, gave up so much in the past four years. I thought if I gave it my all, it would just make sense—that they would give me the promotion. I didn't do enough, I guess. I should have done more. Now, I have nothing. I'm thirty years old with no friends, no life. Just that job which isn't even mine."

She looked at me, her eyes squinted and tainted with pain. Then she fluffed my pillow and guided my head back to the bed. "Listen, baby. First of all, thirty. You're at the prime of your life. There is still so much more ahead of you."

"It just isn't fair. I wanted this so much. I worked hard for this."

"Life isn't fair. You gave this job your all for the past four years, to the detriment of your sanity and your health."

"My sanity?" I asked. Health for sure, but sanity?

"I'm afraid this new development will push you over the edge," she answered. "Listen to yourself—you're still beating yourself up about it. To be honest with you, I think it's only your pride that's been hurt by not getting this promotion. I worried this fast-tracking in your career would come to this. But the quicker you get over it, the sooner you can work on getting your life back. It's not too late. And your dad and I and Steve are here for you, however you want to handle this."

"I know," I answered, sniffing.

I saw my mother's expression lighten and her bleary disposition fade, a sure sign my dad was somewhere near. These people still held hands after thirty-five years of marriage.

Sure enough, in walked my dad with Uncle Don in tow, voices hushed as they approached. Now there were three people standing by my bed. Like a vigil, one hand of theirs on some part of my bed, comforting me.

My dad took my hand and kissed my forehead. "Hi, Princess."

"Hi, Daddy," I croaked.

"Uncle Don filled me in on what's going on. Your mom and I were worried sick about you. Steven wanted to fly here from Barcelona, but we assured him we would stay with you until you got better," he said. "Andie, honey—"

"I know, Dad."

"This is serious, Andie. You passed out and hit your head."

Truth be told, nothing was more important to me than this: "Do you know what I was doing before I passed out?" *Did I make a scene? Break down and cry as I rolled on the floor and threw a tantrum? Tell everyone to stuff it and stomp away?*

Both parents shook their heads. Even that, they did in unison.

Dad sighed and rubbed his forehead. "You're not listening, Andie. Thank God it wasn't while you were on a plane, or worse, in another country. This is a strong warning sign. You need to take a break. I won't lose you, your mother and I, we—" My father choked on his last word. "We're so lucky you're all right. Promise me, honey. Promise me you'll take it slow for at least a few weeks."

Everything they said was true. I had given up so much in the name of my career. I loved the stress, thrived on the adrenaline caused by deadlines and last-minute trips. I slept, ate, breathed this job.

What did I have to show for it? A broken engagement because I'd realized I loved my job more than I loved him. No friends because keeping in touch took too much time. The only reason I had the one best friend was because this person chose to stick with me, even when I made no effort to stay connected.

Here's the thing—when you rise quickly in any career as I had, the expectations grab hold of your entire life. You're constantly running just to keep up, prove you deserve to be where you are.

My attention shifted to the various floral arrangements scattered around the room. Odd, how this room came to life with the colors of spring when there we were in the middle of winter. I noticed my mother's favorites—hydrangeas on one side, birds of paradise on the other.

"Mom, who are the flowers from?"

"All from Hector, the flower guy downstairs."

"Nothing from work?"

Way to deflate my already-weakened sense of self.

"Nothing from work. You would think they'd be filling your room with gifts—since they caused all this," my mother said, defiantly.

Dad glared at Mom, who shrugged.

Just then, two nurses entered and parted my parents like the Red Sea. They moved to each corner of the room and then converged together again. I could hear them, talking about how to convince me to leave work, while the nurses took my vitals and injected more drugs into the IV line.

In a few seconds, I was back with the boy band, numbed to the pain of the past year.

I was reluctantly happy again.

— 3 —
Hold Your Horses

"Hold your horses. Geez, un-bunch your panties for a second." My best friend, Api, exhaled loudly. "Let's get that glass of wine going, first."

"Hold your horses?" I asked. "Where'd that come from?"

"It's my new thing. You know, I'm practicing before I meet James's family. The Southern thang, y'all."

"But you're Hawaiian," I quipped.

"Half. Just half."

"Yeah, last I checked, your other half was from the Philippines."

"Shush," Api answered, throwing one of the silk-tasseled pillows in my direction. It had been a week since my parents had left for Florida, a week since I'd checked out of the hospital and been back at my place.

"Is this new?" Api skimmed her fingers across the velvet couch before I disappeared into the kitchen.

I often wondered what I was thinking, wanting as much space as this apartment afforded. I bought it as an investment. But the potential return didn't alleviate the fact I had four bedrooms I didn't need, and a super long hallway that separated two living rooms and a formal dining room. My decorator, Terri, had invested all my money in drabness. White up the kazoo, white this, white that. When the final *Architectural Digest* photos had been taken, I'd run to the home store down the street and peppered the place with colorful accents.

"This is your forever home and you want to shop at that store?" Terri's voice still echoed in my head every so often.

I'd severed all ties with her, not because she was a lousy decorator, but because I was afraid she'd keel over when she saw the colors I'd added to my space.

I pulled out the glasses and searched the wine chiller for the Hermitage Blanc I'd been saving. It had been given to me as a promotion present years ago, and this was my way of fighting back. How apt. They pass you up for another promotion, the one you wanted all your life—and the way you give them the finger is to drink the wine they gave you. I rushed back to the waiting Hawaiian princess after realizing how much time I'd spent thinking things through while she sat in my living room.

She looked up at me as I approached. "So, new? This couch?"

"Yeah, they had it on sale, finally."

"This place gets more beautiful every time I see it." Api reached out to take a glass before moving to the floor and sitting in a cross-legged position. This was more her thing, always sitting on the floor looking so Zen, her blue eyes a traitor to the rest of her extraordinary features. "You keep changing things up, redoing stuff." She waved her hand and pointed to an antique chest I'd picked up in Paris, blue with gold leaves and ornate knobs. "That's new."

She turned and pointed to a giant painting of Basquiat's *Red King*. "And, oh my gosh. Same with that one—that's definitely new."

"The gallery in New York had an auction and I snatched it up. Believe me, I didn't eat out for months to pay for it."

She rolled her eyes. "Andie, it's me. You don't have to defend the fact that you make a lot of money."

I set my glass down and leaned back on the couch, tucking my feet under my knees. "So now will you tell me what happened?"

Api laughed. "It was nothing, really."

"First of all, who told you, and what are the rumors at this point?"

"Well," she said, visibly tormenting me by slowing down her words and pretending to fiddle around with the coasters on the cocktail table. "Here's. The. Scoop." She smiled and winked.

"Api."

"Okay, okay. I called your office to catch up and your assistant told me you were in the hospital. Obviously, I freaked out and called your parents. But I was told you were at an office event or something."

"And then what did he say happened?"

"He just said you fainted toward the end, when they were toasting to some promotions. That you asked to be excused as they were giving some speeches but you never made it past the crowd. You passed out and hit your head on the table."

"I remember crying," I began. "It was such a shock to me, and I had already been drinking before then. Ugh. I am so embarrassed."

I stood and began pacing around the room. The memory hit

me like a tidal wave, all my emotions felt new, raw. Api jumped up and took me into her arms.

"Don't cry, Andie. It's not worth it. They're not worth it."

"All that work Api. I was so cocky. I thought I had it in the bag. I never imagined—"

"I know, right?" she said, her tone light. "That you'd be scr— uh, passed up." She released me and gently led me toward the couch. "And what the—" She curled her lip. "I mean, by a guy."

I laughed, swiping my hand across my face to get rid of those freshly fallen tears. "Eww. A guy."

We sat side by side for a moment, mutually lost for words, deprived of consolation. After a while, I left to get more wine from the kitchen. She followed, taking a seat on one of the counter stools directly in front of me. I had to admit, this was my favorite part of the house. Terri had outfitted this area with the most modern appliances, not just in singles but in doubles. My walk-in pantry could feed a city if all its inhabitants decided to camp out here during an apocalypse. The counters were made with Calcutta marble that had been shipped directly from Italy. White, of course, like the rest of the house.

I poured us another glass of wine.

"I don't know. I think I should quit," I said.

Api took a swig of her wine. "Well, if anything, you should take a leave of absence. Get your bearings. You never really took time off after …" She paused. "You know."

My broken engagement. The guy everyone said was the perfect one, *The One*. Except he hadn't felt like The One to me. He'd been too amenable, too laid-back. He also had impeccable timing—wanting to have babies during the peak of my career, when childrearing had been the lowest on my to do list. In retrospect, it really hadn't been the peak of my career and I had been fooling myself. "I know," was all I said, acknowledging her unfinished thought.

"Anyway." I reached into the freezer and handed Api a popsicle.

"Anyway," she mimicked, focusing her attention on the number of calories on the wrapper before tearing it open. "I have an idea. I also told your mom and dad about it. Ready?"

I looked at her, squinted my eyes, waiting.

"James has to do a fellowship in Germany for a few months and I want to go with him. But of course, because Daddy put me in charge of the coffee business in Oahu, I have no one to leave the store to. Why don't you take your break in Hawaii? Stay at my place and do me the favor of minding the shop while I'm gone? I could use a business-minded guru like you."

"We both went to Brown. Business program," I said with a smile.

"Yes, but that's not what I want to do," she whined. "Come on, can you help me? It's beautiful there. It will be the getaway you need."

I took the stool next to her, holding her hand as we ate our popsicles. I considered her offer, seriously tried to imagine myself not working. But I couldn't.

"Thank you, my dear friend. But I don't think I should right now. I left so many projects on the table; I need to finish up."

"Shut the front door," she squealed. "They don't care two sticks about you. Why should you stay around after what happened?"

"Api, I need to see this through. I don't run away from my problems," I answered.

"Okay," she conceded. "Okay."

I turned to her, furrowing my brows in jest. "What is happening here? Shut the what? What did you do with my glib and profane friend?"

"I already told you. I'm swearing off swearing for a while. Want to get used to it in time to meet James's family in two weeks."

"Aha. I don't know if I could ever get used to having G-rated conversations with you."

"Well, get used to it." She laughed, slowly rising and pulling me down the hallway. "Because profanity is no longer in my vocabulary. All grown up now. Engaged and all, you know."

— 4 —

Walk of Shame

I did the inevitable—the walk of shame—straight down the executive hallway and into my office. I wanted to lock myself in there forever, or at least until everyone had gone for the day. I arrived at a desk with a pile of print outs—emails I'd intended to respond to the day after the party. But there they were, two weeks later—unanswered and untouched. I felt overwhelmed. My heart was racing. My palms were sweating. Just thinking of everything I'd left behind, all the due dates I'd missed. I shouldn't have taken the time off.

"Andrea?" My assistant, Jim, popped his head in the door. Literally just his head. His lower half bent at a forty-five-degree angle, his shoes two feet away from the rest of his body. "May I come in?"

"Hi, Jim. Yes, please." I motioned for him to come closer while I took a seat at my desk. Jim was the most gregarious guy on the executive floor. But that day, he was somber, quiet.

"How are you feeling? I was the one who called for the ambulance. We all wanted to come and visit but I knew you needed to take time off away from here."

"I'm good, thank you. Got a lot of rest and I'm now ready to get back to work."

Jim scratched his ear, and then his chin. His gaze remained on the pencil on my desk. "Listen, you deserved that promotion. Every single hour you spent at the office. Everything you gave up."

Lesson in life—never give up something in the hopes of getting something in return.

"Thank you. But like I said, there's much to do and I'm ready to move on. Nolan deserves this promotion. He really does." I turned away, kept myself from blinking so the tears would stay in place. I'd given up love for this. And the real shame in this was the pain of losing this promotion was more intense than the pain of losing Nick. This was my back-up plan, the impetus for my accomplishments, waiting in the wings. Now, I was left with nothing. "What about my meetings with Matt? They're no longer on my calendar."

"He canceled everything this week."

"Why?"

Jim stuttered, looked at me with a question rather than an answer. "Maybe because he transferred them all to Nolan?"

My vision blurred. All I could see was red. Not only was I infuriated, I was crushed. My confidence sank. Everything I believed about my success disappeared at that instant. In response, I shot up from my desk and left Jim standing in my office.

As I walked the hall toward the CEO's office, it dawned on me that Christmas was in two weeks. The reception area was lit up in colors of the season, the twenty foot Giving Tree overflowed with presents all around it. Every year, our company hired singers and performers to provide musical entertainment throughout the day. Little angelic voices singing "Silent Night" caused me to pause.

Was I going to do this? What would I accomplish?

Still, I kept going until I reached Matt's door, lightly pushing it in to reveal him sitting at the conference table with Nolan.

"Andrea. Nice to have you back." Matt remained seated. Nolan leaned back in his chair and swiveled from side to side.

"Do you have a minute?" I addressed Matt directly, my emotion in check, eyes blank, jaw tight.

"Sure. Have a seat." Matt motioned toward an empty chair and nodded at Nolan, who stood to leave.

I glanced around Matt's office, settling my gaze on the stately, large, leather furniture that looked like those you'd find in a steakhouse restaurant. The walls were dark, but the pictures of his family—his children and grandchildren—softened the business-like atmosphere and provided some levity.

"Catch up later," Nolan said to me.

"Sure," I answered, turning to Matt.

Once we were alone, Matt began. "You look rested. The two-week break did you lots of good." When I said nothing, he continued, "Listen, Andrea, I was waiting for you to come back from leave. We should set up some time for us to discuss next steps."

"Next steps for what?" I asked, folding my arms.

"Well, with Nolan's promotion, we need to ensure he has a good support team, starting with you. You'll be reporting—"

"But those two most recent sales, I closed them for you. Nolan was in the Bahamas when this was all going on. I know more about these clients than he does. And I assumed I'd keep reporting to you."

"Well, things have changed," Matt said. "We have to follow reporting lines. I need Nolan to take over a few of the open projects."

"Nolan," I muttered. "Not me."

"It was a tough decision, this promotion. But the Board felt it wasn't your time yet."

"My time? My time for what? I gave up—" I started, my voice rising. But then I remembered. It didn't matter what I had given up. No one cares what you do to get your job done. You just get it done. No one cares you chose a business deal instead of a wedding date. Or hours at the office instead of hours building a family. No one cares.

"As I said, the Board—"

I raised my hand. "The all-male Board. Yes, I know. And when will my time come, Matt?"

"Soon. Just be patient. Work with HR to make sure you plan your path, what you want to do."

"What I want to do now that I'm reporting to Nolan? And work with your all-male HR team."

"Andrea."

All I heard was the pounding of my heart, the muffled swishing that felt like water in my ears. I had to stand, but my feet were bolted to the floor. My legs were shaking, my thoughts bombarding me in rapid succession. I didn't feel composed at all. And yet, I had to be. I couldn't allow Matt to see how much of my life this had been. I supported myself by laying both palms on the table and pushing myself up with all my strength.

"Listen, Matt. I don't think I've fully recovered. I'd like to take some more time off; would that be okay?" My tone had completely changed. It was cadenced, measured, like he'd always expected of me. I felt my heart rate slow, pasted a sweet smile on my face. "I love this job and I love working for this company. I will continue to do my best in any role I assume."

"Atta girl. That's what I like to hear. Take all the time you need. And when you get back, let's continue this conversation."

— 5 —

Dead of Winter

"Hi. Yeah. Can you hear me?" I adjusted the volume on my earbuds to combat the sound of the whipping wind while navigating through the 5 p.m. crowd on Wacker Drive. I used to belittle the people who left exactly at quitting time, called them losers and slackers. I would tell Nick all about them after a late night at the office, thinking out loud as I opened up my laptop at the dinner table to do more work. Looking back, I should have taken my investment in time and effort and placed it all on him.

Nick had always said, "Why? These people have families. They have lives."

"And no ambition," I would counter.

And there I was, running with the rest of them. Booting it out of the office as fast as I could.

The razor-thin chill of the winter air and the sting of the wind caught me unaware. I buried my nose in my scarf to hide it from the burn of frostbite.

"Hey," Api answered. "Yeah, I can hear you."

"I did it. I asked for a leave," I shrieked, breathless and giddy.

My skin felt prickly, hot and thawed, despite the cold of the Chicago winter. Imaginary fish were swimming around my stomach. "I'm coming." My tone turned squeaky with excitement. I hurried into the nearest entrance for shelter from the wind, which also happened to be a Soul Cycle location. I stood by the door, in my marshmallow coat and extra-large woolen scarf, while good-looking people hardly wearing anything scooted past me.

"Well, son of a puppy," Api squealed back. "I'm so happy."

I laughed out loud. "Oh my gosh. I forgot you're fasting from curse words."

"Anyway, what happened? What made you change your mind?"

I sat on a wooden bench in the corner of the lobby, disentangling my scarf and laying my backpack on the ground. It was a process, the undressing that happened when you were out and about in the dead of winter. There was the hat and the scarf and the knee-highs and the furry boots.

"It just didn't feel the same after I went back this morning. I think I need to view this from a different perspective, you know? Be a little humble, figure out what I really want. I have so many regrets."

"Oh, Andie," she said sadly. "Everything you've done is because you're true to yourself. No bullsh—I mean no cr—Ugh. You know what I mean."

"I know what you mean," I said, smiling. "Speaking of ..."

"Nick's okay. You know he's dating someone, right? She's actually all right. A friend of mine knows her and says he's found his match."

When I remained silent, she knew.

"He'll always love you, you know that. But we should be happy he's found a way to move forward."

"I know," I answered. And then an afterthought. "Api? Why'd you stay? Why didn't you give up on our friendship like everyone else did?"

"Are you kidding me? First of all, that's what friendship is about. Love, loyalty, growing, staying. But more than that, you're actually pretty awesome as a person. Plus, I'm pretty pushy so when you hide, I push. We work well together."

The lady at the registration desk eyed me strangely. She knew I wasn't there for classes. I put my armor back on and headed back out into the cold.

"Andie, are you still there?"

The wind howled.

"Yes, sorry, I had to leave the building." I shuffled past the pedestrians and turned on Dearborn Street to cross the bridge to my apartment. Chunks of ice coated the river like shards of broken glass. Snow still covered the grates on the bridge, and my breath formed trails of clouds as I spoke. "Anyway, I'm thinking of catching a flight next week. Will you be there to tell me what to do?"

"Well, James has to leave next week, so I'll try to have him delay by a couple of days. But we can do everything by phone. You'll know what I mean when you see the shop. And I still have a few staff there who can help you. The important thing is that you take a break. The new environment will be good."

"I'm not gonna lie, I'm a bit worried that I don't even have a plan."

"No plan is great, my friend. Trust me."

"So, will you just send me all the info? As in where your place is and the shop, all that?"

"Yeah, I'll email you tonight."

"Will your mom be there? I'd love to see her."

"Yes, she lives close to the store. And I can't wait to tell her you're coming."

"How is she doing, you know, with all that's happened?" I was getting close to the apartment.

"Okay, I guess. She has good days and bad days. She misses Maku, but she knows he's at peace."

"So much to catch up on. I'll call when I have my flight info and date. I hope you have at least a day or so at home so I can see you."

"And if not, I'll see you when I get back," Api said. "Oh hey, one more thing."

I paused at the entrance of my apartment. Paddy, the doorman, meandered leisurely toward the door, jangling his keys and whistling a tune.

She continued, "Want to remind you that I moved out of my parents' place into a one-bedroom apartment. It's not that big, but it's comfortable."

"Api, you don't have to worry—"

"Not you, Andie. Your clothes. I may not have enough closet space for your stuff."

"Oh. Ha." I giggled. "Well, don't you worry. I actually decided to simplify for this trip. One suitcase, that's it. Live simply, get rid of all the junk in my life. By the time I get there next week, I'll be a new woman."

"Huh. Really. Bathing suits, maybe? You'll need lots of

bathing suits."

"Maybe. But you just wait. And I'm not bringing any work with me."

My phone vibrated. I swiped out of the call to see who it was. It was a selfie of Api, smirking.

"Apikelia Flores." I exclaimed. "Stop mocking me."

She burst into a fit of laughter. It was music to my ears. Made me feel better that there were little things we could still laugh about.

"Anyway, I'm home and about to get into the elevator now. Thank you for inviting me. You don't know how much this means, Api. I'm so grateful for your friendship. I love you."

"You're the one helping me. James will be so happy. Thank you."

—6—

Leaving on a Jet Plane

I was used to traveling out of O'Hare during the winter months, but that day started out with a blizzard that left me with a white-knuckled limo driver moving at a speed of fifteen miles an hour. I barely made the flight, which, to my chagrin, ended up leaving on time for once.

I made it out of security, wondering why on earth I had opted for pre-check when the priority lanes were completely empty. Luckily, my gate was only a few steps away from the concourse. Boarding had begun but I stayed to the side, despite hearing the call for Group 5. The screen on my phone was flashing as it rolled along the X-ray machine belt. It was a long flight to Hawaii, so I decided to linger for a minute and call him back.

"Andie?" Gosh, I hadn't heard his voice in a few months. I tried to remember how long ago. I couldn't.

"Hey, sorry. I was going through security when—"

"Security? Where are you flying to?" Nick asked.

"Hawaii. I thought I'd spend a few weeks at Api's place. I'm actually late to board."

"I just got back from a business trip. Found out what happened. Why didn't you call me?"

Because I didn't want you to know I'd lost everything?

"Mom and Dad were here. So was Api. I'm fine," I said, glancing up to see two more groups of people waiting. A few people still stood by the rows of seats directly in front of the gate checker. Standbys.

"I just thought I should have known. Something as serious as a hospital stay."

"Why? You've moved on, why would you have to know?" I huffed, annoyed. My carry-on handle made a clicking noise as I pulled it up, looped my purse handle around it, and dragged it toward the gate. "Nick, I have to board now. Can I call you when I get there?"

"I moved on because you made me."

"You gave me an ultimatum." The carry-on wasn't cooperating. I stopped to flip it back on its wheels.

"I asked you," he said, his voice cracking, "what you wanted more than anything. And you said you didn't know. You chose your job. You chose it over me."

I had to board the plane, so I did. Ignoring the sugar sweet greeting from the stewardess and marching directly to my seat.

"And I regret it. Is that what you want to hear?" I squealed loud enough for the other passengers to look up from their cushy little lives. "Please, let's not do this now. I'll call when I land, okay?"

I pressed END just as we were taking off for the skies. Far away from my life. Away from every single thing I'd done wrong. Away from all my failures.

My mood after I got off the phone with Nick was dark.

I didn't want to talk to anyone on the plane.

I was tired and second-guessing my decision to take time off work, filled with disappointment about discarding my relationship in the name of this promotion, and losing both in the end. Frankly, I believed I was cursed. I had lost the man I was going to marry, my job, and my health in a span of ten months.

The woman next to me was old and heavy-set, smiling as she slipped a leftover sandwich into the seat pocket. The smell of tuna fish was thankfully overpowered by a strong and fragrant scent. It must have been her perfume—opulent and heady, deeply sensual. An exaggerated aroma of lilies in bloom.

She kept looking at me in anticipation, like she wanted to introduce herself and start a conversation. I'd rather have my leg caught in a bear trap than indulge in friendly chitchat. I reached for my book, slipped my earphones in, and settled down for the eight-hour plane ride. The window seat on a first-class ticket wasn't going to be too bad.

The woman looked at me one last time as I began reading my book.

Seven and a half hours to go.

The flight was uneventful. Just as we were landing, I was finally ambushed with a conversation. I must have fallen asleep and dropped my book because the woman had it in her hand. She handed it back to me with a sweetness only a grandmother could possess.

"Here's your book, little sister. You dropped it while you slept."

"Oh, thank you," I answered, smoothing its cover over with my hand. "Look at that, I bent the pages."

"I tried to catch it, but it was too fast."

We sat there in comfortable silence. That wasn't so bad.

"Are you visiting the island for vacation or business? I know you don't live there."

There it was, the trap.

"How do you know I don't live there? That seems awfully presumptuous, I think," I said, slightly annoyed.

"People who live on the island move in island time, it's slower. We are never in a hurry, even when we are running late. We take our time. I've watched you since you sat down. You're in a hurry and you have nowhere to rush off to, you're stuck in your seat." She said this last bit with a deep, warm belly laugh.

She was right, I lived my life in a hurry and as recent events had shown me, it had been to my detriment.

"I'm sorry, you're right. My name is Andie and I'm going to stay in Honolulu for a while to help a friend of mine out. She owns a coffee shop near Ala Moana and I'm going take over for her while she travels for a bit."

"That sounds like work. You're a good friend. How long will you be on Oahu?"

"I'm not sure yet. I don't have a plan."

Then something very strange happened; I proceeded to tell her my life story. I'm not sure she knew what she had bargained for, but she soon learned about my broken engagement, how I had been passed over for a promotion, and how I'd almost broken my head open on the corner of a table. She got the entire story, as if purging those words was the only way to cleanse the pain from my heart. All the while, she sat and listened to me, smiling. When I caught her up to the part where I had been running late for my flight, she asked me the strangest question.

"Are you ready to forgive yourself?"

"I ..." I choked on my answer. I wanted to say yes, of course, but it wouldn't come out.

The strange woman went on. "Well, be prepared. The islands are a special place. The Aloha Spirit. I don't know if it's the breeze that blows across the ocean and brushes over the land, or the fact some say the moon hangs lower in our sky. My ancestors believed it was the lava flowing underneath the surface of the ground keeping everything off balance, making it easy to fall over and into love. There is a very special energy on the islands. The old ones say that love itself was born in Hawaii. If you are brokenhearted, the islands will mend it. If you are lonely, the islands will guide you to your companion. The whole world is drawn to them—that's why everyone takes their honeymoon in Hawaii.

"Personally, I believe it has something to do with the waves, the tidal pull, and the constant motion of the ocean. If you stand on the shore and look out at the Pacific, you will begin to feel as if you are on a boat. You become unsteady and unbalanced. My husband used to say it is the ions in the air, charged and bright and full of energy that makes everyone so eager to fall in love. He didn't say it so politely, but you catch my meaning. So, my daughter"—I had graduated from little sister to daughter—"if you stay long enough, perhaps you too will be changed by these islands."

"I hope so."

We sat there silently until the plane landed and taxied. Then with one word—"Aloha"—she walked off the plane and down the steps to the tarmac.

7

Arriving

W e landed on an airstrip perched above water so transparent one could see every sign of life around the coral reefs. The foam forming on the tips of the waves was close enough to touch. The Honolulu airport, with its palm trees and friendly, smiling people, erased my every thought of the freezing Chicago winter. There was something about this place—the sweet smell of the thick, salty air—that made me believe all was good with the world. At least for a minute. Until I reminded myself that like me, everyone seemed to be there because they didn't want to be somewhere else.

Maybe, just maybe. This could be the break I've been needing. I can make sure of that.

As soon as I stepped off the plane, there it was—the world-renowned island breeze. A combination of warm air and humidity, like a heavy slap to the face. It woke me up and soothed me at the same time. Tempered and grounding, that was what it felt like. A sign I was far, far away from the transient cold that has been a part of my life for quite a long time.

"You made it. You're here."

Api's excitement when she met me at the bottom of the steps appeased all my apprehensions. As I folded into her welcoming arms, cringing at the shriek heard throughout the airport, I heaved a sigh of relief.

"Wait, look what I got you," she screeched, jumping as she looped a lei around my neck. "A lei is a symbol of love and friendship and welcoming. It is the true symbol of Aloha. And now you can say you got lei'ed in Hawaii."

"And there's the Api I know and love," I answered. "Aloha to you too."

That overpowering smell. I wondered if that lady on the plane was also wearing a lei. I didn't see one on her, but she sure smelled like one.

She giggled in good humor. "I almost didn't think you'd make it today. That snowstorm in Chicago looked harsh."

"Just my luck, right? Although, not even a snowstorm would keep me from coming to see you."

"Your bags are at Claim Number Eight." Api led me through the throes of animated travelers. Hawaiian shirts in Hawaii. Ha. What a concept.

"We don't need to go there. These are all I have," I answered, pointing to the duffle bag she'd taken from me and gazing at my rollaway.

"No way," she said with a snicker.

"I'm only here for a few weeks."

"You used to pack a whole house just for one week," Api retorted.

We paused for a second and alighted on the moving walkway. "Not anymore. I'm working on relieving my life of all the noise. All the clutter. No more clutter."

"I still don't believe you," she teased, as we approached the double doors leading out of the airport and into the parking lot. "But the shopping is great here, so I'm sure you'll be able to pick up what you need when you run out of your three outfits in that carry-on."

"So, just for your point of reference ..." Api turned to me briefly as we drove down Highway 92E. "We're in Oahu, near Waikiki. I live in Ala Moana, and the coffee shop is a few miles away from the apartment."

I nodded; the lush green countryside against the bluest horizon I had ever seen captivated most of my attention. "Your coffee shop," I corrected. "What'd you end up naming it?"

"Don't laugh," she said. "My dad had a dumber name for it."

I kept my gaze on her.

"Beans and Bites. I mean, we can change it if we want to."

"Hmm," I answered. "Okay. I suppose because ... there are things to eat?"

"Exactly. When my dad first opened it, we only served coffee. But now, I found a cook who makes the meanest cinnamon rolls with a Hawaiian take on the toppings. So, there."

"I like it," I said, touching her shoulder affectionately. "Thanks for having me here, Api. I'm glad your conspiracy worked."

"Yes. I admit, I did conspire with your parents to get you here." She giggled. "But I should be thanking you, e *ku'u hoaaloha*."

We turned into a large condominium complex that was hedged by palm trees. I could see the reflection of the water on the large glass windows that flanked the building. We parked in an underground garage and took two flights of stairs to the lobby. It was all decked out for the season, with huge palm trees lit up with colored coconut balls, a giant red outrigger canoe guarded by angels wearing hula skirts, and dolphins jumping in and out of makeshift cotton waves. This was not like the Christmas I had just left in Chicago—giant wreaths on every door, snow globes on every store window, the Macy's displays of fairytales and princesses, the cold forgiven by pretty, light snowflakes and laughter-filled skating rinks. It wasn't a bad memory, the Chicago I'd left behind. But it made me realize that I was stepping into a very different life.

"Cute, huh?" Api said.

"Different."

We approached the front desk. A young man in a Hawaiian shirt and a Santa hat sat behind a beautiful marble counter, complete with built in computer monitors and television screens. "Hey, AJ," Api greeted with a wave.

"Hello, Ms. Flores. Mr. James stopped by earlier and let me know he'll be picking you up for the airport at eight."

"Thanks," Api answered. "This is my friend, Andrea. She's the one I told you would be staying at my place for a while. Be nice to her, AJ. Take care of her like you take care of me, okay?"

"Of course, Ms. Flores. Welcome, Andrea, to Park Lane. And to Honolulu, for that matter."

"Thank you," I answered, twisting my neck toward him as Api pulled me toward the elevator.

8

Api's Place

A nd, here we are," she said, motioning for me to join her on the other side of the doorway.

It was the kind of apartment you only saw in magazines—wall-to-wall glass windows with a balcony directly facing the ocean. In theory, at least. I had to look past the trail of clothes from the front door through the living room to the other parts of the house.

"I know, it's a bit messy right now, but I'll clean up before I leave tonight. Follow me here." She ran toward what I surmised was her bedroom.

Just like her entire home, Api's bedroom had been professionally decorated. Asian-inspired with chinoiserie style dark lacquer wood cabinets and a headboard with a tapestry of hues. An antique desk with a multitude of drawers filled the side of the room, which was accented by a large blue and white oriental rug.

"It's beautiful," I said, as I lightly trailed my fingers along the edges of a life-sized portrait of Api and her parents. "You must miss him so much."

"I do." Her smile stretched tight as if it might crack.

"I can only imagine, and I'm so sorry."

I followed Api to the living room and watched as she began to pick her clothes off the floor. "I'm mostly packed but I couldn't decide on a few more things," she said, clearing the couch before taking a seat and tapping the area next to her. She stood again to grab a box sitting on the cocktail table. "So, I thought I'd give you some information about the coffee shop. There's a small staff there, namely my cook and one server. I sit by the register every day. Most of the time, I watch YouTube. It's busy season right now, so it may get a little swamped, being the only one close to Wai'alae Beach."

I sat with my hands on my knees, transfixed by the resplendent view of the sky touching the ocean. I'd been there for a mere two hours but already the noise had begun to filter out. I actually heard Api, saw her, admired her crystalline blue eyes and the animated way she gestured with her hands.

"Andie, are you okay?"

"Yes, yes, I was just making mental notes. Want to make sure I don't mess it up."

"I mean with everything. How are you doing?"

"Well ..." I exhaled loudly. "This is the most impulsive thing I've done in my life and I don't want to let you down."

She knelt in front of me and took my hands in hers. "You'll be fine. You've run billion-dollar businesses—this is nothing compared to that." She saw me glance down at her ring finger, the pear-shaped diamond catching my attention. "Seriously, after what you've been through, taking coffee orders and being nice to customers will be a breeze."

"I think there's more to it than that." I smiled. "But we did have some serious barista skills back in college."

"At our apartment?"

"Well, yeah. Mixing Nespresso capsules," I whooped. Then I reached over to touch the protruding, beautiful stone. "Your ring is gorgeous, by the way."

Api held up her hand and wiggled her ring finger. "He did good, huh? Although I didn't want him to spend quite as much. Somehow, he thinks he needs to live up to how my dad took care of me, but I keep reminding him, he's all I need. Just him." She looked at me with a grin. "Considering everything I've been through with all the guys I dated."

We laughed at the same time. Dating at Brown had been a disaster for both of us. Surprise, entitled, over-confident jocks were not our thing.

"I'm just so happy for you, Api. He is perfect."

She jumped up with a sudden realization. "Speaking of, he'll be here in an hour. I have to get packed up. Are you sure you're going to be okay? I didn't have time to stock the fridge but there's a mini-mart two blocks from here—I figured you'd want to pick your own groceries."

"All good. Go ahead and get ready. I won't unpack until you're out of here, so we don't run into each other."

"Okay," she answered. And then as an afterthought, she disappeared into the coat closet and emerged with a big brown box. By then, I was reaching for my duffle bag and unloading my books. I brought quite a few of them, new titles by authors I loved. She sat on the floor and began to unpack its contents.

"If you don't mind, I got some stuff to decorate the store. Will you hang a few of these at the store tomorrow?" She pulled out two sprigs of mistletoe. "Maybe strategically position them around the dining area?"

"Of course." I took them from her and began to unwind them from each other. Api continued, fishing some garland and a wreath out of the box.

"Want to hear my genius marketing ploy?" she said with a wink, pulling out a large sign written in bold green and red letters. *A KISS FOR A CUP.* "If you get couples to kiss under these thingies, they'll get a free cup of coffee."

"And this is why we're not in advertising." I laughed.

"You hate it."

"No. Actually, I think it's cute. I'll do it. Will set up the store tomorrow and run it for two weeks until the end of the year. Sound good?"

"Sounds perfect."

The buzz of the lobby intercom brought a smile to her face.

With that she flitted across the clouds and into the waiting arms of her lover.

— 9 —

A Kiss for a Cup

I *could definitely get used to this.*

There I was, standing in the glory of the most beautiful sunrise I'd ever seen. The sun took its sweet time coasting across the Pacific Ocean, turning the water from cobalt blue to turquoise as it climbed high into the sky. In my hand was a cup of the most delicious coffee I had ever tasted. Or ever made.

Api was long gone, but she'd left me two things: a large burlap sack filled with freshly ground coffee—the only item in her refrigerator—and the stuff she didn't want to pack right on the floor. I had the apartment cleaned up in no time, certain it was nerves that spurred me to keep going until everything was back in its place.

In the meantime, I had an hour before I needed to head to the shop. I glanced at my phone, calculating the time difference in my head. Eleven in the morning in Florida simply meant my mom was at the store. Her bookstore. The one my dad had bought for her when he'd decided to retire and devote his days to a free clinic he'd established. He'd figured it would keep her busy. And it did. In fact, it was the only bookstore that survived the onslaught of ebooks and indie authors.

"Hi, Mom," I greeted as soon as she picked up the phone.

"Andie, my love. How is Hawaii?"

"Don't know yet. I thought I'd call you before I head out to Api's store."

"Did she brief you on what you needed to do? I know you were worried about that."

"Well …" I began tidying up the sheets on the pull-out. "Yes and no."

"What does that mean?" My mother heard me grunt as I pushed the metal bar back into the sofa. "And what are you doing?"

"Pushing." Pause. "This." Exhale. "Thing in." A loud thump reverberated through the phone. "Sorry, Mom. I had a little trouble collapsing the bed."

"Where are you?"

"Oh, I'm at Api's. But I decided not to sleep in her bedroom. She has a rather comfortable pull-out in her living room. Anyway, we talked more about some of the things she wanted to do for the holiday to promote the store. And then she had to get packed to leave with James."

We both chuckled.

"That girl is finally going to settle down," said my mother.

"I'm just so happy Mr. F had the chance to meet James. And he liked him."

For a brief moment, I wondered whether my mom wished the engagement was mine.

I placed the phone on speaker so I could keep putting things away. My mom continued to speak.

"Anyway, Andie, listen darling. You'll do great. Remember that this is just a secondary part of why you're there. You're mostly there to take a break, so leave it to Api's people to handle, manage it a little but most of all, take time to enjoy yourself."

"Okay."

"Promise me, Andie."

"I promise."

"One more thing," she said as a follow-up. Mom was known to make these closing statements after every single phone call. Sort of like a wrap-up. Or a recap. Sometimes they were digs, other times they were words of wisdom. It was her way of getting the last word in, making sure I knew exactly what she was thinking. That morning it was this: "Call Nick."

And so, I did.

He picked up on the second ring.

"Hey."

"Hey, sorry about yesterday. I was with Api, trying to learn about the coffee shop and just missed the time difference," I rambled.

"It's okay. I'm sorry too. I was just worried, that's all."

"I know."

"How is it over there? Beautiful, I bet," Nick said, his tone light. Like night and day from the previous conversation.

"It is. As soon as I landed, everything just melted away. I literally felt the heaviness leave my body. My mind is following suit."

He remained silent. I pictured him pacing around, nodding, the way he did during business calls.

There had been times I'd watch him with so much tenderness,

grateful to have such boundless love. And then there were times I'd felt strangled and restless, finding freedom through my many business trips.

Nick wasn't the man for me.

"Nick," I finally spoke. "How is she? Api tells me you are happy."

"I am. It's still a little new—I mean, I'm not proposing to her or anything like that. But she loves me. She's not looking for something she can't seem to find."

"I loved you."

"I know you did," he responded. "Just not enough. And I accept that now. I gave you an ultimatum because you were too afraid to let me go."

"You're right and I'm truly sorry."

"I'm sorry too," he said quietly. "Hey, listen, Andie. Don't be a stranger okay? If you need anything while you're out there, just call."

"I will," I answered. "Thank you."

"And Andie?"

"Yes?" The sun was high in the sky, shining, confident, strong. I wished I felt that way, wished this despair wasn't looming over me. Instead, I felt horribly alone, knowing this would probably be the last time I would hear his voice. This was the goodbye we'd never exchanged. The rational resignation of a four-year relationship.

"I really hope you find what you're looking for. I have a feeling you are in the right place and this is the right time. I ... Bye, Andie."

At the very tip of Kahala Avenue where the road meets the highway, right by the entrance of Wai'alae beach, sat a lone wooden structure on a gravel parking lot crowded with overgrown grass.

"This is it, I guess," I muttered to myself as I approached a heavy wooden door. A small sign right above it read *Beans and Bites*.

Yep. Interesting little place. This small store couldn't be what had fueled the wealth Api had grown up with. Unless there were a string of them across all the islands—but Api had only mentioned the one shop.

I pulled on the knob, but it wouldn't budge. For a coffee shop to be closed at seven in the morning seemed a bit strange to me. Must be a cultural thing. I mean, this wasn't Chicago where people were hustling on trains and in cars at the crack of dawn. This was a chill place. Maybe people slept in and then went to the beach in time for lunch. Or something. They were all so fit and skinny, they probably skipped lunch too.

A young girl, a teenager, stood by the door after I had turned around to retrieve Api's box from the car.

"Can I help you?" she asked, beautiful brown eyes with her hair in a ponytail.

"Uh, yes," I responded, arms still encircled around Api's box. "Apikelia Flores? She's a friend. My name is—"

"Andie. Andie, her best friend," said the pretty young lady.

"Yes. Yes. This is me." I laughed. "I'm Andie."

She pulled out a key from her back pocket, unlocked the door and gently nudged me inside. The view on the inside was nothing like the outside. It looked brand-new, with freshly painted walls of blue and white stripes, white countertops, and a combination of both colors on high tops and stools scattered in the middle of the shop.

The girl saw the surprise on my face. "Looks different in here, huh? Api had this redone after she inherited it, hmm, about six months ago."

I continued to walk around, still holding tightly to the box.

"I'm Maele, by the way. I'm the server-slash-barista," she said.

I placed the box on one of the tables and reached out to shake her hand. "Hi."

Just then, an older woman entered through a swinging door, which I assumed was the kitchen.

"You are Andie?" she addressed me, her eyes lighting up as she tied an apron around her waist. "My name is Kawailani. Call me Lani for short. I'm the cook."

"Hi, Lani," I greeted, still absorbing the environment. Colored surfboards decorated the walls. To the right by the entrance, a semi-empty shelf housed coffee mugs of different colors and sizes. "I'm sorry in advance for all the questions, but I wasn't really able to get a full download from Api before she left."

"Of course, no problem at all. We are excited to have you with us here."

With that, both women began to work around the store. Lani left for the kitchen, while Maele pulled out a washcloth and started to wipe down the counter. "We open at eight," she said, her attention now on the cash register. "What would you like to do, Miss Andie?"

"Well …" I circled the counter and stood next to her. "I guess you can teach me how to work this so I can help out?"

"And the coffee?"

"That too." I smiled. Then an afterthought, "Oh hey, before I forget. Api had asked me to put some Christmas decorations up." I pointed at the box on the table.

"Sure, let's see what you have."

We dug through the box to pull out the sign Api had made earlier. Maele laughed. "This is so Api."

We proceeded to decorate the store in silence. Maele held the garland up while I tacked them on the wall with pushpins. We lined the countertop with crystalline white lights and hung a wreath with bright colored lights in the center. Each surfboard had a red and green ribbon tied around it. The place lit up like a Chicago Christmas. Festive, bright, and over the top.

When we were done, Maele held up the mistletoe. "And these, where?"

"Well, we have to see them kiss so we can give the free cup. Why not over here?" I stood in the center of the room right underneath the spotlight. "And I think we only need one."

10

What If I Tried

I changed our opening time to seven, of course upon consulting Maele and Lani. They went for it right away, assuring me they would do anything to help make things work. It took a few days for me to realize what they meant. "Making it work" was a new concept. Because the current plan was not.

I had been in Hawaii for a full week, immersed in learning how to make a cold brew, a bullet, a hazelnut latte, and a cortado. I figured out most of these varieties were based in espresso. And this particular grind they had in the store was delicious. Full bodied and crisp, a little sweet and very strong.

I delayed my calls to Api, wrote down my questions and saved them for that call. The hours were long and slow—from 6:30 a.m. to 8 p.m., we served an average of ten customers. I finished three books in seven days. Sometimes, I'd send Mae and Lani home to have dinner with their families. I closed up the store every evening exhausted, not by the flurry of activity but by boredom.

"Hi, Mom." I pushed the button on the register drawer to tally out the cash. "I'm getting ready to leave for the day."

"How are you, honey? How'd your first week go? What have

you been up to?"

"Nothing much," I replied, propping my phone up between the number pad and the transaction screen. My father's face popped up next to her. "Hi, Dad."

"Hi, my love. What's new?" he asked.

"Oh, nothing much. Still at Api's store but heading out soon."

"How is it doing? Busy for the holidays?" Both parents were cheek-to-cheek, their faces smushed together for the camera.

"Actually, no. Not busy at all. The place is great, so modern. The location, not so much. I'm waiting for the chance to speak to—" An incoming call was signaled by a beep. "Let me call you right back. Api's on the other line. Love you."

I pressed the ACCEPT button and Api's bright smile lit up my screen. "Hey, gorgeous."

"Hey, girl," she answered. "Germany is freaking awesome even when freezing."

"And Hawaii is perfect," I said. "How are things?"

"Wonderful. I've had a chance to sightsee a bit while James is in school. Thought I'd call you before my day started. How's B&B? You'll never know how thankful I am that you're doing this for me."

"Of course," I answered. "Maele and Lani are wonderful. I do have a list of questions for you, if you don't mind?" I pulled the notebook from under the counter and leafed through the pages.

Api laughed. "Sure."

"Okay, hold on." I tried to make sense of my scribbles. I had written them in bullet format but the notes I made were barely legible. "Ready?"

"Hit me."

"Menu choices. Have you ever considered other things? Why just cinnamon rolls?"

"No reason, really," she replied. "I just haven't had time to look into other items."

"Okay, what about location? We only have about ten customers a day, Api. Is it low season or something?"

"Ten. Ten is more than we've had in the past few months," she squeaked. "That's great, Andie."

I shook my head in disbelief. "What? Api? That's not enough to make a profit."

"I wasn't in it for that. It was Dad's store, Dad's hobby. I'm just carrying on his legacy. I'm not a businessperson; I don't know marketing and all that. I plan to hire someone to turn it around after this trip. Mom has friends who recommended some business-turn-around people I can hire."

Business-turn-around people?

"Do you want it to grow? Succeed?" I asked. My mind churned with ideas. *I can do this.* But only if she wanted me to.

Her tone turned low, serious. "Honestly, I don't know how to turn it around. You know, this isn't what I want to do. I want to paint, show my work in galleries."

"I know," I countered. "But this place has a lot of potential. You're right by the beach. People just don't see it, I think."

"I'm sorry I didn't tell you, Andie. I was embarrassed and frankly, still grieving my dad. I'd do anything to eternalize his legacy, but I don't know how. I have yet to meet with the accountants, but I think we may have to pursue a sale. The property is prime. There are many buyers."

"Wait a minute. Let's not make rash decisions. What if I

tried?"

"Tried to what?" Api asked.

The bustle of the world outside her window filtered through the phone. Busses revving up, motorcycles speeding by, and a singsong siren.

"Tried to make a go of it, make it grow," I answered. "Since I'm here anyway, let me look into some options."

"The venture capitalist at work."

I wasn't going to deny this was the perfect challenge for me. "How much do we have to play with?" I opened my notebook to a blank page and started to doodle. Doodling helped me get my thoughts organized. My pen automatically drew a circle, and then another, and then another.

"Not much, to be honest. I'll have my bank guy give you a call on Monday. I'm also going to add you as a signatory, so you have free use of the remaining funds. There's not much though. My mom has offered to reinvest but I don't want her to at this point."

"We may not need that. I'll think this over and let you know, okay? In the meantime, enjoy your time in Germany. Don't buy anything I wouldn't," I teased.

"I'm so grateful." Her tone changed back immediately. Shrill, light, happy.

"Maybe by next Christmas, we'll get this place turned around." I thumbed through the first few pages of notes, making sure there was nothing else to ask. All the other questions revolved around the results of the business. And Api's few statements had made it clear. There was, however, one more.

"Oh, hey, Api—one more. If we closed up this place, what would your liabilities be? Any covenants or arrangements I need to know about? Who's your supplier for that amazing coffee?"

"What are covenants?" I could hear shuffling in the background and her voice blew in and out. She was moving around; I could tell she was no longer indoors. "I'm actually hustling to catch the bus," she huffed, seemingly out of breath. "But don't worry—our distributor for the plantation will be able to find new customers to take on the products used in the shop. Okay, gotta go. Muah, muah. I'm so grateful. Love you, Andie."

"Wait, Api. What plantation?" I blurted, only to realize I was in a conversation with myself.

11

Christmas Eve

A plantation?

As in acres and acres of what? Coffee beans? How do you even grow coffee? Do they grow in the ground like potatoes? I mean, this is how much I knew. I knew nothing.

The businesswoman in me had my brain spinning, planning, strategizing. How? Did Mrs. Flores actively manage this? No wonder there were no supplier costs in the books. At first, I thought the costs were recorded as part of overall supplies. But right then, it made sense. Beans and Bites' coffee supplier was itself.

I asked Lani and Maele as soon as they were in the next day. "Oh, yes," they both cried in unison.

Maele continued, "We're sorry, we thought Api told you. The plantation is about forty miles from here. We grow coffee and cacao."

Cacao? Why in the world weren't we serving it here?

Lani jumped in. "My husband manages the plantation. It is half owned by a large company, but the Kona we sell here is owned by the Flores family."

"Can you take me there?" I asked. "Obviously we can wait

until after the holidays."

They both nodded.

"Which reminds me, it's Christmas Eve, ladies. Please pack up and head home to your families."

"But you?" Maele asked, picking up her knapsack and stuffing her tiny black shoes in it. "You should go too. I don't think anyone else will be here this evening."

"You may be right." I laughed. "But I like the quiet. I'm going to do some reading."

A lot of reading. And none of it will be swoony or scary or mysterious.

I pulled out a bag of books I'd recently ordered from Amazon. Books about coffee plantations, Hawaiian soil and how climates related to the quality and kind of coffees around the island.

"There's nothing like seeing the actual thing," Lani said, slowly guiding Maele toward the back door. "Andie, this may sound awkward, but we would love to have you over for Ahiahi Kalikimaka. We have a simple dinner, but the children will all be there."

"Thank you for such a kind offer. But I really planned to stay in and catch up on some reading. I want to be ready to dig in after the holidays."

Maele gazed down uncomfortably before taking Lani's hand. "Come on, Lan, let's lock up and leave Andie to her plans," she said.

I raised my hand and grinned widely at the same time. "No, no need to lock up. I'll stay a while. Who knows? There may be somebody out there who will feel like a coffee and a snack on Christmas Eve."

I tidied up when the women left, counting the remaining number of coupons we had for the *A KISS FOR A CUP* promotion we ran for the holidays. Maele suggested we keep going until New Year's Day. *Don't they all kiss on New Year's Eve?* I took pictures of the Christmas decorations to send to Api and my parents. I'd improvised a little bit, added garland to the coffee cup shelf and a little flocked Christmas tree in the corner of the store. I grew misty-eyed as my gaze took in all of the cheery decorations. The place should be filled with happy holiday makers—not a lonely, failed businesswoman who didn't know what to do with the rest of her life.

I blinked back the tears, took a seat on one of the high tops, and opened my bag of books.

Being that I was less than five foot five, my legs dangled slightly above the ground. There were books on the table in front of me and a laptop with an Excel worksheet behind me. I shifted from the books to the laptop, rotating the stool as I took notes, made calculations, highlighted passages, and repeated the process. Focusing on saving the shop for Api helped me push my feelings of loneliness away. After a while, my phone rang and I fished it out from under one of the hardbound books.

"Mom, hi."

My mom's vibrant smile filled the screen. "Hi, baby girl. Merry Christmas from our time zone. We missed having you here for our Noche Buena." She panned the phone around to show me some happy, stuffed, waving people. A few of them were asleep on the couch. It was really late there. "Everyone says hi. Your *titos* and *titas* are in Florida visiting."

"Hi, everyone. I miss you too, Mom." I swear. This wasn't the first Christmas Eve I'd spent alone. There were times I'd spent the holidays in my office, sleeping on the couch and working through the night. But this night was different. I felt sad and alone. My heart felt heavy and tears threatened to betray my gallant attempt at stoicism.

"What did you have for Noche Buena?"

"Lechon, of course." She smiled.

"Dad's favorite. You gotta watch that man. Did he overeat?"

"Of course. What are you doing tonight, honey?"

I lifted my phone up and scanned it around. "Isn't the store nice? I thought I'd stay for a while and come up with a business plan. This business has so much more potential than we think. Api needs my help right now."

I saw her shake her head, her eyes slanting into a full-on smile. She knew I needed Api just as much.

"What?" I asked.

"My daughter the Problem Solver." She leaned forward, her chin on her hand. "I'm not going to say what you think I'm going to say. I just want you to be happy. And to get your much-needed break, whether it be working"—she chuckled—"or working. Need anything from me or Dad?"

I smiled back, filled with love for such support. They were always there for me. When Nick and I had broken up, my mom stayed at my condo for weeks. I literally had to ask my dad to bribe her with a trip to Paris to give us both some space. I'd worked long days and came home close to midnight to home-cooked meals and a warm bed.

"Nothing right at the moment. I've got to check out how much we have in terms of funds. And of course—"

She interrupted me. "No decisions until you speak with Api. Or her mom."

"Right."

"I love you, *hija*. I'd better go, your dad is picking at the lechon again. I'll call you again tomorrow. Mele Kalikimaka."

"Wow, Mom."

"Jimmy Buffet."

Before I could respond, my attention was snatched by the slight chime of the Christmas bells hanging above the door.

"Did I lose you, Andie?"

"Sorry. Gotta. Go." My train of thought halted by surprise more than anything. "We have some customers."

12

Stranger in the Night

W ell, they weren't customers.

It was *a* customer.

By the time he cleared the door, I was back behind the counter, ready to take his order. He stopped before approaching me, turned and made his way to the corner of the room to look at the flocked tree.

"Haven't seen one like this for a long time," he muttered, reaching out to touch its frosted tips. When he directed his gaze toward me, there was a look of surprise on his face. The awkward double-take and the way we locked eyes caused me to consciously touch the corner of my mouth, to make sure nothing unsightly was stuck to it.

"What can I get you?" I asked. This place was filled with beautiful people. Working in a coffee shop right by the beach made the clientele a little fitter, a little more active, a little less self-conscious, and a lot more self-confident. But this guy was different. He was from here, but not from here. Not a local, not a tourist. Maybe a transplant, just like me. He wore khaki shorts but not beach shorts. His hair was brown, but sun-kissed enough to look golden. Clean cut, not long or wavy. Darker features masked the bluest eyes I'd ever seen, like the turquoise ocean on a really dark night. The look of surprise soon faded, and he walked a few steps closer to the counter.

"I've never seen you here before," he said in all seriousness, his glare too intense I had to look away.

"I'm sorry? What would you like to order?" I rearranged a stack of papers by the register, hoping the rustling sound would break the deafening silence between us. I willed myself to take control of the situation. It was Christmas Eve; I was vulnerable and alone. I also allowed my mind to run rampant for a brief moment. He was just as tall as Nick, but while Nick looked rough-and-tumble Grecian, this one was a mismatched, clean-cut surfer boy. Compared to Nick, he had less angular, more refined features. He was good-looking enough to be a model, well-built enough to be an athlete.

Reality set in. He was a random stranger and I was all alone in the middle of nowhere.

Maybe I just found him quite attractive. Or maybe I was missing Nick. Or the idea of him. Or all three.

"Oh God. I am so sorry." He took two more steps closer to me. "I was looking for Apikelia Flores."

"She's not here at the moment. Is there anything I can help you with, Mister—?"

"My name is Warren. Warren"—a slight pause—"Yates."

He offered me his hand; I took it.

"Andrea Matthews," I answered. "Well, Mr. Yates, Apikelia is currently traveling but I will be sure to let her know you're trying to contact her." I wanted to know why, but I didn't want to push.

I had some theories—he was probably a jilted lover just finding out about her recent engagement.

"Thank you," he said. "I'll check back at a later date."

I nodded as he turned away, leaving the counter to get back to my books. I planned to boot it to the door and lock up as soon as he left. I looked at my watch—7:15 pm and still a couple of hours worth of necessary research. If he left now, I'd be able to get back to my reading.

A few seconds later, he cleared his throat.

There he was standing right in front of me.

"I do think I'd like to order a cup of coffee, please," he said, voice muted, his right hand ruffling through his hair.

"Sure." I headed back to the counter. "Which one would you like?"

He followed right behind me. "Hmm. Just an espresso, please."

I switched the machine on and poured the coffee in a little paper cup.

He handed me a ten dollar bill and placed all his change in the tip box.

"Would you mind if I took a seat?"

"No, of course not," I answered, waving my hand in the direction of the seven empty tables while I made my way back to mine.

Gently, he pushed the books aside and sat at my table. We faced each other, him with his cup and me, well, with a highlighter in hand.

"So, Andrea," he began. "What are you doing here all by yourself on Christmas Eve?"

"It's Andie." A slight tingle ran through me. "And same thing you are."

He laughed. "You're not from here. Are you a friend of Api's? Where are you from?"

He must be an old friend of Api's, for sure.

"I have the same question for you, seeing you made a trip all the way here to see Api," I retorted. "How do you know her, anyway?"

"Acquaintance," he replied.

Aha. Old lover, I bet.

"And you?"

"We went to Brown together. And I moved home to Chicago after that. We've been friends since freshman year."

"And you're here running her coffee shop, because ...?" He was relentless.

"Because she asked me to do her this favor while she accompanied—" Oops. I shouldn't tell a complete stranger my best friend's business. Well, complete stranger to me. "While she accompanied her mom on business," I finished.

There was a flash of doubt on his face by the way he pursed his lips, but he recovered rather quickly, leaned back, and relaxed his shoulders. "How long have you been here? At her store?"

"Two weeks."

"What do you think so far?" he prodded.

"It's doing great," I lied. There was no way I was going to divulge we were going downhill fast. "She's on a prime location."

"That, she is," he agreed. He leaned forward, arms crossed, elbows on the table.

A pleasurable flutter tickled my stomach. "Apikelia has been wanting me to come and visit." I broke our eye contact. I didn't need to defend my presence. But I was like a fish out of water— was I doing this right? It had been too long since I'd been involved in a little flirtation.

"But she's not here."

"Well, she'll be back soon. Like I said, she's with her mom, wrapping up her father's affairs. He just recently—"

"I know."

"So, you're a friend?" I prompted, my curiosity piqued.

"No, actually. Well, kind of. I'm here for business."

I nodded, acknowledging, but not really.

He rephrased his question. "What keeps you in Chicago?"

"The weather, really. The fact that I can dress to four different seasons."

I sounded so shallow. He didn't look fazed. He actually smiled.

"Ah." He chuckled. "Now, all the more I'm intrigued."

"Whatever it is I do, it's nothing exciting, I can assure you. Besides, I can say the same about you. You've been kind of cryptic about walking in here on Christmas Eve, looking for my friend."

"Well ..." He shifted in his seat before taking a sip of his coffee. It had probably cooled by then. "I was born here, moved to New York for a few years, and now I'm back."

"I didn't really ask where you were from, but that's nice. You might as well tell me what you do."

"I'm actually trying to figure that out. I'm in a transition period."

I really wanted to tell him I was there for the same thing, but geez, he was a total stranger. Maybe it was because I needed to confide in a friend. Api had been busy with her engagement lately. And all I really knew was that it was Christmas Eve and I was inexplicably drawn to him. Or to his company.

Or both. Maybe the mistletoe had magic powers. Because all I could think about was kissing this guy. This feeling was literal. I mean, small sparks shooting up and down my body, electrifying me, making me believe that if I touched him, these little flares of yearning would subside. Like an itch. A kiss itch.

He looked up to discover he was right under the darn culprit. The mistletoe. Good Lord. Had he read my mind? "*A Kiss for a Cup*. Has that really been working?"

"Of course," I said, defensively. "It was a brilliant marketing ploy. We've had many winners."

"I suppose any man would take the opportunity to kiss a pretty girl if she were standing right under the mistletoe," he said, sarcastically, I think. I couldn't read him. He stayed pretty much expressionless, save for the slight tilt of his head.

"I would say it's the other way around. What woman wouldn't want a free cup of coffee?" *I'd rather have the kiss, to be honest. How weird would it be to kiss a stranger? And exciting.*

He gently placed his paper cup on the table and stood, grabbing my hand and lifting me out of my seat. My heart was pounding, the floor began to melt and shift beneath me. His blue eyes drilled into mine, looking at me, looking into me. It made me nervous, but it also made me bold. "Well, I want the kiss, you want the coffee," he said, drawing his face closer to mine, leaning across the table. "Let's give ourselves what we want."

With that, he kissed me. A kiss so deep and hungry, it made me want everything. The animal desire to bite his lip, allow him to ravage me. His big hands pressed into my lower back, pulling me toward him, his fingertips on my spine—I wanted this so much. For him to explore me, nothing was off limits.

Suddenly, I was jolted into reality by a loud wood-on-tile screeching noise as he pushed his chair back, creating a few feet of space between us.

"Andie, are you okay? Where'd you go?"

"I'm sorry, I was thinking … about something else. I think I'm just tired," I said, shaking my head, commanding these impure thoughts to take a hike. My back was hot, burning as I stood up. I bet I was blushing. As I gathered the books on the table and shuffled them back into my bag, something spurred me to pause for a moment. That smell. The mistletoe had that familiar fragrance—not pine, nor evergreen but of a warm bed of flowers. I just couldn't place my finger on it.

"Are you okay? You look a little flushed," he said.

"It's late and I still have quite a bit of reading to do. I wish you could stay, but I'd like to lock up before I leave."

"Of course," he said, standing abruptly while squeezing his paper cup. "I apologize—didn't mean to keep you on a night like this."

"I'm sure you have to be somewhere too."

I thought I heard him say, "Not really."

He stood in place for a while, stepping back to give me room to sling my bag over my shoulder. He looked confused, or disappointed. His lips pursed in not quite a pout, while his neck bent and shoulders hunched forward. It was almost as if he really wanted to stay longer. I highly doubted anyone who looked like that would want to spend the night before Christmas in a coffee shop, making small talk with a barista. I felt sorry for him. And then I felt sorry for myself.

I decided to call it a night. For sure, this time.

"All righty," I said definitively.

"Okie dokie," he answered, a loopy grin pasted on his face.

I may have exhaled loudly or rolled my eyes because it finally spurred him to act. "Oh, of course, I should go," he said, with a wave of his hand. Then he smiled at me. "Thank you for the coffee and the conversation, and ..." He looked right into my soul. "Merry Christmas."

— 13 —

New Year's Eve

Api's father owned a coffee plantation, the only one outside of Kona, right in Oahu. Before he passed away, he'd entered into a joint venture with a multinational company to lease their equipment and enlist their help in building the business. The Island Coffee Company had been started by his grandparents. It was a small operation—not lucrative by venture capitalist standards—but a thriving business nonetheless. Until a few years ago, when he'd fallen ill and could no longer actively participate in the business..

I had so much more to learn, so much more to think about.

But for the next few days, my focus was elsewhere.

That guy who showed up on Christmas Eve. If there was someone like him with nothing better to do for the holidays, there must be hundreds more like him. Okay, not hundreds, but at least ten more.

I had five days to pull it off, this grand idea of mine. After spending the holidays doing some research, I decided to plan an event for New Year's Eve.

"Why New Year's Eve when we are a coffee shop?" Lani asked.

"To get noticed, silly. We want people to know about us." We were also too late for Christmas.

Maele knew a local band from Pearl City who was willing to play for seven hundred dollars. They called themselves the Soul City Brothers and played Motown hits. That was good enough for me.

I rented a billboard space right along Highway H1 and asked Maele to deliver flyers on the beach. We would have free coffee and music. Lani created a temporary menu of noodles, ordered a whole roast pig, and told me we had to have poi on the menu. We set up some tables and chairs in the small outdoor space and hung some Christmas lights between two large palm trees. The view from the coffee shop was stunning. Elevated on a small hill, it overlooked Wai'alae Beach and faced west toward the sunset.

"Hey, girl. Happy New Year. I just had to call. The picture you sent—is that the store? Cheese and rice. There are about fifty people in there."

"Cheese and rice, no, but we got poi." I laughed, kicking up the stones underneath my sneakers as I walked around the parking lot. Somehow, the cellphone reception was better outside. Around me, a cacophony of sound filled my senses: the crunching gravel, the whistling breeze, the rustle of the palms. The discord in my head was often muted by the beauty of this place. Everywhere I looked there was an abundance of color, bright nights that signified hope.

"Still on a no cursing kick," she said. "Anyway, how'd you get all those people in there? That's so amazing."

"Ah," I answered. "Long story for another day. But I think we got it done."

"I can't believe it. You are so good, Andie."

"I've got so many more ideas. It's actually quite exciting."

She leaned into the phone, her picture-perfect features accented by the scenery behind her.

"Where are you?"

"Taking a break, enjoying the morning at St. Mary's Square in Munich. James and I have brunch coming up for New Year's Day."

"Love that sculpture behind you."

Api smiled. "But how are you, Andie? How are things? Are you doing okay over there?"

"Yes, yes. Everything is good. I've been keeping busy at the store, always trying to come up with something. I hope it's okay that I've done all this. I didn't want you to have to worry about anything."

"But I don't," Api exclaimed. "I trust you so much and I'm so grateful."

"Hmmm. We'll see. I still don't know if all this will work."

"What. Didn't you just send me that picture? You pulled that off in four days."

"Yes, but—"

"But nothing," she insisted. "I feel bad that you've devoted your entire stay to changing things up, but it's time to have fun now, okay? Take that break you were supposed to."

"This is my break." I giggled. "I'm actually having fun doing it."

"Fun is meeting a hot guy on the beach and having a glorious Hawaiian fling."

"I haven't been to the beach yet."

"Bleh," she said. "Not good."

"Api, that's just looking for trouble." I debated whether I should mention the guy who came over on Christmas Eve. Nah. It was probably a fluke and not worth another second of my time. I could kick my brain for even bringing it up. No one knew about it, not even Lani or Maele. I'd tell Api about him when she got back. He never even said why he wanted to find her, so it couldn't be important enough to tell her—especially as he said he was an acquaintance. Besides, I was trying not to think about him.

"Andie, you there? Did you hear what I just said?"

"Huh? Oh. Sorry, my mind just wandered."

"Well, you'll want to pay attention. I was showing you these earrings." She moved her head sideways to show me her right ear. "I got them at Maximilianstrasse in Munich."

"Gorgeous." Tiny diamonds lined the oval-shaped ring that drooped from her ears.

"I got you a pair," she yelped. "Someone from James's fellowship is heading back to the States. I'm sending them through him."

I noticed more people at the entrance of the store. I had to go. Two hours before midnight and the isolated area around me seemed to come alive. I held my phone closer to my ear, so much so that Api could only see my nose. I could hardly hear her over the fireworks that started to blast off in the distance. "Oh, no. No. I don't need them."

"When did we ever need what we bought? They're a steal."

"Thank you for thinking of me, but I was serious about downsizing. I haven't shopped since I left for Honolulu and you know what? I haven't really craved it." I clicked the button on my remote and got into my Jeep. I let out an audible sigh and smiled at Api through the phone. "There. Better. Now I can hear you."

"Andie, are you wearing the same outfit you had on when I saw you at the airport?" she teased.

"Downsizing, girl." I chuckled right back. "I told you."

"Well, I still say you need these earrings. I'm sending them. You'll go back to your normal fashionista self in no time. You're just taking a break and pretending you're not you."

Ouch. She just called me out. I'd gone from a Range Rover in Chicago to a Jeep Wrangler in Hawaii, traded in my rag & bone and Gucci loafers for a denim romper in Hawaii. Did I feel happier? Lighter? More in tune with myself? Not really. But what I did feel was free. Free to navigate my day as I wanted, without any pressure to prove myself to anyone.

"Hey, Andie. You still there?" Api's voice rang through my thoughts.

"Hey, sorry. You're breaking up. Can I call you in a couple of days? It's almost midnight and I need to check back in the store."

"Sure. I miss you. Happy New Year. This year will be yours, my friend. Don't forget that."

"And yours too. Love you, Api."

— 14 —
Boulder on the Sand

Fourteen steps.

That was the distance between the back door of the coffee shop and the most glorious view I'd ever seen. This was where I watched the fireworks streak the sky thirty minutes before midnight. I had seen fireworks before, but not to this magnitude. Flashes of light all over the sky cast out the darkness, disappearing into the water, and then rising up again. Slivers of color arose from every corner of the earth, meeting in the middle and then spreading out as far as the eye could see.

Maele had told me that tradition called for much revelry and noise on New Year's Eve. "To scare off the evil spirits," she'd said, as she hauled three large pots of jook, a rice porridge with chicken and duck eggs, which she'd insisted was the customary Hawaiian meal at midnight.

I couldn't believe how many people were at the coffee shop for this event. Maele brought two friends to help serve, the band was hopping, and the front door was open to accommodate patrons who had brought their own folding chairs. We were over capacity for the first time. This little out of nowhere coffee shop looked like the happiest and hippest place on the island.

So there I sat, straddling a large boulder settled on the sand, contemplating the events of the past month and trying to figure out what I was going to do after that night. My leave was coming to an end and work was calling, asking me to come back. I tried to focus on the tall grass that swayed with the wind and on the sloping hill that led out to the shore.

My nose began to twitch. I couldn't quite place my finger on it, but all of a sudden, that recognizable fragrance filled the air. Strong, sweet, comforting. Like a field of flowers on a hot, sunny day.

What do I really want? What's next for me?

The sky turned into a movie screen, the past year's memories playing out in front of me. A broken engagement at the beginning of the year, head down, hunkered in work and ambition, in success. A nervous breakdown that changed my narrative. Misguided priorities, a fairy tale that was no longer rooted in truth.

"Penny for your thoughts."

I looked up to see the Christmas Eve guy standing next to me. This time, he wore jeans and a hoodie. I saw his face in between the sparks of firework light.

He bent and sat on the sand next to me, knees folded up, arms around them. "Warren from the other night, by the way."

Of course I knew who he was, but he didn't have to know that.

"Hey." I kept my gaze in front of me. He did the same. We both stared out into the horizon.

"You seemed so deep in thought."

"I was thinking about how different New Year's Eve is over

here. I'm normally all bundled up indoors instead of sitting outside, basking in warm weather."

He chuckled. "It took a while for me too. They're incomparable, actually. Each with their own merits."

"So true," I answered, still looking out ahead.

"Some party you have in there," he said, turning to look at me. I finally met his eyes and smiled back.

"Far cry from a few nights ago, right?"

"Definitely."

"I forgot to ask you the other night," he began. This time, we turned back in the direction of the sky, the dissonant bursts of light more intense than ever. "How long do you plan to be on the island?"

"I guess that's what I'm trying to figure out," I answered. "I really don't know."

He shrugged. "Well, that's hopeful."

I don't know why, but he made me laugh. His voice soothed me, made everything that felt essential seem trivial that night. Even if our words were scarce.

"That's some music in there," he said, looking up at me again with that big, wide grin. "They just played 'Staying Alive.'"

"Is that Motown? They're supposed to be playing Motown."

"I don't think so." He laughed.

"Huh."

A flash of light streaked across the sky, causing us to look up at the same time. Out of my periphery, I saw him glance at his watch before jumping to his feet. He offered me his hand. "11:58. Come with me."

And I did. I grabbed his hand and we ran inside the coffee

shop together, pushing our way through the kitchen door and into the main area where a crowd of people stood around the mistletoe. There were couples cuddled in the corners, single people standing on the chairs. He led me directly under the mistletoe, past annoyed couples who glared at him as he guided me right to the spot where we'd sat a few nights ago.

"Five. Four. Three. Two. One."

"Happy New Year," said the crowd, cheering as loud as they could. The band stopped playing for a second and then jumped in with "Auld Lang Syne."

Then he kissed me.

First a soft touch of his lips, testing our connection. It was chaste but languid, slow and controlled, as he pressed them to mine, his hands gently cradling my face and his thumb lightly skimming my cheek.

I saw fireworks with my eyes closed, felt the morning rush of the breeze even as strangers' bodies pressed against mine.

I kissed him back. With all the certainty of the uncertainty that lay before me, I kissed him.

We swayed to the music, our lips pressed together until the band slowed down and the audience cheered when they segued into a second set. This time a slow dance where words like *love* and *forever* were used in the same sentence, played to the delight of lovers in the room.

"Would it be okay," he said as he pulled away, his blue eyes dancing, his voice breathless, "if you gave me your phone number?"

Resolutions

I stayed in the next day, loaded myself up with information about coffee plantations—how they survived only in Kona because the volcanic soil was at an ideal elevation above sea level. This drainage was perfectly suited for coffee cultivation. The cool, dry season from November to March synchronized the dormant period of the coffee plant with the rainfall that ensued in the spring and summer. I felt like a coffee expert as the day wore on, highlighting facts and passages, and analyzing business projections.

If we invested this, the return would be this.

Would this business be worth saving?

First, I needed to know what the current state was. Maele and Lani were going to take me there the next day.

It was New Year's Day after all, so staying home was only half by choice.

I used to believe in resolutions. Most of them had to do with exercising or the gym or attending Jenny Craig. Shallow stuff like that. Nothing about what I wanted out of life, because I thought I was living it. What a difference a year made. Two sides of a dream had been lost, one driven by the other but propelled in regret, nonetheless. Now, here I was, trying desperately to plan my near future. How much time did I think I needed to help Api turn this business around? What would I do next? Would I go back to life in Chicago?

Definitely.

I had to go back. My life was there. My career was there.

Because of that, I couldn't delay the inevitable.

With a cup of coffee in hand, I stepped out on the balcony and took a deep breath of the fresh sea air. I could see the line of outriggers, bouncing with the ebb and flow of the waves. The beach was full of holiday revelers. Party music drifted up toward the sky, the clouds rhythmically twirling in response. The air was filled with the sounds of vacation, and people looking like tiny colored ants thirty stories below filled every space on the sand.

I dialed Matt's number but it went to voicemail.

Even before I finished my message, he rang me right back.

"Andrea, so nice to hear from you."

"Hi Matt. Listen, I'm sorry to bother you—I was hoping to just leave you a message."

"No, this is perfect," he said. "I've been wanting to talk to you."

"Oh?" I asked, intrigued by his lighthearted demeanor. So not Matt.

I glanced toward the beach and made out a small group of surfers surveying the waves, their backs turned to me, boards under one arm. One of them turned, craned his neck and looked directly at me. I turned my back on the balcony, feeling self-conscious all of a sudden. Lord knows how many times I'd gotten dressed with the sliding door wide open, thinking no one could see me from that high up.

"Andrea, how long do you think you need to stay over there? How much time do you need?"

"Well," I said, hesitantly, "that's why I'm calling. I'm not quite sure. I'd like to ask for an unpaid leave."

"It's not working out," he said.

My knees went weak, I steadied myself by reaching for the balustrade. "Are you," I paused my words, tried to hold myself together. "Are you saying—" *Am I being fired right now?*

"No, no. I mean, it's not working out with Nolan."

"Oh." I raised my arm up and did a fist pump. *Yesssss.* You see, the universe takes care of you if you just gave it some time and trust.

"There's no compassion, people aren't relating to him like they did to you. We need you back. In that position. I can offer you a bonus, stock, plus a fifty percent increase in base pay."

"I'm ..." I swallowed hard, tried to stop myself from saying what I was about to blurt out, even if my brain told me to slow down and think harder. "I'm not ready to go back."

"What?"

"I need more time."

"Like how long?" he asked, his tone timid. For the first time in a long time, I felt in control. The thing is, it did nothing for me.

I wanted to ask for four more months; that would give me time to get the coffee shop on track, get back home, make changes in my life, downsize, simplify, and then get to the starting line of the rat race once again. But who asks for almost a half a year off?

A long pause. It felt like a minute when it must have only been a few seconds. I said nothing. He said nothing. And then his voice came back over the line. "Sorry, I was working out some numbers. Fifty percent on your base plus five percent bonus for every million plus stock. Start date, February 1st. That gives you four more weeks."

It was my turn then. My turn to take it or walk away.

Was I stupid? That would put my annual salary in the seven figures.

I wanted him to sweat a little. *In every negotiation, it's always good to kick the can down the road, as he liked to say.* I turned back around, and that tiny figure was still there, looking up at me. My phone vibrated with a text message, but I couldn't retrieve it just yet.

"Andrea, are you still there? You know what? Let's make the start date May 1st. That's four months, which will give us time to exit Nolan."

"Yes, yes. That all sounds good," I replied. "I'll take it. But you'll need to send me the offer in writing tomorrow via email and courier."

"But do I have your verbal on this?"

I was surprised he really needed my reassurance. "Yes, you do. Thanks, Matt. I have to go."

"Of course, of course," he answered. "But, Andie?"

"Yes, Matt?"

"I'm sorry. It was a mistake and I regret putting you through that."

I had no interest in hearing any more of what he had to say. I pressed END and swiped up to check my messages. There was one from my mom and one from Api, both wishing me a Happy New Year.

The third one was a missed call from an unknown number. I knew the New York area code too well. But there was no message.

— 16 —

That Kind of Kiss

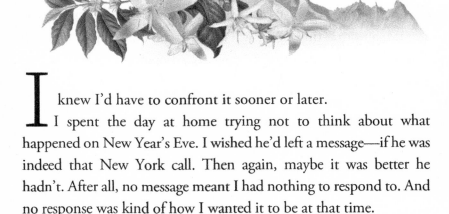

I knew I'd have to confront it sooner or later.

I spent the day at home trying not to think about what happened on New Year's Eve. I wished he'd left a message—if he was indeed that New York call. Then again, maybe it was better he hadn't. After all, no message meant I had nothing to respond to. And no response was kind of how I wanted it to be at that time.

Yesterday, while I was busy mapping out my business plan, visual flashes of our kiss would suddenly flood my head. I mean, I hadn't kissed anyone since Nick.

Nick was an emotional kisser—he was one of those guys who kissed with so much feeling. One of those guys who handed you his heart every time he kissed you. The thing is, I never really recognized it until I started to miss him. And his kisses. It had taken me about one week to break down in a hotel room in Tokyo—when I realized no one would ever kiss me like that again.

Pause and rewind to the other night, when that kiss was familiar and new at the same time. It was new because he was virtually a stranger to me, but familiar because he kissed me exactly the way I wanted to be kissed.

And therein lay the problem. It was the Josh Lucas and Reese Witherspoon *Sweet Home Alabama* kind of kiss, complete with the strobe lights totally replicating the flashes of lightning slicing through the sand.

I knew when he pulled away I was making a huge mistake. Who in their right mind would even entertain a relationship or even a one-night stand, when I didn't even know how I'd gotten here and where I was going?

So that's when I ran.

While everyone else in the world was delighting in the newness and hope that each New Year brings, I was pushing my way through the jubilation and running away from the implications of that kiss. I didn't see him come after me—maybe he expected the drama. I knew nothing about him at all and yet, it felt like I'd known him forever.

Maele and Lani were sitting on one of the high tops, bags on the floor next to them. Their conversation turned into hushed whispers, with eyes shifting side to side as soon as I appeared through the kitchen door. Lani turned to me with a huge grin.

"Morning," I greeted, avoiding her eyes. "I left my stuff in the car."

I grabbed the key from the drawer underneath the register, expecting to lock up before we left. When neither of them stirred, I made my way to the corner of the room to start unwinding the

Christmas lights. The heat of their stares was on me, absorbing my every move. They watched and observed while I straightened the coffee cups, sat cross-legged on the floor, and unplugged the extension cord from its socket.

"So?" asked Maele, gesturing with her hands, two palms facing up.

"How long does it take to get there?" I asked, looking up at them. "We'd better head out."

"Not 'til you tell us what happened the other night," Lani teased in a singsong voice. "Are we going to have to beat it out of you?"

"What night?"

"Andie," Lani and Maele screeched.

Just thinking about him made me smile. "I guess you saw that, huh?"

"It was in the middle of the room. We saw it," Lani said, clapping, squinting her eyes, and showing her teeth. "And it was."

"It was... eeeeek." More shrieking from Maele. "So romantic."

I couldn't help it. My eyes crinkled to the point I couldn't see. It brought back that rare feeling I had when I'd met Nick, before I'd allowed my head to overtake my heart. There was some kind of magic in those early days. The harsh reality is that love shouldn't change who you are. It should make you better, enhance you, allow you to soar, to fly.

"One cup and we'll go. Promise," Lani pleaded, handing me a cup of my favorite, Cortado.

I took a sip of the perfect mix. She made it just right with equal parts espresso and hot milk but knew to add three pumps of brown sugar as well. I remained seated a few feet away from them.

"Gosh, how romantic is that?" Maele gushed. "Kissing a stranger on New Year's Eve."

"Well, he kind of wasn't a stranger," I said.

Both women responded with furrowed brows, confused.

"I met him on Christmas Eve. He walked in here looking for Api."

Lani piped in, "He did look familiar."

"Do you know him?" I asked. The old boyfriend theory.

"It was dark," Maele answered. "Didn't really recognize him. But I did see him earlier when he walked into the store. He was looking for someone, wove in and out of the crowd. Now of course, I know it was you." She giggled. "I noticed him because he turned heads and a handful of women were ogling. But he left shortly after. Went out the back door."

"Tell us what happened on Christmas Eve," Lani exclaimed.

"Nothing, really. He came in. We had a cup of coffee and made small talk."

"Oh."

I was being interrogated by a girl band. Their reactions and comments all in unison. I decided it was the best time to ask the Spice Girls.

"You think it's an old boyfriend of Api or something?"

"Hmmm. Did he look mad?" Maele quipped. "Kidding," she followed up as Lani rolled her eyes.

"Api only introduced us to two guys before James. And I know they moved back to the mainland. So, quite unlikely."

The quite wasn't highly reassuring. There was still a chance. I started an inner monologue about how dumb it was of me to even care. I had other things to focus on.

"We saw you leave shortly after. Were you okay?"

I didn't even know who asked this question. I didn't mind it. These two women had provided me with security over the past few weeks. I knew they looked out for me; knew I could let down my guard a little bit.

"Yeah, it was quite silly, actually. I just left after that kiss. I didn't expect anything like it, and I don't think this is what I should be doing while I'm here."

"Why not?" This time it was Lani. The older, more grounded one.

I was sure she didn't know about my past.

"Because these things need to happen when I'm prepared for them. Right now, we need to get up and leave for the farm," I said, smiling.

"Will you see him again, Andie?" Maele asked, looking straight at me.

"I don't know, Baby Spice."

"What?" she asked, confused.

"Nothing. Seriously, though, that's really not my goal at the moment."

The wiser one came in for the kill. "Things happen when you least expect them to. Life never moves in a straight line. If it did, we would never have met."

I nodded.

"You never told us how you ended up here," Maele added.

"Well," I said, getting up from the floor and crumpling up my paper cup to signal the end of this conversation. "I had reached the end of my line, and I just thought this would be a good place to start."

"It is indeed," said Lani, "a good place to start."

17

What Plantation!

The drive to Waialua from Ala Moana took all of one hour, first on the highway and then a narrowing course through a single-lane road walled in by hills and dipping into the valley. Large tracts of farmland, some lush and green and some rich in crop and soil, alternated in equal parts throughout the journey. Thirty minutes in, there was a marked change in elevation, the winding road leading us away from the coastal town, higher and higher up Mt. Ka'ala. When we reached our destination, we turned right into an unpaved dirt road, billows of dust settling on every surface of my Jeep.

We stopped at a heavy wooden gate, supported by fences stretched out on both sides to a distance I could no longer see. The place looked more like a cowboy ranch—structures unrefined and crudely built, dilapidated log piles held together by wire and rope.

"Wow, how big is this place?" I asked, eyes wide with wonder, the calculator in my brain on overdrive.

"Over three hundred acres."

An elderly man with a great big smile trudged toward us and with all his strength, slowly pushed the gate open. Lani motioned for me to drive through until we reached a battered, old structure standing in the middle of a lot cobbled together by cement and brick.

I know people who know people. We can restore this with the original wood.

I laughed to myself when I realized this had been my first thought. An old sign, lettered in faded blue and white, hung over the rafters, swinging back and forth with the wind. The screen door, left ajar by a misaligned doorjamb, dipped lopsidedly to the left.

"Welcome," Lani said, taking my hand and leading me to the door.

An older gentleman stood proudly at the entrance, chest out, hands on hips, and then extended his hand as I walked in.

"Andie, this is my husband, Duke. He's also the caretaker and foreman for the plantation."

"Welcome to the Flores family plantation, Miss Andie."

"Duke," I said, placing a hand over his as I shook it. His name suited him. There was a quiet strength about him. Noble. Like a duke.

Unlike the store on Wai'alae Beach, it was evident this place had suffered from neglect. The foundation itself had integrity— thick wooden planks that held up through the years, painted and peeled and painted again. The floors creaked as I made my way around. Even in broad daylight, it was dark and musty. Thick oak shelves lined up in the middle of the store held a hodgepodge of souvenirs—some in baskets, some in Tupperware. Plastic leis, puka shells, leather bracelets. But what caught my eye was a colorful array of coffee bags that lined a glass counter by the door. Yellow, orange, pink, and blue—dark, medium, light, and cocoa. The aroma of coffee beans filled my nostrils as I moved closer. Unfortunately, I also let out a sneeze from the dust that lined the counter.

"It looks quite dirty, I know. But no one really comes in here. During the tours, we leave the things outside for people to purchase," Duke pointed out.

"Why is that?"

"Oh, I don't know. We haven't been able to renovate after Api's father fell ill."

I nodded before attempting to lighten things up. The place alone reeked of loneliness and loss. No wonder Api didn't like coming here.

Duke read my mind. "Mrs. Flores has not been here either."

I rubbed both hands together, trying to look as excited as I could. "I'm ready for our tour."

Just then, Maele walked in. For the first time since I'd met her, I noticed how alluring she was. Her untied hair fell softly on her shoulders. She had light makeup on, her round brown eyes accented by her thick black eyelashes, her full lips shined and glossed. On her neck hung a tiny blue diamond set on a silver chain. It looked so delicate, just like the way I saw her. She held hands with a boy on her left and a preteen girl on her right.

"These are Lani's children," she said. "Milani is fourteen and Keoki is eight."

Their proud mother stood behind Duke.

"Did you know that Mae is my brother's daughter? He works at the plantation as well."

"Your children are beautiful. What a beautiful family." I

touched Keoki's shoulder affectionately.

"Thank you," Lani answered.

"Shall we?" Duke asked, gesturing us toward the door. "Wait for me at the entrance. I will pick you up in the truck."

"These were former sugarcane lands," Duke said, as we drove down a dirt road toward the coffee fields. His face, aged and weathered, had the most remarkable lines, each layered with its own story. The color of his skin matched that of his floppy straw hat, hands on the steering wheel thick, strong, and calloused.

We bounced around in a red 1950 Chevy truck, over a wooden bridge and into a thicket of trees that crowded in as we neared the plantation. He parked the truck, motioned for me to wait, then opened my door, and offered me his hand. I took it, hopped down from the elevated cab and landed on thick, red soil. On either side of us stood rows of trees, grouped together, maybe one hundred at a time. Before us and behind us were mountain ranges, majestic and breathtaking.

"We seem to be on a plateau?" I asked, trying to keep up with Duke, who was now a few feet ahead of me. He moved from tree to tree, running his hand along the branches, as if in greeting.

"Yes, if you look this way." He turned directly toward the trees, finding a sliver of space that opened up into the horizon. "We are locked in between the Waianae and Ko'olau mountains about eight hundred feet above sea level."

We walked in silence between the trees.

"The elevation makes for good drainage," he continued. "That's why these plantations normally thrive in the mountains, Kona, most especially. Volcanic soil and cool seasons help during the dormant period."

"Now until spring?"

"Yes," he answered. "The buds will open in—"

"Time for the rain. And harvest season starts in September?"

"Exactly." He smiled. "You've done your research. It's refreshing. Although the way the girls described you, I expected no less."

"Ugh." I exclaimed, smiling. "That's not good."

We walked a little farther, Duke leaning down every so often to pull out a branch or a weed or piece of stone on the ground, tossing them into plastic bins that lined the road. To my surprise, he stopped to turn to me. "We need help, Andie. And I'm hoping it will be you. Mr. Flores was just getting started in modernizing our operations."

"How do you mean?"

"He went into a partnership with a company called Apex. They were going to help supply funding to buy harvesting machines."

"Currently, you're still in manual mode?"

"We have one piece of equipment. But the difference is very obvious. Our workers can pick about two hundred and fifty pounds of berries a day. With machines, we can do about twenty-five thousand pounds. We can't harvest fast enough, as we only have a limited time."

I nodded, deep in thought. It must have been hard for Api's

dad to allow investors into the family business.

"How many workers are there now?" I asked, not wanting to make any assurances. I was there to listen, to learn. I was the girl with no plan—how could I provide anything at that point?

"Let me show you," he said, walking back to our pug-nosed truck. We climbed in and drove back toward the main entrance. Duke turned left instead of right and stopped in the middle of a group of tiny homes. Each was identical to the next, about twenty-five in a neat row, wooden porches, little front yards, iron thatched roofs.

"There are forty of us right now. Our families have lived here for over thirty years. When Apex bought half of the company, they wanted to tear these homes down to make room for more trees. Mr. Flores wrote it as part of their agreement that we would remain untouched. He also provided for college funds for our children. I'm afraid that with his passing"—he paused and looked at me, his eyes drooping down—"this will all change."

The reality of a business, its ebbs and flows, its culture, its owners, its ability to survive through the years—I knew all too well. I also knew all too well how heartless and cruel business and the bottom line could be. Harsh, as I remembered how even I had stuck to my guns on so many occasions, making decisions that would benefit big business. But that callousness catches up with you, becomes a natural part of you if you let it. Nick had helped me to realize that. In the past few years, I had tried to be someone who looked out for the people no one else would, people who could use a hand up, people exactly like these people. And in that moment, I made a choice to do all I could to take care of Duke and his family.

"I heard there was a drought a few years ago. You survived that. You'll survive this, Duke. I just know it."

18

That Playlist

I'd been here before. These obsessions with business ventures, helping people out, turning their dreams into reality. The project that did me in had been similar to this. A rideshare app, a monthly fashion subscription, a collaboration between gamers and their favorite sneaker brands. Whatever it was, it was always an all-consuming venture that didn't allow me to have a proper life.

My choice. All my choice.

Nobody made me do it. I did it all on my own.

I made it home from the plantation and spent the evening waffling between wanting to swoop in and save the Flores legacy and knowing I couldn't save the world.

I guess it was the quiet that made all that noise in your head. I hadn't really had that in the last four years. In the silence of that night, and for the first time in two years, I felt regret. And I cried for the missed opportunities of friendship and of love, because I'd had them right within my reach, and I willingly sacrificed them.

I let emotion overtake me for that first part.

Then I sat up on the couch and made a plan.

The first visit to the plantation filled me with so many options and ideas. I'd decided to immerse myself in a business that was totally unfamiliar to me. No amount of graphs or charts could mitigate the fact that weather, temperature, seasons, and people were all the moving pieces with a stake in this game.

People. That's what got me the most. Digging into this, figuring out what worked and what didn't, meant delving into the future of the people who had lived their lives on that farm for many years. Generations had been made in that place.

I had four months to make this work.

I paused for a minute to witness the sunrise over Waikiki Beach. As the orange sun spread its rays over the island, the warm breeze wrapped me in its embrace, assuring me everything happened for a reason. With outstretched arms, I breathed in the kaleidoscope of colors that reflected the sky, the sun, the sea. For the first time, I knew what I wanted. I wanted to live my life in color.

With that, I strapped on my running pouch, slipped on my shoes, cranked the music up, and headed out the door.

"Good morning, AJ," I greeted, waiting for him to begin his daily weather forecast.

I had only started going for runs a few days ago, but AJ would jump out of his seat with a daily forecast. "Eighties and sunny, Miss Matthews."

Nothing today, except extreme eye contact with his lips pointing to the left.

"Everything okay?" I stopped in front of him, pulling out my earbuds.

No word, just an intense stare with a sideways puckering of

his lips, directing me to the side of the lobby. In my mom's culture, people pointed with their lips instead of their fingers.

"Waiting," AJ whispered.

There he sat. On the pea pod shaped metal bench, looking up as I approached.

"Hey, Warren."

"Hi," he answered, jumping to his feet.

"How can I help you?" I asked, trying to mask my surprise, his presence quite unsettling, considering I had not a single shred of makeup and hair frizzed up to the nth degree.

"I was here the other day and AJ said you went for a run. I decided seeing you in person was better than trying to call you again."

"That was you, the New York number," I said, confirming what I already knew.

"That was me." He hesitated, taking a deep breath. "I thought I'd ask to join you today, if that's okay."

"Where do you normally go?" I responded. "I don't really do anything, just a loop around the trail leading to Diamond Head and back, about five miles."

He laughed. "That isn't nothing. I'm cool with that if you don't mind some company."

I shrugged. "And I normally crank up my music."

"Understood," he said with a nod.

I kept up with him. Or at least he made me think I did. I suspected he may have shortened his strides a little bit, because there we were, running the trail together in perfect cadence. At one point, I looked over to find him jamming to his own tunes, lips moving, eyes closed as if relishing the words.

"Looks like you have a great playlist." We slowed to a walk at the five-mile mark. A large garden filled with tropical flowers flanked both sides of Api's condo. Birds of paradise, plumerias, and gardenias crowded every single square inch of the ground. I had never seen such an abundance of colors.

"Oh." He laughed, looking embarrassed, squinting from the glare of the sun. "It's a compilation of cover songs by some local bands. I can share it with you if you'd like."

"Sure, thanks."

"Andie? Would you like to sit out for a while before heading back? I can run inside and get us some water." He pointed toward the wicker benches scattered across the way.

He ran inside before I could respond. I glanced at my watch. It was almost eight in the morning. The shop would be open by now and I didn't want to text Maele about running late. Being late was a huge no-no for me, especially when I was the one who had asked for an earlier start time.

But then again, no woman in her right mind would resist an invitation to sit and have a bottle of water with the stranger she kissed on New Year's Eve.

He was back, two plastic bottles in hand.

"Andie, about the other night," he started, facing me directly as he handed me a bottle. "I can't explain my action, and I want to apologize for—"

"Oh." I reacted quickly, swatting my left hand in the air. "Nothing to worry about. It was the moment, you know? We were caught up in it."

"I didn't want you to think—"

"I haven't thought about it."

"You haven't?" He took a big swig of water, pausing and then downing the whole bottle.

"Nope. Too much going on right now," I explained. "You know, the business."

"The event the other night was a success. Are you sure you're not in the event planning field?"

"I've never planned an event before." *Except maybe my wedding.* I had mastered the art of catching myself when thoughts or words brought me back to the past. "But thank you."

He smiled. "No, seriously, maybe that's all you need. A good marketing plan."

"I think it's more than that. I'm told the farm needs more than just a good word of mouth. There's some modernization that needs to take place."

"I thought it was partly owned by Apex?" he asked. "Wouldn't they make the investments?"

I did a double take. Shot him a look of surprise. "How do you know so much about this?" I asked.

"Everyone knows that. It's common knowledge."

"I suppose," I said. "Can I ask you a really weird question? Not for anything, but are you one of Api's exes?" I felt weird when I uttered those words and my belly tightened. I was nervous.

"What?" he asked, raising his tone a notch. "No. No. Of course not. Why would you think that?"

"Well, showing up on Christmas Eve looking for her … That was weird timing."

"Okay, I can explain that. I'd been trying to reach her for a few weeks. I was in the neighborhood visiting my … I mean for a personal thing, and just on impulse decided to stop by her store."

He grinned at me, looking smug, raising both eyebrows in jest. "You see, there is a logical explanation."

"Why have you been trying to reach her?"

"It's purely business. Let's wait for Api to get back. It's not a big issue, really."

My phone buzzed. It was a text from Maele, worried that I hadn't arrived at the store. "Oh, no," I said, typing a message back. "The girls are worried about me. I'd better get going. They need me at the store." I stood and he did the same. "Thanks for the company and the water."

"Of course. It was nice to see you."

"I'll see you around. Thanks, Warren." I turned away and started to walk toward the building lobby.

"Andie?"

I paused, twisting my neck in his direction.

"It wasn't just in the moment."

He registered the surprise on my face—mouth agape, stumped. So, he tried again, fumbling with the right words, hands weighing down his pockets. "For me, I mean. It wasn't. For me."

— 19 —

Family

I don't usually take stock in what people say out of impulse. In a high-stress environment, there are times when people behave like boiling cauldrons, constantly exploding with the right amount of heat and pressure.

Warren was definitely being impulsive.

Most importantly, I'd come to Hawaii to find myself. Not to have someone find me. Then again, that's being presumptuous. He probably just wanted to be friends. And since I can count my friends with half of one hand, I could really use another one in this foreign place.

"Andie? Did you say something?" Maele lightly nudged my elbow, while her whole family had their eyes trained on me.

"Sorry?"

"I thought I heard you say something—did you want more rice?" she asked, shaking her head at her family, urging them to stop staring.

There were ten of us sitting in Lani's home, in a simple kitchen adorned with nothing but necessities. Pots and pans overflowed the edges of the narrow Formica counters and jars filled with food were piled next to the stove. The kitchen table, a long picnic table with benches on both sides, was heavy and sturdy, made of thick unpolished wood.

Warmth manifests itself more in simplicity. No trappings to absorb it, no distractions to take you away from the love.

Surrounding me were some new friends I'd made—Duke, Lani, their two children, Maele and her parents, Haku and Lolana, and the farm's assistant foreman, Kukane and his wife, Waiola. I'd spent the day at the farm, walking around with Duke and getting to meet the families who had built their homes within the property.

"Oh, no, I was saying how delicious the SPAM was with the sticky rice."

"Did you try the kalua pork?" Duke asked, passing me the plate of roasted pig.

"Oh gosh, yes, it's delicious. My father would have loved this dinner. He loves lechon, which is more or less the same as this in my mother's country."

"Yes, of course, that makes sense," answered Duke. "We have a heavy Filipino population here in Hawaii. Your people were recruited to work in the sugarcane plantations here as far back as 1906—that's how Mr. Flores came to be here. This is why their food is a large part of our culture."

I nodded, taking another serving of poi. This creamy, purple-colored pudding made out of taro root was a great palate cleanser—not too sweet, a little nutty, and with a pleasing smell.

"What did you think about your day on the farm, Andie?" asked Lani. "I know you've been doing so much research."

"Well, first of all, the real thing is better than all the books I've read," I said with a laugh. To begin with, coffee trees looked more like coffee shrubs. Their leaves were so much bigger in real life—heavy and waxy, droopy almost. The stems were skinny, like bamboo stalks, and the plants grew in pairs. I'd also learned from Duke and Kukane that although the pods bore seeds in pairs, sometimes when a plant was less fertile, only one seed—called a peaberry—was produced.

"I'm afraid we tired you out a little bit." Duke laughed and then turned to his wife. "We kept Andie on the field with us while we checked on the trees. There's not much to do during this hibernation period. The blooms don't come until March. And then the party starts."

"Well, then let's not talk about work anymore," said Maele. "What was the best part of your day, Andie?"

"Having dinner here, with all of you," I answered, making eye contact with everyone as they smiled back. "It means so much for me to be here."

"Our humble home is yours—you are Api's family—you are our family," Lani said. The rest of the guests nodded. She stood and retrieved something from the refrigerator. "Have some Haupia. In case you don't know what it is, it's only made of coconut and sugar."

"Oh. I'm obsessed with coconut."

Everyone laughed, but my attention was interrupted by the ringing of my phone. I shut the ringer off, although not before I saw who was calling. I knew who it was by then. It made me smile.

"You just lit up," Maele whispered. "Is it him?"

"No, no," I whispered back. "It's my mom. I'll call her later."

"Andie, how was it, growing up in Chicago?" Lolana, Maele's mother, asked. "I don't know how anyone could last in that cold."

"It's not so bad, really," I answered. "You go from one heated place to another. There's about four weeks of extreme cold, but other than that." I paused, closing my eyes to experience that memory. "I actually love the season. It reminds me of hot cocoa, marshmallows, snowflakes."

"Api used to be so excited about buying coats and boots," Maele piped in.

"That too."

"Are you an only child?" Waiola asked, handing me a plate of cheesecake bars. These guys were determined to resurrect my repressed sweet tooth. "Try this. You can really taste the crushed pineapple. It's from our backyard."

Everyone laughed. There was lighthearted banter about how lucky they were to have the rich plantation soil where they grew a variety of fruits and vegetables.

"Andie has an older brother named Steven," Maele began. "Right, Andie? Is he much older?"

"He's four years older than me. He's a doctor, like my father, and working in Barcelona as an oncologist. Because of our age difference, it felt like I was an only child after middle school. But he's an amazing person and the best brother I can ask for. He's been with me through—" There I was rambling once again. I thought I'd stop while these people still liked me. What I'd learned in the past year was that sometimes it's better to keep things to yourself, better to stay quiet and have people think you're wise, than open your mouth and prove you're a fool.

Their silence urged me on to continue. No one said a word—they were waiting. I guess they were trying to get to know me, and I was still holding back. "Through stuff. You know. All the stuff we all go through."

"Yes, yes," answered Duke. "I'm not sure how much you knew about Mr. Flores, Api's dad, but he was very fond of you, Andie. Every time Api said she'd be going to Chicago to see you, he would say—'if it's Andie, that's okay. No one else. You are not traveling to Chicago for anyone else.'"

"He would fly us to New York for long weekends," I said, remembering him fondly. "His favorite place to eat was Tavern on the Green. And he was obsessed about that show on Broadway?"

I knew Duke would know, because Api used to tell him to stop talking about it so much.

"*Cabaret.*" Duke clapped, pleased with himself. "He always said, 'Duke, come to New York and we'll have a ball watching *Cabaret.*'" He lowered his eyes. "I miss that man."

Lani laid her hand on his. "We all do."

Duke cleared his throat. "Anyway," he said, lifting his glass. "Let's toast to our new family member, Andie. Welcome, Andie."

"*Ke aloha,*" the group raised their glasses in response.

"*Ke aloha,*" I answered, thinking about all there was to celebrate about life. A tightness in my chest complemented the wave of guilt that washed over me. I had missed so much in the past few years. Most importantly, I felt like I played the villain in everyone's life—first Nick's and now Api's. I hadn't been there for her when her father died.

"To good times," Lani followed up. "There is so much more to come, I know it. Andie is our gift from Mr. Flores. She will make everything all right."

20

Let's Make a Deal

"Andie?" Api asked, bringing the phone so close to her face that her left eye and her nose were the only things I could see. The apprehension in her voice was clear. "All okay?"

There I sat, in my favorite place, on the boulder behind the coffee shop. I swear, sometimes I really believed I could see the world from there. There was no wind at all, no breeze rustling through the tall grass. But the water was a different story. The waves rolled toward the shore, despite the low tide. They spun around in tight, never-ending loops.

"Yes, yes," I said, cradling the phone in one hand, knees up with one arm holding them in place. "Had dinner with Duke and his family and I just missed you, that's all. Why are you holding the phone so close to your face? I want to see you."

She wore a white turtleneck and a thick furry coat. It was winter, after all. "Oh. How are they? To be honest, I hadn't been able to see them after—"

"I know," I interjected. "I know." I stared blankly ahead of me, visions of her dad and our families during happier, more carefree times. "We talked about New York, remember those trips?"

Api made a failed attempt to laugh, a throaty croak. I could feel her pain through that sound, saw her downcast eyes and her wan smile. "Yeah."

"Api, listen. I'm calling to say I'm sorry I wasn't there for you. I was so selfishly engrossed in my career and in figuring out my life with Nick, I totally left you alone. I'm so sorry." I choked on the words, fighting back tears.

Before I could finish my sentence, she gasped. "No, no, no. I don't feel that way." Her voice was thick with emotion. "You were going through so much too, and I don't fault you for it."

"Was James there for you? Did he make up for my absence?" I asked.

"He was there for me, yes. But he didn't make up for you. Because you fill my life in a different way, Andie. And you always will. I might not have had much of you at that time, but you're here now. Friends make up for the different parts of who you are. Everyone serves a purpose, fills a gap. One person isn't enough to fill your life."

"Gosh, who would have thought you'd become so philosophical?" I teased, still swiping my teary face.

"Loss does that to you."

I nodded, and she smiled back. For a while, it felt right to just let the silence overtake us. She kept her eyes on me and I kept mine on her. No words were necessary.

"I took the day off today."

"Woot, woot," she yelped, both hands in the air. She had the phone pointed toward the sky. "What are you going to do?"

"I think I should check out the beach."

"Great plan. You know the one across from the condo is the best one, right?" Api asked, her face in full view, grin as wide as can be.

"So I've been told."

"Well, tell me all about it tomorrow. You deserve this break. Go for it. Have fun, okay? No more of these sad calls."

"I love you, Api."

"I love you too, Andie. Go find that hot guy on the beach and report back to me."

There he was. The hot guy. On the beach.

Warren stood with his back to me, light blue surf shorts with a faded yellow line going down the side. His hair had grown out since I'd first met him a few weeks ago, and he'd had a Yankees cap when we went for a run. Without it, natural curls cascaded over his ears and the back of his neck. In front of him were four rather friendly women tossing their hair and batting their eyelashes. Between the women were young children, boys and girls, who couldn't be more than ten years old. Two boys started chasing each other in circles. Amidst the commotion, he turned around and caught me watching him.

Awkward.

"Hey," he greeted with a wave before taking wide strides toward me.

I ran down the sandy hill to meet him halfway. "Hi."

"Thanks for coming," he said, raking his hand over his hair before dropping his arms to his sides.

"Sorry I wasn't able to call you back. I left the plantation quite late and reception wasn't the best."

"That's okay. I'm just happy you thought of calling me back," he said with a chuckle. An excited shriek called his attention. By the time we looked over, two of the mothers were holding their boys back, while another mother was busy squeezing out the water from a little girl's braids. "Listen. I'm almost done with my lesson. Would you mind if I just finished up? I'll come get you here in fifteen minutes."

I watched him conclude the lesson, asking five children to hop on their surfboards and hop off immediately after. They repeated this step over and over again. After they had mastered the hopping off method, he made them lie on their bellies and push up on their hands in a downward dog position. Ten times, they repeated this, each child had his or her own interpretation, leaping, skipping, spinning around in jest. Warren laughed each time, gently coaxing them to pay attention.

"Sorry about that," he said breathlessly.

I must have tuned out for a bit, because he paused, as if waiting for me to snap back to attention.

"My brother, Adam, asked me to fill in for the next few weeks while he's in LA working on a script."

"He's a screenwriter?"

"Aspiring." We made it to the bottom of the hill, a few feet from the tide, still low but slowly creeping in. "He just turned twenty-one and is so sure he can conquer the world."

"Didn't we all at that age?" I answered.

He turned to me and smiled before stooping to pick up his surfboard. It was larger than I thought it would be, from the ones I've seen in movies, I mean. When my dad was starting his practice, we would drive from Disney to Cocoa Beach, stay at the Hilton for a few days before heading back to Chicago. I had everything from Ron Jon's Surf Shop: skimmers, surfboards, boogie boards. They sure weren't as serious looking as this one.

A blond-haired boy approached and tugged on Warren's shorts. He must have been about five years old.

"But we didn't even go in the water, Mr. Warren," he said, eyes beginning to water. His mother took off after him.

"I know, Chase. This was our first lesson. I have to make sure you can stand straight on the board and keep your balance so when you're in the water next time, you'll do great."

"When is that?" Chase asked, stepping away when his mother tried to grab his hand.

"Tomorrow."

Chase looked up and smiled with delight.

"I'm so sorry, Warren," said the mother, who had now taken hold of his hand. Chase seemed more mellow now.

"No problem, Annie. We'll see you guys tomorrow."

"Hey, Warren," Annie said, motioning for him to step away from me. He didn't move, but I backed away to give him space. "We still on for drinks tomorrow night?" she asked shyly.

"Absolutely, it'll be nice to catch up with you."

Warren smiled at the mother and then rolled his eyes at me before nudging my elbow and leading me in the opposite direction. "She and I went to elementary school together. I've known her for a long time. She's going through a pretty nasty divorce."

We walked in silence, one arm around his board, our footprints marking the sand, until he stopped at a point a few feet away from the high tide waterline. "Would you mind waiting here for a minute? I have to go to the car really quick."

When he returned, he laid a red and green blanket on the sand and held up two mugs of coffee and a brown paper bag. "Breakfast," he offered. "Hope the coffee isn't too cold—I asked a friend to drop it off and leave it in my car about fifteen minutes ago. I also brought you some malasadas. Have you had them?"

"No, I don't think so. What are they?"

He took one out of the bag, a round fried donut ball.

"Yum, looks awesome," I said, taking it from him.

We sat side by side on the blanket, legs outstretched for him, crossed for me. It was breezier by the water. The hum of the wind, the flapping sails, the lull of the tide rushing in and out—unfamiliar sounds that relaxed my senses. For the first time in a long time, my head was quiet. And the malasada? It was the best I'd had so far—chewier than a donut—somewhere in between a bagel and a pastry. I knew I had to cut back, but raw sugar and cinnamon? Anytime.

"Good, huh?" Warren said in between bites.

"Delicious."

"A Brazilian guy named Emerson makes them and sells them out of the back of his truck."

"Oh, they are so good." They really were a perfect breakfast treat. "Do you think Emmerson would let me sell these out of the coffee shop? I'm looking for ways to add some bites to the menu and these would be perfect."

"I'm sure he'd count that as a blessing, yes. I'll ask him."

I took a sip of the coffee. "Oh, nice. Island Coffee Company."

"Nothing but." He laughed.

"It's the best, actually." Another sip and my mind went back to what we were talking about before breakfast. "So, your brother, he goes to school on the mainland?"

"NYU." His eyes became the ocean. Bright, light blue. "But he decided to take a sabbatical," he said, using air quotes. "Now, he's home for the semester. A friend called him to help pitch a screenplay in LA, so he's flown there for two weeks. How about you? Do you have siblings?"

"An older brother. He's a doctor practicing in Barcelona."

"You close?" he asked. By now the malasadas were gone and the atmosphere was light. There was a haze of clouds and sun floating lazily across the sky. He was leaning on his elbows; I was upright with my arms around my knees.

"Quite."

"And your parents?" he asked, taking another sip of coffee. "You see them often?"

"I try to. Life has honestly been nuts for the last four years, so our visits have been less frequent lately. But they did come to see me before I came here," I said, halting my words at exactly the right time. No point in sharing too much. "They're semi-retired in Florida. And I say *semi* because I don't think my dad will ever stop working."

He exhaled loudly. "Same with my dad. My brother is my half brother, by the way. My dad remarried twenty years ago. My parents were divorced when I was in high school and I lived with my mom before and after I went to college. This thing with Adam, it's new. About five years."

It was sad to hear about his parents. Any divorce or loss was devastating. But I also understood how people are constantly evolving and eventually, time can leave one of them behind. That's what had happened, I thought, to Nick and me. I kept running at full speed and we didn't have the right kind of love to keep up with each other.

"Mom passed away five years ago," he continued. "We were close. She raised me. I connected with my dad after she died. My brother and I have a relationship now."

"I am so sorry for your loss." Those were the only words I could muster.

He shrugged and looked away.

"So, you've avoided telling me what you do." This time, he turned back to face me, playfully lifting his eyebrows as he tilted his head.

"So have you."

"Touché," he answered. "Except that seriously, I'm not into anything right now. I'm in between careers, trying to figure out what I want to do in the long term. In the short term, I work for my father. Long story, but it is what it is."

"I think I'm in the same boat," I said.

"Well, with what you pulled off on New Year's Eve"—he looked straight at me—"I bet you're in some kind of marketing career."

"Close," I said with a laugh.

Our conversation was light, happy. We talked about everything, really. How he spent his teenage years in a small apartment in Jersey with his mom. How the divorce settlement from his father had been generous enough that she had not had to start her life over. In her later years, she finally picked up on her passion and began sculpting and painting, showing her work at some of New York's top galleries. Before she died, Warren had made her dream come true. He had taken her to Paris where they'd rented a small apartment by the Louvre. There, she had been able to experience an artist's life, filled by what she loved most—him and the world's most beautiful works of art, in her words—before succumbing to breast cancer. He'd studied economics at Wharton and worked for one of the top consulting companies in the world.

We talked about team events and gatherings and all the consultant-type idiosyncrasies of our past jobs. You could tell he was focused and driven just by the experience he'd garnered by the time he'd turned thirty. Which still led me to the same question— something I didn't dare to ask just yet.

What was he doing in Hawaii, teaching little kids to surf and sitting in the sunshine with a woman he hardly knew—when there was a lot of conquering yet to accomplish?

"There you go again, in deep thought mode," he teased.

I looked over to him. "Nah, just feeling really relaxed."

"Have you decided how long you're going to be here, yet?"

"A few more weeks? Or months?" I questioned myself. How long would it take me to turn the plantation around?

"Well," he said, jumping to his feet, "in that case, I have a few more weeks, or months, to show you around this beautiful island. And with that ..." He picked up his board, laid it flat on the sand and began to rub wax on its back. "We should be getting on the water."

"Where are we going? I don't surf," I argued, quite weakly, shedding my T-shirt and shorts and tossing them on the sand. Wow, I hadn't worn a swimsuit in years. This one was black, a bikini that fit a little loosely because of the weight I'd lost last November. In a way, I didn't care what we decided to do. For the first time in a long time, I was willing to go with the flow.

Warren took my hand and led me into the water. It was warm and calm. Like us.

"We're not surfing. I want to show you something. We'll paddle out to that rock," he said, pointing to some sort of formation a few hundred feet from where we stood. He held the board firmly on the water, using his weight to keep it steady. I climbed on top of it, straddling it and finding it difficult to maintain my balance at first. Because he was much taller than me, he stepped over and got on the board with ease. We began to move farther from the shore.

"Would it be okay to put my legs up on the board?" I asked, nervous about having my legs dangling underwater.

"Sure," he answered from behind me. "You'll have more balance with your knees on the board. Don't worry, it will get a little deep but after a few feet, it will get shallow again. We'll be able to stand if we wanted to."

He was right. As we moved on, the water got deeper, but also so much clearer. An array of colors appeared below us—fish of all shapes and sizes and corals abounded. Warren pointed them out to me.

"They're reef fish; they feed on the reef that's right in front of us. Most of them are types of butterfly fish—there's a bluestripe. And there's a long nose. Oh, did you just see that puffer? One day we should snorkel out here, so you can see them up close."

I dipped my hands in the water but withdrew them immediately after. "Ugh, I hate the unknown. I always have this weird feeling that something else is under there."

"Always listen to that feeling when you're in the ocean," he said. "Most of the time, you're spot on."

I listened to him talk, turning around every now and then to smile at him. Then the water turned shallower as we approached the rock formation that towered above us.

"That is beautiful," I exclaimed. "Does it have a cave underneath it?"

"Yes, it actually does, but you have to be an experienced diver to be allowed to explore. They call them stacks. Or sea stacks. This one is actually a large rock that was shaped by wave erosion. You can see more of these in places like Thailand or Scotland or Canada."

"Hmmm. Yes, makes sense."

"You've been to all those places."

"Uh-huh," I answered comfortably. No humility needed. I felt so open, so free to just tell him who I was or what I'd accomplished in my life. But not yet. Not yet.

"Me too."

We laughed at the same time. He stopped paddling and allowed the board to gently bob up and down as we sat about a hundred feet away from the sea stack. I felt his hand touch my arm, gently at first and then holding it firmly while he pointed over my shoulder.

"Look," he whispered.

In front of us was a pod of dolphins, at least seven of them, playing in the shallow water, diving gracefully in and out. Their chirps and squeaks varied in pitch but were loud enough to fill the air. I sat motionless, mesmerized. I was awed. The way they glided beneath the water's surface, reappearing only to come up for air. The symphony of their movement, so in tune with one another, it almost seemed like they were carrying out a well-rehearsed dance.

"Warren. I've never seen anything like this before."

We sat still and watched, lost in the sound of the sloshing waves and the spectacle in front of us. Suddenly, two of them practically laid their noses on the board, startling me and causing me to lose my balance. The board dipped sharply to the side.

"It's okay," he whispered, pulling me close and encircling me with both arms until my back leaned on his chest, my skin warm against his. The dolphins splashed and squealed and played, spinning around close enough to rock our board. Warren paddled backward, ensuring we kept a safe distance. We sat in silence for about ten minutes more until one by one, they swam away.

Don't go. I thought. *Make him hold me for a little while longer.*

"I found them the other day and thought of you. Wanted you to see this."

"Will they stay? How long will they be here?"

"Each pod is different. Some migrate, some just stay in one territory. It's hard to tell whether these are the ones that I saw the other day. The reef makes for an abundance of food around here."

"What an experience. I've never been this close to anything

like that. Thank you for bringing me here."

"This is what I want, Andie. I don't know much about you. I know you're probably just passing through. But while you're here, I'm going to make sure that moments like this make it hard for you to forget me."

I smiled from ear to ear, excited about what I'd just witnessed and amazed at the comfort I felt with someone I hardly knew.

"In fact," he said, holding out his arms to make sure I didn't fall while I turned around to face him, legs crossed in applesauce. "I'd like to give you a moment like this every week, no questions asked. We don't have to explain anything to anyone, you don't have to tell me anything you don't want to about who you are or what you've done or didn't do. No past, just the present. We can offer each other a fresh start." His head moved closer, until my nose almost touched his. There was an undulating rhythm in the water. I rose up, he went down; he rose up, I went down. It only served to heighten the voltage that ran between his touch and my skin. His eyes turned dark and ominous. "And every weekend, until you leave, you're mine."

"Um, so weekends are really busy at the coffee shop," I said with a flirtatious grin, trying to resist his charm. That smile was getting to me. I couldn't tear my eyes away from his mouth.

"Not so fast, pretty lady. Fridays then. We go on a Moments Tour every Friday. Deal?" He offered me his hand. What did I have to lose?

"Deal."

21

The Lighthouse Keeper

W arren picked me up at 8 a.m. that first Friday. He told me to wear a one-piece bathing suit under my clothes because he wanted to show me something uniquely Hawaiian to start our grand "Moments Tour." I obliged with a stunning white one-piece and raised the ante by providing the beans and bites. He picked me up on a black Honda Elite scooter and held out two helmets. It maxed out at forty-five miles per hour, but it gave us a chance to see everything as we slowly cruised by.

"We're going to explore the island, every side of it, and I'll show you things nobody even knows about or ever has the time to see. First stop, the south side."

We zoomed over Diamond Head where he stopped to show me the white lighthouse with the red roof that hung off the side of the mountain, warning sailors that they could run ashore.

"It's run by the Coast Guard. They say there is a ghost that haunts the lighthouse. On certain nights, at exactly 3:03 in the morning, the light will begin to blink in Morse code, spelling out the name Angela. Rumor has it that when the lighthouse was first built, the lighthouse keeper had a wife named Angela, who was one day swimming in the water below."

We looked down to see the bottom of the sea floor reflecting white in the sunlight and creating a brilliant turquoise color.

Warren continued, "And, as he watched, he saw her being pulled out by a riptide. Despite running down the steep cliff as fast as he could to try to swim out and save her, it was too late. She was carried out to sea, never to be seen again. It happened at 3:03 in the afternoon, so every night at 3:03 in the morning, he would signal her name with the lighthouse light, hoping she would see it and be able to find her way back home. He blamed himself for not jumping off the cliff to save her. Sadly, a few years later, on the anniversary of her death, he took that leap and perished in the same ocean that swallowed his wife. That's why they say it's haunted."

"Oh goodness, that is so sad. What a terrible way to start your Memories Tour." I slapped his arm playfully and he overreacted, pretending like it hurt.

"The story goes, he loved her so much that when she was pulled out to sea, she took his heart with her. To me, this lighthouse reminds me of how achingly beautiful love can be. I want that kind of love, don't you?"

Before I could answer, he revved the throttle and away we went, down the backside of Diamond Head, through a tasteful neighborhood where he stopped the scooter again. He pointed to a brown house adorned with Asian accents in the roofline and trimmings. Its large, white double door was enclosed by tall windows on either side.

"This area is called Kahala and we are on Elepaio Street. This is the house my parents lived in when I was born. I grew up in this house."

It looked like a lovely place for a childhood. I couldn't see Warren's face, but the melancholy in his heart seeped out through the silence. We sat for a while, before he sped off again. Soon we were on a much busier street, looking at apartment buildings, and long stretches of busy beaches.

"This is East Honolulu. It's where a lot of the successful locals live, mostly."

We made our way up a hill that overlooked the most beautiful bay I had ever seen.

"Wow."

"That's Hanauma Bay. It has world-class snorkeling. If you are ever in the mood to swim with the fishes, you must go here."

"Is that on the Moments Tour?"

"It could be, but no, not this time. Just you wait. I've got something much better planned for you."

We rode in silence. My hands firmly gripped his waist—his core was tight and strong. My legs held on to his legs, our skin touching, sweaty; the hairs on his thighs tickling me. The Honda slowly crested the hilltop where we were hit with a warm wind and a blinding view of the sea. Suddenly the island became dry and almost desert like. A totally different terrain on this side of the hill. Further on, we made our way past a golf club and Warren pulled us up to a beach. There was a deafening crash as the waves pounded the shoreline.

"Welcome to Sandy Beach, otherwise known as Breakneck Beach, or affectionately as Sandy's. This was President Obama's favorite place to body surf, and it happens to be the first stop on our Moments Tour."

"I don't body surf though."

"Remember our agreement—no questions, no saying no."

"No saying no to things that won't kill you. You just said it was called Breakneck Beach, for crying out loud."

"Andie, trust me, I'm going to show you how to ride a wave with just your body and you will feel more freedom than you've ever felt in your life. Have you ever flown?"

"In a plane?" I asked.

"No, not in a plane. With just your body?"

"Of course not. Have you?" That was ludicrous.

"When I ride these waves, I have. It's that good."

He ran down to the waterline over the hot sand like a child, free from worry, with nothing but joy. It was joy I recognized from my childhood. I used to run like that and seeing him do it made me want to do that again.

"Wait for me!" I chased after him, shedding my shirt and shorts as I went.

"Now, on this beach is a seal named Lucy. If Lucy is in the water, then it's safe for us to swim. If Lucy is on the beach, then that means Calvin is in the water. Calvin is a bull shark that lives off this beach. He is not so nice when he's hungry, but don't worry about Calvin today. Lucy is nowhere to be seen."

Off went his shirt. Holy. Cow.

They don't make them like that in Chicago. His body was tanned, lean, and tight. He had muscles in his stomach I didn't know humans had, and his back and arms were firm and strong. Although I could see he was in the sun a lot, there were no tan lines. He wore yellow trunks with a little blue and orange rainbow that arched across his perfect bottom. He walked backward toward the water and waved me on to follow him. I did.

The water was cold but refreshing. The sound of the waves was even louder this close, and the light, misty spray of the break on my face frightened me. Warren took my hand and gave me some very easy instructions to follow. He led me to a place where the waves weren't as scary, and then we got in the water and I began to fly.

It was the most exhilarating experience I'd ever had in my life. I would turn my back to the ocean and wait for a wave to roll in, and when I felt the water draw back, I would get ready to swim as hard and fast as I could. As the wall of water rushed by, I would catch it, allowing it to pull me toward the shore, making me swim to the top of the wave as it broke into froth and foam. I was ten years old again and free from every worry I'd ever had.

The water washed everything away. The salt dried you out and healed you up at the same time. That didn't include the fun of it. My goodness, this was how a beach bum was born.

After two hours in the water, we were done. You'd have to be an Olympic athlete to stay in any longer. Even runners like me, who were in shape, couldn't sustain the energy after a while.

"It's almost three o'clock," Warren said, handing me a towel. "We've been gone all day. I should get you back."

I was hit with a wave of nostalgia; I didn't want our day to end. But I knew I had to pace it out. I was not here for a grand Moments Tour. I was here to clean up my mess and find myself. Alone.

We dried off and drove slowly back to my apartment as the sun began to dip into the western sea.

22

Dancing Queen

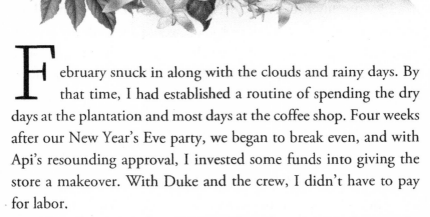

F ebruary snuck in along with the clouds and rainy days. By that time, I had established a routine of spending the dry days at the plantation and most days at the coffee shop. Four weeks after our New Year's Eve party, we began to break even, and with Api's resounding approval, I invested some funds into giving the store a makeover. With Duke and the crew, I didn't have to pay for labor.

The place turned unrecognizable—that wooden framework, old and dilapidated—was re-boarded and replaced by vinyl siding. We matched the roof in ocean blue from a local metal roof manufacturer. The best thing about it was it stood out among all the other structures. With the help of a billboard along Highway 72 and flyers Maele and her little helpers delivered to patrons on the beach, we began to thrive.

Our new name? Beans and Books. I okayed it with Api and she thought it "elevated" the coffee shop to literary proportions.

Valentine's Day was coming up and we planned to give away candy hearts and serve strawberry-flavored coffee. What better way to introduce a festive Chicago favorite to the locals?

It was late that night. Lani had left for the evening, while Maele and I stayed on to tally our weekly reports. I was busy sorting books on the built-in shelves we'd had installed. They formed a border around a reading nook filled with couches and ottomans, a round cocktail table with bonsai trees and a sprinkling of children's furniture. Mysteries and suspense books were aplenty, but romance books were the most popular ones. When I first started this, I made a mistake by allowing patrons to take one to read. Now, we did an exchange—one book out means another book in. There were duplicates in each genre—most authors I knew, some I didn't. I walked over to Maele while secretly admiring the sprucing up we'd done on the inside. Everything was painted white with blue accents; the counters had been upgraded to stone, the high tops changed to round dining tables with blue wooden tops and thick, white metal legs. Each chair shaped like a quarter moon formed a circle when stored together. Really cool and modern.

"Oh. My. Gosh. You won't believe this," she said, stooped down and hidden by the pile of receipts and twelve column worksheets. I was halfway there in convincing her to use the accounting software I purchased. A few more of those grueling nights of manual calculations would get her on board, I was certain. She held out her tally for me to see, causing me to move closer so I could read.

"Look what we did for the very first time."

"Stop it," I teased, my tone light. "Are you serious?"

"Yes. Look," said Maele, handing me the ledger. "If you take all the expenses against what we made this week, we're up three hundred dollars. We made money today."

"Wait. Let's see." I punched a few numbers on the adding

machine. Yes, adding machine. The antiquated gray box with number keys and a roll of tape attached to it. And she was right. We made our first profit.

"Yes." I raised my hand in the air and she met my fist bump.

"Let's call Api," Maele squeaked.

"It's three in the morning there. I say maybe we should wait."

"Okay. Let's celebrate."

"Yes, let's," I agreed. "Except you're only twenty so alcohol is out of the question." I sauntered over to the jukebox. Yes, we had one of those too. A full-sized edition complete with a digital touchscreen and Bluetooth. To be honest, it was on loan from the manufacturer—I promoted their product, they gave me free music. Too bad this one was orange and black. It didn't match the decor, but I figured when we made enough money, I could get one custom built just like it.

"What music shall we play?" I scrolled through the list.

"This one." Maele jumped in, placing her hand over mine and guiding me to Lizzo.

Music filled the store—hip-hop, dance music, one about feeling good as heck. I twirled around and started to dance. Arms in the air, fingers snapping, feet sliding across the floor.

"Andie," she said, swinging her hips to the beat. "Can I ask a question?"

"Not if you don't dance. One move per question." I kept going, in between tables and chairs.

She raised her hands upward and pumped her fist. The little blue diamond defying gravity as she spun. "Okay. That guy from New Year's, do you still talk to him? I know you probably haven't seen him. I mean, you're either here or at the farm so—"

"Sometimes." Another twirl. "We text."

"But you haven't seen him?" This girl could dance. It was a shuffle of some sort, with arms doing some scissor thing. "From what I remember, he's gorgeous."

"Nope." So, I lied.

She looked like she was doing the chicken dance, her elbows were folded. "Why did you break up with your ex-boyfriend?"

"It's complicated."

Then she surprised me with a ballerina-like kick and a pirouette.

"Whoa. Where did you learn that? You get two questions for that."

"Ten years of ballet lessons. Oh, and piano too," she said, while doing another kick turn. "How complicated? Api said he was gorgeous as well."

I frowned at her. "Looks are boring. You can't live your life staring at each other."

She responded with a jeté, leaping up with one leg in front and landing with the rear leg in the air.

"Honestly, I messed up. I wasn't looking at the right things, so focused on my job. So, don't do that, don't do that." I laughed, out of breath, yet continued to twirl.

She followed suit. "I won't do that." She laughed before she offered me her hands.

We locked fingers and swung each other around. Spinning around so fast while holding on to each other. We laughed hysterically, my hair lapping around my face, Maele's hoop earrings and her sapphire blue necklace coming to life on their own. Then her face changed.

Her eyes widened and she took an involuntary breath right before she let go of my hands and grabbed the back of her neck, as if in pain.

I fell back, thrown a few feet away, fully expecting to land on something hard. Instead, I stumbled backward into someone's chest and two arms that held me up.

I threw my head back, not understanding what just happened. The chairs and tables were strewn around the store, music still blaring, and Maele fidgeting with the controls to turn it off.

"Warren?"

I pulled away, stepping back to face him with a look of confusion.

"Hi." He dropped his arms and raked a hand through his hair. "I thought I'd stop by."

— 23 —

What Drives You

"Andie. I'm so sorry," Maele burst out. Her face flushed with embarrassment and she combed her hair with her hands and massaged her neck. "Are you okay? I got startled. I didn't mean to—" She stopped in her tracks after taking a few steps toward me.

"I'm okay," I answered, still rooted in place.

There we stood, a triangle, me in the middle with one on either side. The silence was so ticklish, it made me want to laugh— the way the three of us stood so stiffly with our gazes on the floor. Warren moved closer, I moved back.

Finally, to break the lull, "Maele, this is my friend, Warren Yates."

"It's very nice to meet you." Maele stepped forward to offer her hand. He nodded, as if in reverence, and shook hers. She drew away. "I should get going. Andie, okay with you if I get going? I'll lock all the papers up."

I nodded. "Thanks for your help, Maele. I'll see you tomorrow."

Maele bustled about for a few minutes and left through the

back door.

Then it was just me and him.

I was delighted to see him. I couldn't explain it, but he exuded this warmth that made me feel safe.

I smiled.

He smiled back.

I pointed to the couch in the reading nook and he obliged.

"Did you want some coffee?" I asked, making my way to the bar.

"Black, please."

"Cheers," I said, after handing him his cup.

"You're a great dancer," he said with a wide grin.

"We made our first profit this week."

"I'm not surprised," he said, glancing around. "This place is a far cry from the way it was a few weeks ago."

"Did you see our new roof?"

He shook his head.

"Too dark, probably. But it's so pretty. The flyers, the billboard. All a part of making this work."

He leaned back, draping his arm behind the couch so it almost touched me. "That's great."

"Enough about this. How was New York?" I asked, genuinely interested in learning about his trip.

"My dad sent me to attend a stockholders' meeting. Uneventful. Although I did enjoy the restaurants the team took us to. I'm sorry the trip made us miss our Moments Tour last Friday."

I wondered whether he was there with someone else. I pushed those thoughts away.

"It's okay. Work is work. I used to love spending the weekends there during work trips. Since I had to fly there so often, sometimes, I'd stay the weekends and just work straight through."

"What did you love about New York?"

"The buzz," I replied. "Being in the middle of everything. Like the whole world converged in that city, an active vibe that was constantly alive. I used to spend so much time walking down 57th and 7th, people watching outside MOMA. Weird, I know. But in that chaos, I found so much peace."

"But you lived in Chicago?"

"I grew up there. Chicago is different. It's got soul. Midwest values. The people are warm and friendly, and relationships are key."

"Ah," he said, squinting. Either he had bad eyesight or was deep in thought. "So, there was no one waiting in Chicago for you? You had the luxury of spending weekends away?"

"Well, I wouldn't call it a luxury," I answered. "I worked."

"You're avoiding my question, I think."

"You're trying to get to know me by assessing my previous relationships," I answered, unable to hide my irritation. I didn't want to act irrationally by moving to the edge of the couch. I felt like a failure, having to talk about Nick and my past.

"On the contrary ..." He took a sip of his coffee and placed the cup on the cocktail table before moving a tiny inch closer. "I'm floored as to why someone as intriguing as you hasn't been snatched up by now."

"Snatched up." I laughed.

"Okay, wrong words. But you know what I mean."

"I could say the same for you," I countered.

"Ah, that's a sweet compliment. But to be honest, I saw what my mom went through during her divorce, so I've been very careful about pretending to find 'the one' when she's not the one."

"Huh?"

"Despite the pressure to be married at thirty-one, I'm holding out for the one. I haven't found her yet. And I'm not going to settle. Because I would never put anyone through what my dad put my mom through. He married his assistant."

"How long ago?"

"Hmm. Let's see," he said, looking away, as if trying to coax the memory to return from somewhere in the distance. "Adam is almost twenty-one, so I was twelve. There was an overlap, as you can see."

"I'm sorry to hear that," I said truthfully. It would kill me if my father ever did something like that. The way he looked at my mother, the way they were when they were together … It would be like my whole life was one big farce. And I didn't think I would ever survive that.

"Yeah, well. For a while I was really angry about things. First her husband leaves her and then she dies. And he gets to live a neat little life with his new wife and his son. Not fair."

"Sorry." I took his hand. He jerked his head in my direction, surprised. But he held on, intertwined his fingers in mine and stayed.

"Don't be," he said, holding my gaze. "I've healed for the most part. I have a fantastic younger brother and my dad and I get along now." He paused and then chuckled. "Most of the time."

I nodded, at a loss for words. I had this strange urge to kiss him. Again. It must have been the dim lighting or the moonlight streaming through the windows, or the intimacy of what he'd shared.

Where was this kissing spree coming from? His strong hands? His long limbs and broad shoulders? His eyes? His lips? Dimples. Good Lord, he has dimples.

"What drives you, Andie?" he asked in an almost whisper, reaching out to graze his finger against my cheek without letting go of my hand.

"What do you mean?"

"What moves you? Inspires you? Makes you tick?"

"It used to be success."

"And now?"

I paused, trying to find the right words. "Impact. I want to be remembered for changing someone's life."

"You want to save the farm."

"Yes," I said quietly.

"Eventually, we're going to have to tell each other what we did in our past lives. So, I'll start."

"No," I countered, taking his hand. "Don't. We'd be breaking our own rules."

He laughed. "You gave yourself away when you revamped the state of this coffee shop. A left brainer with an artistic kick. You're in some sort of business."

"Actually, all I did was channel my interior decorator's all white policy," I said with a laugh.

"So, any ETA on how much longer I'll have you?" he asked, leaning forward, lips curving up in a sly smile.

"You're breaking the rules, Mr. Yates."

"And so be it. I have to know, Andie."

"I have to be back before May 1st, so I would say, ten weeks?"

Warren leaned back, exhaling loudly. Showing me his relief.

Uttering those words, defining how much time I had left, spurred me to separate myself from this. A tightness in my chest screamed, *I can't do this right now.*

Instinctively, I looked away and loosened my grip in an attempt to disconnect the force that kept pulling me to him.

"What's the matter?" he asked.

"Nothing. I have to get up early tomorrow to meet Duke at the farm. I think I'm going to call it a night."

"No," he said, gently pulling me toward him, urging me to sit back down. "Don't get up. Stay for a few more minutes."

"Okay, but—"

He draped his arm around my shoulder, held me to him while resting his chin on my head.

"Listen," he whispered. "Can you feel it?"

"Feel what?"

"This. Right here. We're having another moment, Andie."

"We are?" I asked, turning my head so his lips brushed against my ear.

"Yes, we are. Let's just take a few minutes to enjoy it."

You Can't Fight Fate

In all honesty, I looked forward to the 6 a.m. trips to the farm. With my windows rolled down and the sunroof wide open, I savored the scenery, especially the winding road that brought me closer to the clouds. As the air grew thinner and the lush greenery turned to tall trees and layers of brushwood, the only sounds left by the time I turned into the neglected pathway were those of birds and barking dogs. As expected, I was distracted that morning. My focus was off. I was anxious about meeting some bankers at the farm.

Warren had taken over my thoughts.

That moment we'd had? It lasted longer than I expected. It was midnight before we called it a night, a mere hour later, a lifetime of stories richer. We shared the same childhood experiences: road trips, summers at the Outer Banks, cousins, extended family, days in the sun, high school mean girls-boy jock drama. The amazing thing was that his life hadn't stopped at fifteen. His mother had made sure his experiences were as colorful as they were after they lost his father to someone else. She was his hero.

"Andie?" I heard the crunch of gravel. Lani approached my car and rested her arms on my window. "I saw you from the inside and worried when you didn't get out of the car."

"Oh. I was just getting my thoughts together. The bankers are coming today."

"You look really nice," she said, referring to the pink pantsuit I'd managed to put together for that day. She didn't see the four pairs of shoes on the car floor—two pairs of sneakers and two pairs of heels in varying heights. I decided to wear the heels; it was just a matter of risking an ankle injury on the uneven grounds.

"Come inside and we'll have a cup of coffee," she said.

"If you don't mind, I'd like to sit here for a while," I answered, pointing to a pile of papers neatly stacked on the passenger seat. "Organize my pitch."

"Let me bring you out a cup of brew."

She returned less than a minute later and handed me a mug of the sweet, roasted variety.

"Thank you," I said.

Lani leaned in, this time resting her chin on the rubbery part of the window. Her smile was infectious. It lightened my mood. "Mae says you had a visitor last night."

"Ah, I knew this would come up sooner or later." I smiled at her and nodded. "Yeah, he stopped unannounced on his way home from work."

"So, he's been in your life since New Year's Eve."

"Yes," I said, glancing down at my feet. Lani reached for my chin and gently tipped it upward.

"Missy, there is nothing to be embarrassed about. It's a good thing. Have you looked at yourself lately? You are the whole package."

"But—"

"No buts," she countered.

"It's just that I came here to release all expectations. Both for myself and that of others. I just want to do what I came to do and then get back to my old life."

"You hated your old life. And you didn't think you'd be here to work the farm either."

"That," I laughed, "is true. Okay, I guess I'm afraid I'll mess up again. My head isn't in the right place just yet. I need time."

"Then take it," she said. Then she removed herself from the window and stepped back. "But, girl, fate is fate and you can't fight it."

And then she walked away.

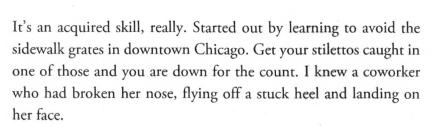

It's an acquired skill, really. Started out by learning to avoid the sidewalk grates in downtown Chicago. Get your stilettos caught in one of those and you are down for the count. I knew a coworker who had broken her nose, flying off a stuck heel and landing on her face.

There were times when those grates were unavoidable. There was no choice but to learn level two, which consisted of walking on the tips of my toes, lifting the heels off the grates.

Level three, which I'd mastered in Italy a few years ago, was the most dangerous one of all. Walking through the cobblestone streets in high heels while keeping up with Nick, who had taken three of my strides with every one of his.

Block heels.

They were the best things that ever happened to career women like me.

The bankers were thirty minutes late. Said they couldn't get through the access road without having to take the route across the mountains. They gushed at the landscape that led them from the city to the farm.

How lucky could I be, they said, to be witnessing such splendor every single day.

The bank had sent two men and two women. They said that for a loan as large as this, many more compliance departments would be involved. We slowly baked under the sun. With rains as fresh as the day before, our shoes were caked with mud. None of us seemed to mind it, because everyone was transfixed on Duke and Kukane's animated narrative of the entire harvesting process. The lady in the navy-blue suit and a large silver clipboard took furious notes while questions and answers were volleyed back and forth.

"And your elevation is only eight hundred feet? That's low, no? We've seen plantations as high as four thousand feet."

"Yes, but there is something about the soil in this place and the location that attracts afternoon clouds that shield us from direct sunlight. Rainfall is also quite heavy—more than fifteen inches a season," Duke explained.

"What type of coffee is this?" asked the lady in the blue suit.

"Coffee grown for commercial production has two major species—Canephora is robusta coffee which is strong, disease resistant, bitter, and has a high caffeine content. It is found in Africa and Southeast Asia," Kukane began, pausing to make sure she was still with us. When she nodded, he continued. "Hawaiian coffee is mostly Arabica. It is very susceptible to drought and adverse weather conditions. Also to disease. It tastes better because of its lower acidity. It requires much handpicking because—you see this? This green cherry is immature. It needs to ripen some more."

Duke lagged behind with the other two men who seemed to take their time admiring the hillside views.

"Are you still processing and drying beans manually?" asked the other woman in black pants.

"Our harvesting process is manual. It is very slow. We allow the harvested beans to ferment and depulp on their own. Machines can pick up to three hundred and fifty thousand pounds of cherries a day. Our irrigation process is also manual. The drying process is tedious, as we must constantly turn the beans to avoid developing mold. Mr. Flores had partnered with Apex to deliver some machines before he got sick. It never materialized."

The tour lasted three hours. It seemed like every tree was touched, every row was checked, and soil in different areas was collected for testing. The growers and harvesters were interviewed. Many were required to demonstrate their use of the hand tools for pruning, digging, and caring for the plants. Our last stop was the processing facility where the beans were washed and dried.

The bank representatives looked satisfied when the time came for them to leave. They thanked us for a very informative tour, said Duke and Kukane's knowledge was impressive.

Duke and I stood outside the store while we waved them

goodbye, his attention shifting to my foot as I placed my weight on one and then the other.

"Are you okay, Andie?"

"Yeah," I said, lifting one foot straight up and rotating my ankle. "Four hours in these heels was a little brutal."

"Well, if it's any consolation, I think it was worth it."

"You think so?" I asked. "I couldn't get a read."

"Did they give us anything to read?"

"Oh no, Duke." I smiled and gently touched his shoulder. "What I meant was, I couldn't tell one way or the other if we convinced them."

"Well, whatever it is they decide, we did our best," he answered.

"Yes, we did."

"Andie, I just want to thank you for managing this for us. I know the Flores family has been distraught over the loss of Mr. Flores. This is a wonderful thing you're doing, in his name."

— 25 —

Shave Ice

"Happy Friday, Andie. It's our second stop on the Grand Moments tour. And for today, the North Shore."

"Yes. I've heard so much about the North Shore, the waves, the beaches."

"The shave ice," he added.

"What's shave ice?"

"It's a Hawaiian delicacy. You'll just have to taste it to find out."

He was driving an old convertible Rabbit this time. Faded red, with a black ragtop. Stick shift. I was impressed. I hadn't seen a Rabbit on the road in as long as I could remember. He said to bring a suit for a beach day, not a water day, so I wore an aqua blue bikini top and cute white jean shorts. I tied my hair back in a ponytail, and away we went.

He drove up the H2 and we passed the turnoff to the plantation. I thought about my friends at the farm and how proud I was to be working with them.

Our first stop was an overlook to Waimea Bay.

"This is Waimea Bay. It's a very special place. Do you see how narrow the mouth of the bay is?"

"Yes," I answered.

"What you can't see is that the ocean floor is making a rapid rise almost at the same place as the mouth of the bay, so it's a perfect combination for some of the biggest waves in the world. I've seen days where there were sixty-foot swells." He paused for effect. "That's about two school busses stacked on top of each other. One year there was a record eighty-foot swell. They called a 'condition black' and closed out the entire North Shore. In 1957, a guy named Greg Noll was the first white man to surf big waves. Before then, only a few Native surfers handled this break here and on the west coast. I'll take you there soon. Greg Noll changed surfing for the whole world. He practically invented it for everyone who wasn't Hawaiian, but it was a Hawaiian named Buffalo Keaulana that taught Greg how to surf the big waves. Buffalo took him out on the west side, and he learned how to charge down the face of a wave. It's pretty amazing history and it happened right here."

We sped over to several other beaches that day and met some of his surfer buddies. On Sunset Beach, we collected a handful of tiny white shells that looked like flat pearls. We saw the world-famous Banzai Pipeline and watched a few of the world's greatest surfers getting in some sets.

Then came the highlight of my day—shave ice.

We drove to a little hut called Aoki's Shave Ice and I ordered ice with coconut flavor.

"You need to ask for cream," he instructed.

"What's cream?"

"Andie, if you haven't learned to trust me yet, then please do so now. You won't regret it."

"Okay. Can you make that with cream please?" I asked the server.

"And I'll have the same."

How sweet. We ordered the same flavor of shave ice. I felt like a schoolgirl falling all over her boy crush.

"What?" He looked back at me.

"You ordered coconut flavor."

"Yeah, it's the best flavor and if you spill it"—then we said at the same time—"you won't stain your shirt. Jinx. Jinx. One, two, three, four, five, six, seven, eight, nine, ten. You owe me a Coke."

We laughed at our foolishness and our silliness and our freedom.

Yes, Warren, you did it. You gave me another moment that I will never forget. A story about surfing and a fistful of shells, and a game of jinx over coconut-flavored ice with cream. Which by the way, was the best tasting thing I'd ever had in my mouth.

26

Marigold Loop

Api lived thirty minutes away from her parents. And although I knew they'd settled in an affluent area in Kailua, the opulence of it still astounded me. Their Marigold Loop home was nestled among acres and acres of beachfront homes with yards that looked like golf courses.

"It's Andie Matthews for Mrs. Flores." I said to the guard who stared at his computer screen before flitting his fingers across a keypad.

In front of me, a large imposing iron gate with a gold *F* insignia remained closed. Ahead of his response, a vibrant, melodious voice crooned through the intercom.

"Andie? Is that you?"

"Mrs. Flores?" I asked, neck craned over the car door. The guard reluctantly handed me the speaker, reaching out his hand, but not really.

"Auntie Mel, to you," she said. "Drive on in, Andie. Don't park in the lot. Come straight up to the entrance."

"She's in the greenhouse." The lady in a white uniform met me with a smile on her face. "Andie, I'm Juana, Api's nanny from the time she was one."

"Nana Juana. Yes." I stepped into her open arms, disappearing in the warmth of her welcome. I couldn't help but notice the things around me. Every intricate detail—from the coffered ceilings inlaid with bamboo to the walls made out of coral and stone.

"I've seen your pictures, but you are even more beautiful in person," she said, holding my hand and leading me through the foyer. We stopped at an indoor pond, circular in shape and edged with stone. Around us were orchids of different varieties—green, purple, and red, interspersed with copious amounts of Chinese antique jars and life-sized wooden statues. Peeking through the lilies that covered the water's surface were enormous koi happily being hand-fed by a gardener on the opposite side of the pond.

"Mr. Flores' passion," Juana pointed out.

I bobbed my head up and down, speechless.

"You see that one?" She pointed to a giant fish about two feet in length with orange spots on its head and tail. "That was the last one Mr. Flores and Api bought in Japan last year."

We crossed a stone bridge over to the other side of the house. Dark, antique barn doors led to another area—this time, a greenhouse lined with rows of white countertops, each empty space filled with plastic pots with labels and markings. Sitting at a table in the middle of all the greenery was Api's mom, wearing gloves and holding a pair of shears. The sound of snapping reverberated throughout as she pruned and repotted her flowers.

Even at home, she was dressed exquisitely, a yellow sundress and white open-toe sandals which complemented the color of her long, blonde hair.

"Andie," she said, standing up to greet me before kissing me on both cheeks. Her eyes were moist with tears.

"Hi, Auntie Mel."

"So nice of you to come over. I was asking Api when I would be seeing you." She motioned me to follow her to another marble table set tastefully with matching blue and white dinnerware, wine glasses, and silver cutlery. "Jane is going to be serving us lunch in here. I hope it's okay with you. Somehow, this has been my place of refuge for the past few months."

I understood what she was saying. This woman lived her life for her husband and daughter. She'd become an award-winning horticulturist after Api went away to school. An orchid had been named after her. I took a seat and allowed the server to pour me a glass of white wine.

"How are your parents? How is Lourdes? We were supposed to meet in Paris for this year's Fashion Week, but that's when your uncle Ramon fell ill."

"Mom and Dad are fine. They were in Chicago before I came here."

"Api told me what happened. I was very sorry to hear about Nick. How are you doing now?"

"Hawaii has done me a lot of good," I answered. By now we had salad plates filled with endives and arugula, topped with pine nuts and a light-yellow dressing.

Auntie Mel read my mind. "Banana vinaigrette. Good, no?"

"Delicious," I answered, smiling.

"So, your mom. What's she up to these days? Did you know I sent her a few hybrids from here?"

"Yes. She told me. She's been growing a lot of philodendrons and bromeliads like those." I pointed to a group of orchids on hanging planters. "Her favorites are still the red plumerias."

She beamed with pride, her eyes beginning to moisten again.

"I'm sorry," she said. "I've been so emotional lately. Seeing you just now, just reminded me. It's Valentine's Day. I met the love of my life on Valentine's Day, 1942. Your uncle used to make this day such a big deal, bigger than Christmas. This is when Api and I would get all our gifts. He would joke and say they were cheaper after the Christmas season."

"I'm sure you miss him," I said, desperate to comfort her. Finally, I decided to scoot my chair close to her so she could lean her head on my shoulder.

"I lost the love of my life," she cried. "What good is all this? I'm without my love for the first time since I was seven years old. We were just little children when we met, during the war. It's a wonderful love story."

"I'd love to hear it someday."

Nothing I said could relieve her sorrow. I was alone too. There we were, our hearts abandoned, one by choice and the other by destiny. The pain of loss experienced in varying degrees, hers more than mine. It wasn't fair for me to even try to fathom what that felt like. The saddest thought that crossed my mind was this—over the last few weeks, my heart had slowly been mending. I no longer thought about Nick.

I held her for a while, gently kept her face close to me, until the server approached with two plates for our main course.

Mrs. Flores sat straight up, dabbed her eyes with the tip of her napkin, and pulled away. "Pan seared mahi-mahi. I hope you're okay with that."

"It's perfect," I assured her. "By the way, I have to tell you how stunning this home is. Everything is absolutely elegant."

"Uncle Ram was never comfortable with this house. It was way too big, way too extravagant. 'What are we going to do with nine bathrooms, Melanie?' he used to say to me. But our advisers told us to make this investment. He was adamant about living here. He said that if we were going to invest this much money, we might as well live in it."

"Well, as far as I know, it is a great investment."

"But you know the funny thing? Some crazy, young businessman just bought the house on 145 Marigold for twenty-three million dollars. These houses aren't that big. Crazy, but I'm happy our property value has gone up."

"Wow."

The conversation turned cheerful after that. We caught up on life in the last year, including Fashion Week and my mom's disappointment with the current collections. Mrs. Flores laughed when I told her my mom had reverted back to classic Saint Laurent because she complained that the runway was dominated with styles for "young people who couldn't even afford them, excluding the old people whose bodies wouldn't work, even if they could in fact, afford them."

When the topic changed to the plantation and the farm, Mrs. Flores expressed her gratitude for my stepping in and helping with the business.

"Andie, that friend of yours. I worship the ground she walks on. She is my miracle baby. But she has no business skills. Your uncle knew that too. After he got sick, we seriously considered selling it. But he had qualms about letting Duke and the families down. I'm not sure whether he meant to keep it going."

I thought for a minute before responding. I didn't want to take on anything I couldn't handle, give false hopes when I wasn't sure how far this could go. My tone turned serious. I slowed my words down, careful not to commit or too much impulsivity. But it turned out I knew what to say all along. "It's become personal to me, Aunt Mel. Getting to spend the past two months with Duke and Kukane and their families. Watching the trees grow and change over the seasons. It's been my therapy."

"We are grateful," she answered. "Don't pressure yourself too much. I will wait for your final recommendation." She poured some hot water into our cups. I asked for green tea, she asked for chamomile. "Now, tell me. How is your heart doing, *ku'u aloha?*"

She called me her love. In Hawaiian.

"Healing," I answered. "I handled it all wrong with Nick. I pushed myself too much, wanted to conform with the norms, get engaged, have a family. When in reality, I wasn't ready. You know, I spent so much time focusing on my career, and then when Api lost her father, I was dealing with my own stuff with Nick. I feel like I wasn't there enough for her and I regret it so much."

"At some point, you're going to have to forgive yourself. Nick will do the same. As for Api, you can still be there for her now," she said. "She hasn't mourned yet. She's been so busy with the engagement—she's hidden her sorrow in the joy of the occasion.

It will hit her soon, and you will be there."

"I will," I promised, reaching out to take her hand.

"Speaking of," she said, taking her phone from the table and leaning it against her wine glass. "My baby."

"Mommy. Is today the day of Andie's visit?"

Mrs. Flores angled the phone as I tipped my body sideways. Api looked refreshed and rested, her hair pulled up in a bun with tendrils framing the sides of her face.

"I'm here. Hi."

"Hi. My two favorite ladies," Api gushed.

"We are missing you," Mrs. Flores piped in. "How are you and James doing?"

"We're good. James just got an offer to practice here in Germany."

Mrs. Flores turned away, afraid to show Api her immediate reaction. Then she pasted a smile on her face, eyes frozen, lips in a made-up curve. "Congratulations to James. What lovely news."

"He's turning it down. He wants to practice at the Queen's Hospital." That was home for her. Queen's was the largest hospital in Honolulu.

Her mother sighed with relief and looked at me, her expression softened.

I nodded in affirmation. "Oh."

"Yeah, so we'll be home in a few weeks. Andie, we can spend time together before you head back to Chicago."

"That would be perfect," I answered.

"Api, I was wondering," Mrs. Flores began, resting her chin on her palm in a relaxed manner. Her reprieve was obvious. The way she leaned forward with her head tilted, jaw slack. "It would be great to have you and Andie stay here when you come home. Just spend time together, the three of us."

"That's a great idea. Andie, what do you think?"

Api wiggled her eyebrows. Her mother beamed at me.

I would have had enough alone time by then. "I would love it," I said, clasping both hands together.

"That's great. Nana Juana will be ecstatic when I tell her."

27

Hitachi Tree

Friday morning. The sun was already hot and bright as it hung low in the Hawaiian sky. I was excited about the day that lay ahead of me. I had asked Warren if there were any waterfalls on Oahu.

"Sadly, not too many, but I'll show you the ones I can," he'd said.

That was the plan for today—another trip to the North Shore for a hike along the Waimea River. He pulled up right at eight o'clock. Not that I was complaining. His punctuality was one thing, but truth be told, I couldn't wait to spend those Fridays with him. Part of me expected a surf bum to run on island time, but he always managed to surprise me. Of course, I had the beans and bites waiting in hand, something he never asked for but had come to count on.

We hit the road, back on the scooter this time. Back up the H2, passing the plantation on our way. I was overcome with a yearning to see the people at the farm—a sign of belonging, of being rooted in their midst. Hawaii was starting to feel like home to me and I knew my time here was running out.

We pulled up to a little parking lot at the beach on Waimea Bay. Warren locked his helmets to the scooter, lifted the moped up and over the kickstand and parked it. He tucked the little key in the pocket of his camouflage cargo shorts, which he'd paired with a black T-shirt. He looked good this morning. I was wearing short shorts and a white tee. Apparently, we were going to do some hiking today so we both had on sneakers.

"Waimea Bay is fed by the Waimea River and when it rains, all sorts of food for sharks gets washed down the river into the bay. So, note to self, when it's raining, and the river is flowing, stay out of the bay. I've known sharks in there to follow surfers all the way back to shore. But, if the river is running fast, it actually makes a really fun wave where the river meets the bay. You can ride on it for as long as you can stand on your board. There's usually a line to drop in, but if you come out here when the weather is really nasty, you'll be the only brave soul."

"Note taken. Next nasty storm, I'll grab my board and head to the mouth of the river," I teased.

That was something that had recently found its way into our friendship—my humor. It could be a blend of sarcasm and wit; either you get it and think I'm funny, or you don't. Warren got it. And his bite was even more fun.

"Good, just make sure you don't fall off your board and end up as shark food."

Our laughter filled the air. We crossed the road and headed onto the trailhead. The path was paved, but the asphalt was wet from an early morning rainfall. Within minutes, we were towered over by a lush canopy of trees, changing the atmosphere to dark, cool, and wet. We were inside a rainforest.

"One of the most ignored aspects of Hawaii is her trees. Everyone is taken by the beaches, the waves, and the volcanoes, but the trees on these islands are so weird and exotic. I've traveled all over the world and I've never found such a wide variety of trees as there is here on this island."

"You're an arborist too?"

"No, I'm no expert. I just know a good thing when I see it."

He put his hand on my lower back to let me pass in front of him when the path turned narrow. His touch was warm. It filled me with confidence and tingles.

"The most famous of the Hawaiian trees is the banyan tree. That's this one here."

A massive, ancient-looking tree with a thousand branches shooting in every direction towered above us. I could have gotten lost staring up into its arms. It looked almost human in design and wise in attitude, regal and aware. Warren then pointed to another tree.

"This is a monkeypod tree." Then he pointed to something else. "And those are tree ferns. It's a native fern that grows ... in the trees. Hence the name," he said, smiling. I laughed; I was giddy.

We stopped on a sun dappled rise and looked toward another tree.

"And this is a Hitachi tree." Warren pointed to what looked like a giant mushroom, or a spaceship hovering off the ground. Its shape was a perfect dome, sort of like an umbrella. We observed a thousand different types of ferns and rainbow colored Eucalyptus trees, and a red flowering tree called the Ohi'a tree, sacred among Native Hawaiians.

We walked along the Waimea River, intrigued by the sound

of a hundred different bird calls, until finally we came to a small pool of dark water with a thin waterfall cascading into it from about fifteen feet above.

A perfect moment.

Warren took his phone out of his pocket and snapped a picture of me standing in the shadows of ancient, sacred trees. I could feel the sunlight like a prism reflecting and dancing across my face. I was drenched from the humidity, but I didn't care. He studied my face, and gently moved a strand of hair that had fallen out of my ponytail on our walk. And that smell. It persisted once again, filling the air with the sweet smell of citrus. Then Warren took a selfie with me, both of us wearing huge smiles. I felt at home and the thought of leaving this paradise caused a pain in my stomach. That feeling and a million other feelings I couldn't define, made me suddenly unsteady and off balance. As if the very ground I was standing on was undulating like waves. This was what the woman on the plane had meant when she'd told me I'd be wavering.

Just as I reached out to Warren, he caught me. For one brief moment, our eyes met, and I felt anchored once again. The light behind his head shimmered through the branches, reminding me of heaven and saints and angels and everything out of this world.

28

Watch Out for the Fins

"**I** have a very special treat for you today. A really good friend of mine, Brian, lives on the west side. He is a waterman, born and raised in the sea."

"In the sea?" I asked, confused. Who was raised in the sea?

"Well, almost, he spent as much time as he could in it, so he's practically been raised in it. Are you ready to go?"

He'd told me to wear a bathing suit, so I was in my white bikini today. This one fit me perfectly, thanks to the healthy weight I gained back while staying on the island. He didn't look so bad either, rocking a gray T-shirt and Kelly-green swim trunks. We took a moment to eat the bites and drink the beans, and I brought him up to speed on my week at the coffee shop. Then I hopped onto the back of the Honda, strapped my helmet on, and away we went.

It was a chilly dawn. The sounds of the rain had kept me up all night, and I was tired. Warren's body was warm. I held him tightly that morning, my bare legs pressed against his flesh, my arms wrapped tightly around his waist. *What was on the tour today,* I wondered. It didn't matter, really. It was so refreshing—this feeling of losing all control. Of not being in charge.

The passing scenery on the west side was different than the east side and not as lush and green as the North Shore. It never ceased to amaze me how different each part of the island was.

We arrived at a beach where the paved road ended.

"Do you remember that story I told you about Buffalo and Greg Noll? Well, this is that beach I mentioned, and this is Brian, Buffalo's son."

A fit, older Hawaiian man reached out his hand to me.

"Aloha, Andie. Warren has told me so much about you."

Warren has told you about me? I thought we weren't telling anyone about each other? Or was that my rule? The details of our agreement had gotten so blurred these past weeks. I wasn't sure they even held up anymore.

"Hi, Brian. It's an honor to meet you. Warren has told me a lot about you and your dad, too."

"Do you know what we are going to do today?" Brian asked.

"No. I have no idea."

At this, Brian smiled a huge smile and let out a little laugh.

"Nothing like a surprise. This is Makaha Beach. It's one of the last beaches on Oahu that is left alone by the tourists. It's a hidden beach and these waters are teeming with sea turtles. They use this cove like a car wash for their shells, so you will see a lot of turtles today. What we are going to do is run rocks."

That did not sound fun. What did running rocks entail—moving rocks from one side of the beach to the other or running away from Brian and Warren as we hurled rocks at each other?

"What is that?" I asked, sincere in my curiosity.

"Well, my family has a tradition of big wave surfing and one

- 153 -

of the most dangerous things about big waves is how long they can keep you underwater if you fall into the wave break. So, over the years, we've developed a system of training our bodies and lungs to prepare for that."

Warren chimed in, "Brian invented the tow in system, using a Jet Ski to tow surfers into big waves."

"I started using a Jet Ski to get guys out of the path of the wave and bring them to safety."

"That sounds really dangerous. Have you ever been hit by a big wave while on a Jet Ski?" I asked.

"Of course, a few times, it's never fun. But because I've trained my whole life in the water, it's manageable. Today we're going to train you."

He walked across the beach, away from the water and toward a hedge of bushes on the far side. Before I knew it, he was throwing a few rocks onto the sand. Warren followed him and I followed Warren. Brian held up a softball-sized rock.

"Andie, I think I found your rock. Is it too heavy?"

It wasn't too heavy, but too heavy for what? I was in the dark. Brian handed Warren a rock.

"This one is calling out for you, bruddah."

Warren took his rock and held it in both hands in front of himself, chest high, as if he was in church and his rock was a sacred relic.

Brian found his rock and he hopped toward the water, entreating us to follow. At the shoreline, he knelt onto the sand. Warren did the same. So did I, for that matter. Brian said a prayer, thanking Pele for the rocks and asking her to bless them. He apologized for moving them and promised to return them to where he had found them.

We were about to do something serious. I just had no idea what it was.

Brian pulled three scuba masks from his bag. One was black, one was clear plastic, and one was purple. I got the purple one as it was the smallest of the three.

"Okay, Andie. This is what we're going to do. Are you a strong swimmer or no?"

I had been on the swim team from sixth grade until eleventh grade when I'd known my chances of getting any faster were slim to none. But I always placed because my coaches said I had heart. Apparently, according to Nick, I lost that heart somewhere along the way.

"I'm a strong swimmer. I can swim."

"Good, then I'll skip to the end. Here's what we're gonna do. We are going to swim with our rocks to about thirty yards offshore—the water is about twenty feet deep out there—and we are gonna drop our rocks to the bottom. Then we're gonna run those rocks. We swim down, grab them, and the weight of the rocks will keep us underwater, but you'll take a nice deep breath and hold on to it as long as you can. When you feel like you can't hold your breath anymore, you drop your rock, kick up to the surface, grab another deep breath, and we do it again."

This was a workout. Warren has put a workout on the Moments Tour and it was only nine in the morning. Additionally, it was kind of chilly. This moment was not ranking high on my list.

Warren must have seen my concern.

"Trust me, Andie. I know what you're thinking right now, but try it once and then we'll talk."

The three of us made our way into the water. The water was calm that morning and Brian kept scanning the horizon, looking for something.

The rock was heavier in the water than it had been on the beach, but I tucked it onto my hip with my left hand and swam with my right, while kicking like a frog. In no time, we were thirty yards off the shore.

"Okay. Now drop 'em."

We dropped our rocks, then put our masks over our eyes. All the while, Brian kept searching the horizon.

"Okay, now it's time to run our rocks."

We each took a deep breath and simultaneously dove under the water, kicking toward the bottom. My ears began to feel pressure and my lungs became tight. Fear gripped my body, but I resolved to fight through it. Suddenly, thoughts about work and Nick and the memory of my panic attack came flooding back. They weighed me down, trying to prevent me from this experience.

It's funny how failure wants you to keep failing.

Not that morning.

I kicked with all my might, found my rock and picked it up. I saw how Warren and Brian were just standing on the bottom of the ocean floor with their rocks in their arms, cradled like babies. Brian gave me a thumbs-up, I returned the gesture, even though I was nowhere near a thumbs-up. What was I doing, twenty feet below the surface of the Pacific Ocean, standing on the sea floor?

And then I saw it.

I was standing on an underwater hillside. To my right, the slope of the sand descended into the darkness of the ocean; to my left, the sand climbed and climbed until it met its reflection at the surface and became the beach. The sunlight was in shafts, like pillars of light in a watery cathedral, sparkling as the columns made their way down to our league. The world to my right was terrifying, but to my left, I saw a way home.

And the turtles. There must have been fifty of them swimming on the rocks to the right of us, before the sand plummeted into unimaginable depths. Like guardians of the deep, the turtles stayed there. They were rubbing their shells on the rocks and swimming lazily upside down.

Warren and Brian were running with their rocks parallel to the shoreline, and so I began to run too. The air in my lungs began to burn and I felt like my chest was sinking. Before I knew it, Brian was suddenly behind me. I let the rock drop to the sea floor and he lifted me toward the surface of the water. Warren broke through soon thereafter.

"Oh. My. Gosh," I yelled "That was the most beautiful thing I have ever seen in my life. Oh my gosh."

Warren and Brian let out huge laughs. Warren high-fived Brian, then they both high-fived me.

Brian scanned the horizon again, then turned to me. "Are you all right?"

"I am. I just have one question—Brian, what are you looking for?"

"Fins."

We all laughed.

"You ready to do it again?" Warren asked.

"Yes. Again and again."

We had rocks we'd promised to return, but before we did, we

ran for hours that morning. Every time I dove down to find my rock, I became more and more comfortable in my new environment.

Warren was right—this was better than snorkeling.

— 29 —

Pink Bikini

Warren picked me up in front of the apartment building bright and early at eight. I was creating my own tradition of having beans and bites waiting and ready. Today, I had been instructed to wear something I could meet people in and not feel underdressed, but make sure there was a swimsuit underneath. I chose a pink bikini under blue jeans and a button-up shirt. We were off toward Sandy Beach again, where the landscape was windswept and brown, but this time we made our way to the east side of the island. Things suddenly got much greener again. I was amazed at how much empty, wild land there was on Oahu.

We arrived in a small town called Waimamalo. The houses were different here, much smaller and not as tidy as the homes in Kahala. I suppose an area built for wealthy residents wasn't a fair comparison.

"Waimamalo is where a lot of middle and lower middle-class Hawaiians live. There is actually a pretty big problem that Native Hawaiians are facing; their land is becoming too expensive for them to live on anymore. In fact, on the west side, near Makaha where I took you to run rocks, there is a part of the island where

Native Hawaiians are allowed to live as they once did—outside and in villages—where there is no construction. We aren't allowed to go there, otherwise I'd show you."

"What are we doing here?" I asked.

"I'd like you to meet a few of my friends and then we are going kayaking."

He took my hand and led me into a YMCA where we were greeted by an elderly woman and fifteen happy children. When they saw Warren, they ran to hug him. He stood there in the middle of the kids, smiling like a saint, and I didn't know what I wanted to do—roll my eyes or swoon and faint.

"Andie, this is Maineialoha. She runs the youth programs here at the YMCA and I come out here one Friday a month to play a few games with these young bloods. Don't I, guys?"

"Yes, and you always leave upset because you never win," said one of the younger boys in the group.

"I don't get upset. Do I?"

"Yes you do," they chorused in unison.

This was a comfortable and familiar friendship, earned over time.

"Hey, little cousins, do you mind if my new friend, Andie, joins us today? She's really good at these games and with her help, I'm gonna win."

I couldn't give in that easy, so I joked, "I'll play, but only if I can be on the kids' side."

"YAY!" The kids circled me and for the first time in my life, I thought about what it would be like to be a mother. Not an aunt or a big sister, but a mom. To have a child I would live and die for. Maybe they'd look like Warren, their eyes so sparkling and bright, their hair as light as the sun.

What was happening to me?

We played a few hours of games, flag football and a game called Koa Koa Ball—which was kinda like a blend of dodge ball and soccer—and my favorite, Rover Red Rover. After the games, the kids sat down to have a snack. Warren said his goodbye to Maineialoha, who was delightful and fully committed to loving those children. And then we said goodbye to the kids.

"You know you are forgetting something, Uncle Warren," said the leader of the pack.

"Oh yes? And what's that, Momo?"

"You know you have to race one of us before you go."

"All right, all right. I'll race one of you, but I get to pick this time."

"Deal," agreed Momo, the boss boy.

Warren looked over the kids, noticing a little girl hiding in the middle of the group. She was no more than eight years old. Tiny. Like a bird. "Rose. I want to race Rose."

A roar of dispute erupted. Claims that she was too small to race, too slow, too shy, but Warren insisted. He said it was his chance to break his losing streak and no one had the right to take that away from him. I thought that would hurt her feelings, but he must have known something I didn't, because she stood tall and accepted the challenge.

"I will race you, Uncle Warren. Let's go," she said bravely.

Warren put on a very good show, running his heart out, but in the end, Rose won. He managed to push Rose to her fastest speed and then make it look like he couldn't go any faster. It was well done. Something my father would have pulled off perfectly.

Yes, he reminded me of my father.

"I've never shown the kids how fast I can really run, so they think I'm super slow. When they get older, if they see me on the beach, they will chap my hide for sure. But in the meantime, I think it's good to let kids know what it feels like to win. I push them, and for their prize, they get to win."

"I think it's wonderful, Warren. Thank you for showing me that."

He just showed me that life wasn't always about winning.

"Well, that's not all. For playing along with me today, you get a prize. I'm taking you kayaking to a very special place. Let's grab a quick bite to eat then hit the water."

After a tasty lunch at a roadside fish taco hut, we launched our kayaks off Lanikai Beach and made our way to the Mokulua Islands. They were usually closed to the public, but sometimes the north island would open during the day. The islands served as bird sanctuaries.

The water was darker and choppier, as we were on the windward side of the island, but the thrill of being on the water allowed me to ignore those factors. I could see twelve, fifteen feet below the surface. I spotted giant sea turtles and a long, narrow, spotted shark. We saw more dolphins and paddled out farther, reaching North Mokulua Island after about forty-five minutes of paddling.

We pulled the kayaks up on the beach and took a seat on the sand. We were alone, just Warren and me. The call of ten thousand sea birds wailed behind us, somehow it was harmonious and enchanting. The sun was high in the sky now and the island protected us from the winds.

I was warm and sweating. I wanted to touch Warren—his arm, his hand, his face. I wanted to feel him. I wanted to feel him inside of me. It had been a year since I had last been intimate and my body was in revolt. I thought of our kiss on New Year's Eve and how simple and good it had been—how naturally we fit together. I thought about the night he'd walked into the coffee shop and my inexplicable urge to kiss him under the mistletoe. I'd never wanted a man as desperately and urgently as I wanted this man. My body pulsated with nerves. It wanted what it wanted. I started to throb and ache. I wanted him so badly I was about to burst.

"How was the trip over, Andie? You okay?"

"I'm fine, yes. A little tired, but wow. So pretty."

I wasn't making sense. I couldn't speak. Then—right then, I wanted him to kiss me. Why wouldn't he kiss me?

"Warren?"

"Yes, Andie?"

"Ah … I think I'm going to lie down and rest for a bit."

I stretched my body out. My pink bikini was glowing in the midday sun, my tan skin shimmering with sweat. My heart raced, my chest visibly heaving. I moved my legs, felt the friction of rough sand as I rubbed my thighs together. I dug my feet into the hot beach. Time slowed to a near standstill as a seagull shrieked in the distance.

I could feel Warren's eyes on me, taking in every inch of my glistening body. What was he thinking? I wished he would make a move.

Why won't you kiss me?

30

Aries

"Haaaaapppeeee Birthday."

Lani and Maele, together with Duke, Kukane, Milani and Keoki, clapped their hands frantically. Balloons filled the room—red and blue and pink and white. Two giant ones in gold, a three and a zero were pasted on the wall. Confetti strips graced every table, votive candles did the same.

A year ago on this day, I was sitting at the Ritz Carlton with my mother, my fiancé, and my future mother-in-law, tasting pastries and deciding on the color combination for the tablecloths and napkins. And because it had been my birthday, a group of waiters emerged from the kitchen with some sort of Baked Alaska, complete with fireworks and singing candles. I recalled how Nick had been so into it; tasting every single thing they served him. Having an opinion about everything, when all I wanted was for someone to make all the choices for us because a very important work meeting was taking place without me.

What a difference a year made.

That morning, I'd woken up renewed, refreshed, purposeful. I opened my eyes, smiling and thinking of Warren.

"Thank you," I spouted, choked up and rendered speechless. "How did you know?"

"Api told us," Maele said, opening up the fridge and laying a yellow cake topped with a confetti of coconut on the counter. "And look. Mama made you a pineapple cake."

Lani hustled about, assembling some plates and silverware for everyone and serving the cake in nice-sized pieces. We gathered around the reading nook, with the two children grabbing books to read. I sat cross-legged on the floor, the others scattered around the sofa.

"When did Api call?" I asked, taking a mouthful of cake. "Mmm. This is great. Please thank your mom for me, Mae."

"Api called last night to remind us, which is why the balloons are kind of mismatched." Lani laughed. "She said she told us a long time ago, but the girl was imagining things."

We all laughed.

"Andie, does Api know about the guy you're seeing?"

Baby Spice did it again.

I swear, I heard all five necks snap up, bones cracking and all. All four pairs of eyes drilled into me. No one moved, no one said a word. So I, in turn, ignored them. Took another bite of cake and then a sip of my coffee.

"Andie," Mae squealed.

"It's nothing and there's no one. We need to focus on getting the equipment for the farm. Has anyone stopped by the farm or called?"

"Not yet," Duke shrugged. "And if someone were to call, I think they'd call you."

"Good point." It was plain to see they were trying to get back to the other topic. I reached under the couch and pulled out a large cardboard sign. One I'd made at home a few nights ago. A surprise I wanted to give to Mae and Lani. "The best news is still to come. Look."

WE ARE HIRING. INQUIRE INSIDE

Mae jumped up with her arms in the air and Duke followed.

Then Kukane held on to his hips and wiggled them, making him shimmy like a Hula dancer. "Yay. We are growing. Thank you, Andie. You've turned this place around."

"We all did it. We're a great team. And listen, guys, about the other thing. I know you're all looking out for me. But there's really nothing to tell. It's been a confusing year and being here—" I emphasized my point by looking directly at each of them. One by one. "Being here with you all has been so good for me. But I'm leaving in a few weeks. So, I'm going to enjoy every minute that I can, here with you, with Api, and with her mom."

"Sorry for being a pain, Andie," Mae said with downcast eyes.

Gently, I reached for her hand and squeezed it. "It's okay, Mae. You and my mom both."

What sounded like a cough was everyone's attempt to force out a laugh. But once we got that over with, everyone began to relax. I wouldn't have expected my love life or the lack thereof to be a stress trigger for everyone involved. I thought it was just my mom. Apparently, I was mistaken.

When we were done eating our cake, we bustled around, tidying up before opening the store for the day. Then we stuck the sign up, right by the window next to the front door. Already, a line had formed, spilling over into the parking lot. Lately, cinnamon rolls and breakfast bagels had become a staple for some regulars.

It was the best birthday gift of all, seeing our hard work come to fruition. No matter what happened to the farm, this store would no doubt be saved. We could build on it, make it bigger, and create a name for Mr. Flores' lasting legacy.

"Hey, guys, I think I'm going to head out in a few minutes," I said to Lani and Maele after scanning the shop's activity. Customers had converged by the bookshelves, the low murmur of voices and the clanking of plates and silverware still permeating the air. Two men in business suits and earbuds paced around separate corners, one eating our now famous Emerson's malasadas, the other slurping a glass of mango shake through a straw. It was still quite busy for a late afternoon.

"Of course, Andie. What are you doing for your birthday evening?" Lani asked.

"Oh, well, let's see," I teased, tapping my temple like I was in deep thought. "I've got so many options, but I think I'm going to have a glass of wine and catch up on my episodes of *Life Unexpected*."

"Good plan. I have a celebrity crush on the guy who plays

Baze," Maele answered with a girlish laugh. "Let me take this garbage out and I'll help take the cake to your car."

I'd hardly finished stapling together the receipts for the day when Maele came rushing in, twisting her little blue diamond necklace, a wry, feline smirk pasted on her face. "Hey, Andie," she said, loud enough for Lani to stop what she was doing in the kitchen. "The 'nothing' guy," she said, making an exaggerated air quote. "He's outside waiting for you."

Sure enough, there he was. Sitting on the hood of his car, arms crossed, legs long enough to fold as they touched the ground. I felt like Molly Ringwald in *Sixteen Candles*—surely he wasn't standing there waiting for me. He was unmistakably handsome—perfect features—but a contradiction of sorts. Clean cut yet unshaven, slender yet well built.

I took my time, walking toward him in slow, calculated steps. *Because I knew that every moment with him brought me closer to falling.*

"Hi."

"Hello there, Andie, you look beautiful. I hear today's a special day," he said, smiling.

"What on earth could be so special about March 23rd?"

"Okay, to be honest—I walked in this morning as people were celebrating your birthday with you."

"Oh. You should have come in and joined us."

"What? And freak out that young lady like I did the other night? Just now when she saw me, she jumped and turned tail inside." He had this thing about little touches here and there. This time, it was to tuck a piece of hair behind my ear and then a light graze of his finger across my cheek.

"You do. You freak her out."

He smiled and slid off the hood. "So, what are your plans for tonight?"

"Tons, actually. I just haven't figured out which one to choose yet." He took my hand and …

31

Where the Hands Move

I wished I'd paid more attention to where we were going. But the conversation in his car had been so animated—I spent the last thirty minutes yakking about our hiring status and my growth strategy. He listened, gave me some advice, told me to build the business value, and maybe think about franchising.

Handsome and smart. I had to admit some parts of the exchange felt like the Charlie Brown movie, where all I heard was gibberish and all I saw were his bright blue eyes.

We exited HI 62 and walked a path shrouded in coconut trees, down a small grassy hill filled with sand and stone. A few steps later, our view opened up to powdery white sand on a crescent-shaped shoreline that ebbed and flowed into the unbounded sea.

"Over here," he said, draping my hand on his arm and showing me to a small square table, lined with a large mat made with woven leaves. In the middle of the table was a centerpiece of ferns and flowers, set with gold-rimmed plates and champagne flutes. "Happy Birthday, Andie."

"Warren, thank you. How did you pull this off?"

"Called in a few favors," he said with a lopsided smile.

I gave him the side-eye.

"Kidding."

"Where are we? This is absolutely stunning. Is this private?"

"We're on Kailua Beach. And it's public. Just not tonight."

I smiled. "Well, thank you. This is amazing." And then an afterthought. "Kailua, you said? I think Api's family lives somewhere around here."

"Look," he whispered, pointing to a group of people coming toward us. About five hundred yards away, half of them stopped by a sand pit and began to dig. The other half continued over to us.

I grabbed Warren's hand with excitement. He beamed from ear to ear.

"Are they here for us?" Their colored costumes stood out in the fading light. Three women in grass skirts and floral headdresses moved close and slipped leis over our heads.

"Dendrobiums," I gushed.

Warren held a blank look.

"Orchids," I explained. "My mom's really into them."

Three men clothed in tattoos and bright-colored sarongs approached.

"Good evening, Ms. Matthews, Mr. Yates. Welcome to your very own luau. The other guys are now removing the roast pork and vegetables from the ground," explained one of the men with fiery red hair and penetrating eyes. He saw me turn toward the group digging in the sand. "The imu is an underground oven that cooks meat with coals."

"It takes all day to cook and as I didn't know it was a special day until this morning, so hopefully they improvised," Warren explained.

"I'm sure it will be delicious," I said, still transfixed on the women with the costumes and the men approaching us with large wooden trays of food.

"For now, we will serve you dinner while you enjoy the sunset. And then, we will have a little show for you."

As the men walked away, the women began arranging our table. They were extraordinarily beautiful, long straight dark hair and deep-set eyes. Their skin was the color of the golden sun, honey, and brown sugar. They set the plates aside while offering us a choice of wine or champagne.

"I think we'll start with the champagne," Warren instructed. We both turned at the same time toward the sun, as it began its slow descent, first a myriad of colors shooting out in all directions and blanketing the sky. In a few seconds, it spread its fire across the sea, skidding across the water like a ballerina and her swan song, bidding the world goodnight. And then the ocean swallowed her up, light turning to dark, dark turning into night.

"Hold on," he exclaimed, pointing right at the sun. "Can you see it?"

The sun's rim, its very edge, was no longer visible. In its place was a green line, directly above the horizon.

"Yes," I answered. "What is that?"

"It happens all the time, but it's hard to see. The clearer the water, the more the blending of the colors of the setting or rising sun appears to look green. It's called a green flash."

"I can't believe I saw it tonight."

He lifted his glass and looked straight into my eyes. "Happy birthday, Andie. What a privilege it is to spend this special night with you."

Before I could respond, he turned away, leaving the silence to take my mind elsewhere—somewhere between the glow of the sky and the twilight of the sea.

"My mom used to say that sunsets are proof that endings can be beautiful."

I nodded, lost for words. A reminder to me that sunsets are inevitable. That whatever this was, it was temporary.

Who was this man, what did he want from me?

We ate most of our dinner in silence, savoring the delicious pork, which was cooked to perfection, with rice and poi and a variety of vegetables. Warren told me about the history of the luau, when men and women had their meals separately. Common folk and women of all classes had been forbidden to eat certain Hawaiian delicacies, which represented a man's characteristics such as strength, virtues, or aspirations. It was King Kamehameha who had decided one day to abolish that rule, a grand gesture of societal change. Since then, luaus had always been cause for celebration.

"I'm just so amazed by everything on this island. It is so unlike anywhere else I've ever been. There's a mystical vibe that I can't explain. An opposition, really. Old and new, fire and water. Losing oneself to the wild beauty of the island, only to find yourself in the tranquility that envelops you. That sort of thing." I wanted to find a more poetic way of saying it, but I was overwhelmed.

Warren nodded emphatically. "This is what I've been saying all along. I have a friend back in New York City who talks about how he doesn't like the Pacific Ocean, that it's too dark and cold and foreign to him. He prefers the Atlantic because Europe rests on the other side, and as America was engineered by Europeans and Africans, both who crossed the Atlantic to get there, it was tamed and safe. But having lived here as a boy, and again now, having lived near the Atlantic and across it in Paris, I see it differently. I love the Pacific Ocean precisely for its wildness and unpredictability, for the fact that it's surrounded by a ring of fire, and that the faces on the other side of the sea are different and offer a totally distinct view of life. Two cultures crashing like those waves on the barrier reef, creating a new life. A new way. And I love the idea that before the first European sailed these seas, the men and women of the islands were sailing all over the map, hopping from one to the next, establishing different tribes, languages, and cultures, and yet they are all cousins. This ocean is a rolling contradiction and I love it for that."

After dinner, the three women lined up in front of us, a band assembling a few feet away. Each one had a different colored grass skirt; each was adorned with a different style of leis and necklaces.

"And now we have a little presentation for you. Happy birthday, Miss Andie. We hope you love Hawaii as much as we do."

"I do," I said, turning my head toward Warren. "Thank you."

The youngest woman stepped forward. *"Kuhi no ka lima, hele no ka maka.* Where the hands move, there let the eyes follow."

With dainty movements and swinging hips, the women danced the hula. Each one had a personal expression through the movements of their hands. The dancers exhibited extraordinary grace and posture. Each movement, although controlled and balanced, was fluid and mesmerizing. After a few slow songs, the young girl stepped forward again.

"Now, upon the request of Mr. Yates"—she glanced toward

Warren and smiled—"we are going to perform the 'Coffee Cantata' by J.S. Bach."

I looked at him, not knowing what to expect.

Another woman and two men stepped forward and began to act out in song. It was a change from the previous ones, upbeat and fast paced.

Warren leaned forward, his lips lightly brushing my ear. "It's a story about a father and daughter who argued all the time about her coffee drinking habit. He forbids her to drink, saying she will never find a husband if she continues to do so. She agrees to quit drinking coffee but secretly she tells her suitors that they can't marry her unless she can have three cups a day."

I giggled.

He continued, "And then she had it written in the marriage contract."

"Smart girl."

We clapped with delight ten minutes later when the song was over, and the performers took a bow. Out of the shadows, two fire-knife dancers ran in, twirling and juggling batons of fire, throwing them and catching them at breakneck speed. It was a heart-stopping finale that had us on our feet, clapping, whooping, whistling.

Just then, Warren pointed over to the band who started playing a catchy tune. He walked toward the shore, in the middle of the other dancers and performers, and with a big smile, held out his hand to me. I kicked off my shoes and ran to him.

"It's the band from the coffee shop."

He nodded, pleased with himself. "The amazing Soul City Brothers. I don't think they ever played Motown." Warren twirled me around and then wrapped me in his arms while we danced.

"Oh, wait," Warren said, leading me closer to the shore. "There's a legend that says that when a visitor tosses their lei on the shore and allows the current to carry it through the sea, it is a sign that he or she will return one day."

"Here I go," I yelled, lifting the lei off my neck. "I'm throwing this into the water." How apt it was that I saw the face of the lady on the plane. She was in my thoughts, her fragrance as strong as the first day I met her. In my mind, she had become a steady fixture of the islands. Her words had lingered, made every moment with Warren more meaningful.

I couldn't recall how it all happened, but slowly, our party began to thin out, and I never saw the band pack up. While the music continued, I failed to notice the transition from a live band to the speaker on a stand anchored in the sand. I felt the vibrancy of the night slowly dissipate, the light growing dimmer, the sounds getting softer. Then a song, a familiar one, played so softly and sweetly, its rhythm blending with the push of the tide and the rustle of the leaves on the trees.

"Do you know this song?" Warren whispered, gently pulling me close, his big, warm hands firmly on my lower back, while I rested both hands on his shoulder.

"I do."

"Tell me the words."

It was a popular song. One normally sung at weddings, actually. I knew because it had been Nick's choice of song for our wedding. I was so engrossed in the excitement of the evening; it took me a while to realize it. Someone threw a ton of bricks at me, placed their weight on my chest. I was sick with emotion, I couldn't breathe. My knees felt weak. It was like a sick joke. I began to burn up with heat.

"I—" I began, drawing deep breaths while he held on to me, supporting my weight as I dipped slightly forward. In a flash, a green flash, a wave of relief washed over me and, just as quickly, I cooled down. I understood why that moment was meant to be. It was my second shot, my fresh start. I didn't know where this would lead, but I knew I was ready to live in the moment. And so, I straightened myself up, held on to him, and steadied my feet on the sand. I began to quietly sing.

"I want to hold you in my arms tonight,
I want to feel you, here by my side.
Don't worry honey, it'll be all right.
And anything that haunts you as you go to sleep at night,
Just let it die."

With that, I lay my head on his shoulder, his fingers lightly brushing the small of my back, a gentle touch spinning me out of control. Making me feel every touch, every breath, every beat of this sad song. When it was over, there was no one there. Every evidence of the luau before, gone without a trace.

Unlike the first night he kissed me, I didn't run away. We moved to the silence, looking up only once to gaze at the moon and the stars. They begged us to stay, promised to light up the night if we gave love a chance. And we did. In the stillness and in the calm, my heart broke out of bounds, soared above the sky, high enough to touch those stars.

On that night, I knew without a doubt Nick wasn't the one

for me and it had worked out the way it was meant to. I could forgive myself at last.

"Andie?"

"Hmm," I answered dreamily, my eyes closed, lost in my own story. Thinking of all the moments we'd had, the close calls, the times I'd thought I would burst from all those pent-up feelings and wishing he would just. Kiss. Me.

"Can I kiss you now?" He brought his face to mine until our foreheads touched.

"Do you always have to ask permission?"

"With you, yes. Always." Slowly, he tipped my chin up to align his mouth to mine. Lips close.

"Kiss me," I begged, gasping for air, certain only he could breathe life back into me. "Please. Kiss me."

32

For So Long

In my dream, I was in Paris, the Tuileries Gardens in full bloom on a sunny spring day. Runners clogged the lanes between the rows of chestnut trees, and I was merely one of them. The trees weren't lined up the way I knew them to be. Instead, they zigzagged through the pavement like hedges in a maze, blocking every outlet and making us run around in circles. The leaves of the trees weren't paper-thin and light. They were large and droopy, like the coffee trees on the farm. As the runners disappeared, a rain of cherries came rushing down, strong winds causing them to spin around.

What was it with thinning crowds and disappearing people?

My heart was pounding, I was out of breath. I couldn't see past the trees. What's worse, there were no exits. Only dead ends. The running seemed endless. No matter where I went, there was no way out.

"Andie," I heard him say, his voice thundering above the swish of the wind and the slapping of the leaves. "I've been looking for you."

"Nick," I shouted, running toward the voice, relieved when I saw him at the end of the entrance. Everything looked normal—the Ferris wheel, the fountain, all in the places I knew them to be. "Thank goodness. I was so afraid. I couldn't find the exit; I'd been lost for so long—"

When he turned around and held out his hand, I realized it wasn't Nick. Nick with the features of the sunset, the one I left out in the dusk. It was someone else with the sunrise in his hair and the ocean in his eyes.

As I ran to him, a siren went off. Loud and shrill at first, and then foggier and fuzzier as he stood within my reach. I opened my eyes to the vibrating phone on my night table.

"Hello?" I croaked, sinking into my pillow and pulling the covers up to my ears.

"Hey there, it's me."

"Good morning," I greeted. Happy, content—at peace.

"You still in bed, huh?"

"Yeah, I had the weirdest dream." I cut myself off when I remembered he was in it. "I have to get up soon and get to the bank. They left a message last night for me to stop by." I sat up and leaned on the headboard, glancing at the clock to confirm the time.

"Was that before or after the kissing?" he teased.

"Probably before." I laughed.

"Are you—are you okay?" he asked, pausing between words.

"Yes, I am. Are you?"

"I'd like to see you again tonight. Can I see you?"

"I have to drive to the farm today. Let me text you if I make it back at a decent time?" I wanted a way out, in case it wasn't a good idea to see him so soon. Last night had been perfect. I wanted to leave it at that for a while.

"Sounds great."

Duke's heavily starched suit made scratching noises as he shifted in his seat. We waited patiently for the loan officer who was finishing up a call.

"What's his name again, this guy?"

"Paul Ma," I said, running my hand over to smooth the crease on his collar. "Okay, so, Duke. Remember, I'm going to need your help when it comes to the technical info on the equipment. I know nothing about that. No one knows this business better than you do. You are the lifeline of the plantation. Let's make sure everybody sees that."

"Okay, okay," he answered, fidgeting with his wedding ring this time, and holding up his hand. "I don't know why Lani made me wear this."

"It's the finishing touch on such a dashing look," I said, smiling.

Years ago, I'd interviewed with a design agency that specialized in sprucing up bank lobbies and offices. Their work was modern and contemporary. When I went to check out one of their client national banks, I had been amazed at the difference the decor made in the mood and disposition of the employees and customers. The idea was to introduce brightly painted walls, one point of focus, open concept and minimalist design, promotional materials and banners strategically poised but not overbearing.

This bank looked like it desperately needed their help. The office looked like your grandfather's library. Heavy oak, dark decor. Intimidating. No wonder it made Duke nervous.

Twenty minutes later, Mr. Ma was back at his desk.

He opened up a brown accordion folder and began pulling out papers. "Miss Matthews, on behalf of Apikelia Flores for The Island Coffee Company," he said, reading the heading aloud.

"Yes, and this is Mr. Duke Aquino, foreman of the plantation. Do you have any questions about the equipment we'd like to lease and the loan we'd like to apply to capital improvements?"

"Not really."

Now, it was my turn to shift in my seat. I hated to admit this, but I had my power suit on. The only one I'd packed—just in case—the navy blue one with a high-waisted belt. It did nothing to assuage my lack of self-confidence.

Mr. Ma continued to review the papers, shuffling them back and forth, refiling them, resorting, highlighting some words. It felt like forever before we heard a peep. My underarms began to sweat. I wanted this loan more than anything I'd ever focused on before. Duke kept looking at me with his dark, soulful eyes, his gaze halfway down, humbled by this man. I shook my head at him, gesturing for him to look up. Thankfully, he understood and sat up with his shoulders pulled back. "Good," I nodded.

Mr. Ma made a loud whistling sound. "Okay, so. Ms. Matthews. It looks like the share of the Island Coffee Company isn't enough to collateralize a two-million-dollar loan." He turned to a second page. "But if you combine the future share of the Apex company, it will put you well over and above your loan amount.

In other words, you can even borrow more."

I leaned forward, tilted my head, confused. "And who is Apex again?"

"They were the people your dad, I mean Mr. Flores, was going into partnership with," Duke answered.

"Ah. Okay." I crossed my legs and leaned back.

"Apex has agreed to fund as well, Ms. Matthews," Mr. Ma added.

"No, no. I want to do this on my own. I have a condo in Chicago that's fully paid for. I have placements well over the amount of the loan. Let's change the guarantee to my personal assets. Would that be possible?" I wasn't exactly prepared for this, but it was game time. So many people had their lives hanging in the balance.

Mr. Ma scratched his head. "Hmm. Let me find out. Mr. Martinez is here for a meeting, so let me go to him. Give me a minute."

Duke turned to me as soon as Mr. Ma was out of the room. "Andie, what are you doing?"

I placed my hand on his arm and smiled at him when I felt the sleeves hanging loosely. "Let me."

Mr. Ma was back in a flash, this time with more papers. "Do you know Lucas Martinez? He's the owner of our bank."

"No, I don't."

"Oh, I thought you did. Because I didn't even finish what I was saying and he said, yes. All I would need"—Mr. Ma pulled out a checklist—"is a copy of bank statements and investments."

"I can get that to you by tomorrow."

"And an appraisal?" he asked.

"You can get it done anytime. But let me show you on Zillow, the property in question."

He jerked back, surprised when I walked over to his side of the table and took hold of his mouse. When I found my property, his eyes grew large with excitement. "This will work. This will work."

"Would it be safe to say that we've got the loan?" I knew there were more documents to process, but a verbal was good enough. I knew I had the funds.

"Unless you were previously arrested or have had credit problems," he said with a smirk. "I would say, yes."

"Well then," I said, knowing that the equity had shifted. Duke was now in control. "I'd like to get the contact information for Apex from you so I can thank them personally. From here and going forward, Mr. Aquino here will be your contact."

Duke looked at Mr. Ma and then at me before clapping his hands once and letting out a giant, warm belly laugh. He seemed three inches taller. Through a huge smile he simply said, "*Mahalo*."

Instead of sitting out on the boulder overlooking the world, I walked a few steps down the hill to Wai'alae Beach. The night was dark—clouds formed a layer that covered the moon and the stars. I was still in my navy-blue suit, barefoot and digging my toes into the sand. Little blue crabs and hermit crabs crisscrossed on the beach in front of me, washing away with the tide and rolling back in with the waves.

I snapped my head up as someone approached, announced by the crunching of dried up palm fronds.

"Andie? It's just me."

Warren. I needed this time to process everything that happened the night before. I had questions. Lots of them. I had been so caught up in the emotion last night, I hadn't had the words. But anyone who knew me knew how long that lasted. Now, there he was.

"Sorry I didn't text. I ended up staying until ten o'clock and just needed to get some things at the store on my way home."

"I just left work too. I saw your car from the highway and decided to see if you were here."

I nodded. Pulled my knees up and wrapped my arms around them. He wore dress pants, a black leather belt, a pink polo shirt, and glasses—blue-rimmed and square. They did nothing but make him look sexier.

"I can leave if—"

"No, no. Stay." I offered my hand. He took it and sat right next to me.

"You look nice," he said. "How'd it go?"

"We got it. I had to use some of my personal property to get the loan amount, but it worked out."

"Oh, Andie. I'm not sure that was the best thing to do," he said, looking at me, kneading the palm of my hand with his thumb. "I could have helped with other options."

"How could you have helped? You hardly know me. Why would you do that? Besides, I feel really strongly about it. For the first time in so long, I feel I'm truly making a difference. I know this decision is coming from my heart more than my head, but it feels right."

He stayed silent. But I was comfortable with that. It felt good to be in the quiet. With him. I felt him squeeze my hand and tug it slightly, as if to get my attention.

"Can we talk about last night?" he asked, lightly grazing his thumb across my wrist.

"That's why you're here, isn't it?"

"Partly, yes. I had to ask you," he admitted. "When you became emotional about that song, was it because of your past? Is that past still a part of your life?"

"In February of last year, I broke off my engagement to someone I was with for five years. He chose that song for our wedding dance and it just caught me by surprise. But it was just a short-lived lapse on my side. I didn't want to ruin the night because of that."

"Do you regret breaking it off? Is your heart still with him?" Warren let go of my hand and slightly moved away. Somehow, I didn't blame him for putting his guard up. After all, I'd had mine up for the same reason.

"To be totally honest, it's more guilt that I feel. He loved me, Warren. He wanted to have a future with me. But I was too selfish, too focused on my career to take the time to fall in love right back. I thought that if I planned well enough, if I did all the right things, love would happen eventually. When he threatened to break the engagement, I was juggling so many things in my life, removing that one obligation was a relief for me. How bad was that?"

He turned to look at me. Searched for my eyes and held his there. "Did you ever love him?"

"I did. I really did. Just not enough at that time. Being here—spending time with Lani's family and Maele, seeing the Floreses and the love they had, and the time you gave to your mom—I'm changing. Then with my parents and their perfect love story—through them I am inspired to live with an open heart. In the past, I took love for granted. But then meeting you—I'm learning about what's important and I want that now. But I'm afraid I'll never have it."

"Me too," he said, still holding my gaze. "I'm afraid too."

He draped his arm around me, pulled me close so that my head nestled itself on his chest. Every time he touched me, I saw stars, I felt the light. It didn't matter how dark it was.

"Can I be honest with you? I knew you wouldn't want to meet me at the store during business hours."

"What do you mean?" I asked, lifting my head and turning to face him.

"It's bothering me that you haven't told anyone about me. Do they know about me?"

"No, why should they?" I challenged. "First, I've been focused on saving the business. Second, that was part of the deal. I'm your secret, and you're mine."

"Do they know I'm pursuing you, because …?"

"Are you?" There we were, volleying back a question with a question. "Because you shouldn't be. Today, the loan was approved, which means my job here is almost done. I leave in one month."

"Oh, Andie. If only you knew. My instincts tell me to run as far away as I can from this. Yet my heart tells me to keep going. That maybe there's a chance you'll stay a little longer, that something will keep you here. You've awakened the fire in my heart and there's no turning back for me. I don't know what to do with it. How to tame it. How to ignore it. And maybe I don't want to."

"I'm a mess, Warren. I don't know what I want. All I know is that I love spending time with you. That I've never felt so comfortable with anyone else. That our moments together have brought out feelings I've never had before."

"Feelings are good," he said, his eyes the only light in the dark. "Maybe we should just stop overthinking this."

"What do we do?"

He was about to say something but then he took a long pause, the air suddenly became full of anticipation. He met my gaze and held it.

"We spend every chance we can together while you're here. Take every opportunity to see where this goes. And you don't make any conclusions until we talk about it."

"Okay," I said, leaning into him.

He took my hand and brought it to his lips. "One more thing."

"Yes?"

"I'm breaking the rules. It's your turn. Tell everyone about me."

Chiquita's Confession

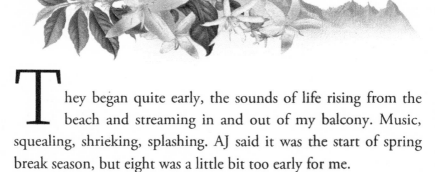

They began quite early, the sounds of life rising from the beach and streaming in and out of my balcony. Music, squealing, shrieking, splashing. AJ said it was the start of spring break season, but eight was a little bit too early for me.

I had taken the weekend off, planned to lounge around in my pajamas, clear my head, write up a plan. With the loan approval process just a matter of formality, it was time to figure out a real business plan to keep the farm going in perpetuity. New equipment to help during harvesting season was just the beginning. Innovation would have to follow next—thinking of new products and ideas to keep sales constant. Research and development would follow. I'd have to hire a small team or a consulting firm to do this. Small-scale marketing had worked so far, and I planned to suggest waiting for a bigger campaign as cash flow stabilized.

First things first. I'd made a promise to Warren that I intended to keep. My mom and dad didn't have to know—no sense in getting my mom all excited for nothing. But my family here, that was a different story.

"Hi, Chiquita," Api answered the phone on the first ring. She walked over to the kitchen and rested her phone against something so she could sit and talk to me. "What's up?"

"Nothing, really. Just want to touch base on a couple of things. I can't wait to see you next week."

"Me either," she answered. "What are you drinking?"

"Nothing but the best coffee," I said, raising my mug so she could see it. "I don't plan on getting off this couch or parting ways with these pajamas today."

Api laughed. "Proud of you."

"Also, we hired two people. Lani and Maele have more help now." I took a sip of my coffee. "And we're still making money."

Api rubbed her hands together in delight. A voice in the background grabbed her attention. She muted the phone and pulled James into the frame. Her tall, dark, and handsome Prince Charming was all dressed up in a suit. He blew me a kiss.

"Mom said the loan was approved."

"Yes. That was next on my agenda to tell you about."

"Of course, you have an agenda," she teased. "First of all, we're so grateful to you for everything you've done for my family, my dad's legacy, Duke's family. Let's talk when I get back there— Mom wants to make sure we help as much as we can. She's insisting that we take you off the hook financially. This wasn't your cross to bear, Andie. How lucky are we that you have devoted all your time and energy to this, instead of truly taking your much-needed time off."

"Let's not worry about the details yet. This experience has helped me more than you will ever know," I said.

"So, I'll see you next week at Mom's?" she asked.

"Yes, I'll come get you at the airport. And I'll pack all my stuff up as well and lock your place up. Haven't made up my mind when I'm heading back, but it will be shortly after you get here. Two weeks tops."

"I'm sad to hear that, but I know you have to get back," she replied. "While we're together, I'll take you wherever you want. Maybe we can hop around the islands or something. You haven't been anywhere."

"Well," I said. *Should I tell her?* I tried to hide my giddiness by controlling my tone. "That's not exactly true." *If I didn't say something, someone else would and Api would be hurt if she didn't hear it from me.*

"Oh?"

"I've been kind of seeing someone."

"Jiminy crickets. I should have known. How could someone as gorgeous as you not meet anyone? Oh my gosh. I am so happy. How long?"

My heart beat faster as a thought hit me. "Wait a minute." She knew Warren. Or at least they were acquaintances from what he said. "How's it going over there, by the way? The no swearing thing?" I said the first thing that came to mind. *What if she didn't like him?*

"As expected," she said defiantly, blowing air through her lips. "They think I'm weird. But who cares?" She looked directly at me. "Don't change the subject. How long?"

"Technically, since Christmas Eve. Realistically? Since New Year's Eve."

She shook her head, confused.

"I mean, I met him on Christmas Eve, but he kissed me on New Year's Eve."

"What?" she screamed. James came running back on camera. She shooed him away.

"Your darn Kiss for a Cup thing," I said, rolling my eyes, pretending to be upset.

"Oh." She laughed.

"Well …" I sighed. "I'll let you go. It looks like you guys are going somewhere." I wanted to end the call before she told me my prince was a toad.

"They're throwing a party for James tonight," she said, flicking her hand dismissively. "Who cares if we're late? I want to know more. Like who is he, what does he do, what is he like? Spill, girl."

"He's amazing, Api. Of course, I'm just getting to know him, but really smart." I couldn't help gushing about him. "He doesn't push, is always respectful of my priorities. But I have to tell you, it's been fun. He's taken me out a couple of times, but he goes to New York on business quite a bit. So, we've been seeing each other when we can."

"And you're leaving in a few weeks?" she asked.

"How do you know, Api? How do you know when it's worth investing in?"

"It's not like the business world. Sometimes, the ones with the least returns are the ones you invest in. Because you can't control what your heart wants. You follow your heart, whether or not it feels right."

"It's too new. I've got to start that new position in Chicago. He knows that."

"What's his name? What does he do?"

"I don't know what he does," I laughed, embarrassed. I made

a mental note to find this out immediately. "But his name is Warren. I'll get back to you on the job."

"Yeah, but you can tell if he's got a good job. His car, his clothes. Can he support you?" Api looked away as she opened a compact and began applying lipstick.

"I don't know about all that. I've been so focused on the farm and work, I never noticed. Besides, I can support myself, Ms. Flores."

"Huh," she replied. "Last name? You do know his last name, don't you?"

"Of course. Yates. Last name is Yates."

She shut her compact with such a force, I thought she'd broken it. Then she looked straight at me, before standing and taking the phone. There was a long pause. I saw the floor, her thighs, her blue skirt. I heard the click clacking of her footsteps on the floor; I could have sworn she was pacing back and forth.

"Api? Api? Where are you?"

"Sorry, sorry. I'm trying to find my shoes," she answered, laying the phone down so all I saw was the ceiling. Seconds later, she brought it so close to her face all I saw were here nostrils. "Reeeeeeeeeally."

"You know him." Once again, that feeling of dread.

"I went to high school with him."

"Whew? So, not an old lover like I originally thought?"

"What? No. Why would you say that?"

"Because he came looking for you."

"Andie, have Maele and Lani met him?" And after a pause. "I mean, do they like him?"

"Maele saw him at the store, but she rushed out," I said with a chuckle. "So, the general answer is no. More like, afraid of him?"

James was back in focus, this time telling her they had to get going.

"Okay, okay. I'll see you outside," she said to him. "Okay, Andie, I gotta go. But I can't wait to catch up on this next week in person."

"Okay, Api. Have fun at the party."

"Thanks."

"Safe travels back."

Just as I pressed END, the phone rang again. This time there was no video, just voice.

"Hey, it's me. You hung up too quickly. I was going to say— I love you."

I couldn't help but snicker. "I love you too, Api."

"Andie, one more, actually. I want you to be happy. So, be happy. But don't rush things, okay? You deserve only the best. One day, there will be this super terrific guy who will be worth all your love and trust. Don't give up on love, no matter what happens.."

PART TWO:
Warren

Life is a prison
We are each other's freedom
Do not be afraid

The M Word

I just met the girl I'm going to marry."

In the strangest of circumstances and on the fifth anniversary of the saddest night of my life.

Five years ago, fate chose to kill my mother on Christmas Eve. Fate used cancer, but it felt like murder. And Christmas Eve, a night reserved for hope, joy, and visits from Santa, has since been forever stained in my mind and heart. Every year, the anniversary of her death hits me like a steam train, tearing through in brutish contrast to the mirth and cheer of the season.

She had asked to be buried in the place where she'd found love and that's what had brought me back here. Before the ugliness, the betrayal and the divorce, my mom had spent the best days of her life with my dad on this island. I was born here, in a small house in Kahala, where I'd lived the first half of my life. The latter half of my life called New York City home.

Like any other year before, I paid my mom a visit on the afternoon of the anniversary of her death. After spending time there, I planned to do what I'd always done these last five years—wallow in sorrow. In earlier years and before the need for NDAs, this night mostly involved drinks and women. For the past two years, it had been only drinks. The biggest constant? Paddy's, the bar across the street from my father's downtown office. Except that evening was different. I was filled with resentment for my father once again. Not an abnormal feeling, but I felt pressured into doing what he'd been on me to accomplish that particular night and for weeks leading up to it. He called it my last big challenge. A carrot he dangled over my head. If I did this, and before the new year for tax reasons, he would release the rest of my shares to me so I could be free to pursue, well … and that's my other problem, I don't exactly know what to pursue.

I had been tasked with taking over a business from this young woman who was running it into the ground. Her dad had recently passed away and she had no idea what she was doing. My father thought it was the perfect time to increase his ownership to one-hundred percent, divide the assets, and sell it for a profit.

I passed on an evening at Paddy's and decided to swing by her shop instead. I knew the place well. It's a charming, albeit in need of some serious TLC, standalone tucked in a quiet area off the highway and right on the beach.

Apikelia Flores, who was also a looker, had gone on a trip with her mother.

But her friend was there, minding the store for her.

In that pitiful place—that dark, sad place where no one ever ventured despite its prime location—was Andie Matthews. Gone were the unswept cobwebs, the disarrayed shelves, and the mismatched furniture, though I barely noticed any of that because of her. She was a vision with her light brown hair, straight and thick, her brown eyes and perfect nose. She'd worn overalls, for heaven's sake. But it was her skin, her lips, everything aligned in perfect symmetry that lit up the place like a burst of stars.

I'd wracked my brain, thought of every excuse to stay. She felt like home to me, and I hadn't wanted to leave.

I'd almost kissed her that night. I'd wanted to so badly. In a strange moment of mishaps and awkward conversation, we had been pulled together, bound by an invisible energy.

The thing is, I was the broken one, the one with a host of issues. Trouble for anyone who crossed my path.

I'd been going to therapy ever since mom passed away. And on that particular night, I was looking to find a way to cut ties with my father. I'd exited from a large deal we made on a resort island in Southeast Asia, taken my share, cashed in and invested it in my house and on stocks and bonds. The profit and dividends I'd made were enough for me to retire. But Father had used some sort of sappy story on me about how I needed to carry on the business for Adam's sake. Even though he was my half brother, we looked alike. I always said it was because our moms were the same type, which speaks volumes about my father, who was, of course, our sole sire. He acted like a king, in a kingdom of his own making. My father's problem was that I didn't care. In fact, neither of his princes did. My father was the only subject in his imaginary kingdom. Adam, half brother of a prince, was a pretty laid-back kid. Got good grades in high school, was well behaved. I hadn't really known him until five years ago, when he'd showed up at my mom's funeral, all by himself, the king and his current queen didn't show "out of respect." He'd been with me ever since, going from a gangly sixteen-year-old with braces to a vivacious, opinionated, passionate young man. It was then I realized just how much of his life I had missed now that he was in mine.

Adam had his head stuck in the fridge when I walked into the kitchen that morning. More often than not, he would crash at my place either when Father and Marta drove him crazy or he wanted to play video games.

"Did you just say something?" Adam looked at me before taking the pint of milk and walking across the lanai, past the pool, and back to the guesthouse, which was his whenever he wanted it. Clothes were strewn all over the floor and an open suitcase sat on top of a pile of shoes. He saw my eyes dart around the room. "Don't worry. Those will all end up in the suitcase." He took a swig of milk and sat on a large rattan chair facing the pool. "Let's talk about the issue at hand, shall we? You just spewed out some really weird words."

"You heard what I said."

"Yes, but do I believe it?" he snorted, leaning back and looking at me with a smirk.

"I needed to tell someone, and you're the closest thing that fits the description."

Adam made a face. "You said that about—wait, what was that girl's name? Julie, Julia?" The milk jug was on the floor; now he was munching on some chocolate chip cookies.

"I did not," I said, grabbing a can of sparkling water from the mini fridge next to the TV cabinet.

"No, you didn't. I was trying to make a point."

"Which is what?"

"Um, I don't know. I just had a brain fart," he said, licking the chocolate off his fingers.

"That's nasty. You're nasty, and now you're gonna touch my

couch with those nasty fingers? Where did you get those cookies, anyway?"

"I went to the Hilton last night. Rooftop. They have amazing cookies when you check in."

"Are you gonna keep partying like that in LA?"

Adam switched on the TV and grabbed one of his game controllers before taking a seat on the leather sectional. A seventy-five-inch curved TV spanned the length of the wall on the opposite side of the bed. "Want to play?"

"Not really."

Adam sat a few feet away from me, pushing buttons while he spoke. "Come on, you look like you need some stress relief." And under his breath, he said, "Which is what you look like every day."

I rolled my eyes.

"And no, LA is really for work. And I truly appreciate your doing the surf school for me. You'll love the kids. The mothers, not so much. Unless you're into that, 'cause some of them are gonna be into you, big bro. Watch yo'self."

"I probably went to school with all of them," I said, matter-of-fact, dismissing his attempts to get a rise out of me.

"Yeah, one actually told me that." He winked. "She asked if you were dating anyone." He looked at me. "I told her you've taken the vow of celibacy. But I guess I was wrong, Mr. I Met a Girl."

"One game," I said, hoping it would segue into what I wanted to talk about.

Thirty minutes in, amid hunting, horse riding, gunfights, and train robberies, he paused the game.

"Hey, I was just about to shoot that sheriff," I said, turning it back on and breaking into the Bob Marley song, full voice.

Hanging out with Adam was my chance to feel young again, no cares, no responsibilities. I loved being a big brother,

That time, he turned the console off. "Hold on. You just traumatized me with the 'M' word, so now you have to totally explain what you said."

I leaned back on the couch, sank into the seat, and stretched out my legs. "Do you remember the coffee shop on Kahala? The one Father sent us to that afternoon a few months ago?"

"How can I forget? The dump that had the really pretty barista."

"Do you recall the owner?"

"Yeah, she was hot too. Except she had these really big eyelashes that could have blown us away if she decided to bat them. She was too princess-y for me. Typical Daddy's girl, accessorized to the hilt."

I laughed. "Yes, Apikelia Flores."

"Kind of like the ones you used to date," he teased. Adam knew how to get my goat. In such a short amount of time, this boy had mastered the art of annoying me.

I tossed a cookie at his head. Perfect shot. "I stopped by the store again after visiting my mom at the mausoleum."

"Before or after Paddy's?"

I let that one slide. "I skipped Paddy's that day."

Adam stood and grabbed a bag of tortilla chips from under the cocktail table and a bowl of salsa from the counter. "This is going to be a long one, I need fuel."

"How long has that salsa been there?" I asked, seriously concerned about his disregard for refrigeration.

"Bruh, don't worry about it. This is yours. I got it from your fridge last night."

"In that case—" I took a chip from the bag and dipped it in the bowl. "Okay, so anyway, I went to the store looking for Ms. Flores that night and lo and behold, she was traveling with her mother. But," I said wagging a finger in the air, "her friend was there. Andie Matthews from Chicago. Stunning. She had these soulful brown eyes, long, sexy neck. We talked for a while. And then, I went back on New Year's Eve and kissed her."

"Whoa. Smooth. The doctor is in," Adam said, turning an imaginary basketball shot into a high five while making a *swoosh* sound. "Does she know who you are? What is it about her that makes you utter the forbidden word? I mean, dude, you've been single for so long. Not to hurt your feelings or anything, but you're kind of getting old. A good-looking, successful guy like you, still single—people think you have serious issues."

"Dude, I'm only thirty-three and I do have serious issues," I said. "Dr. Norman will attest to that." The sounds of crunching and munching filled the room. "Anyway, we've been really cagey about our pasts, specifically what we do for work. I'm sure she's looked me up because I've done the same on her. She's a big-time venture capitalist who's worked on huge contracts with social media giants and auto entrepreneurs. But dig this." I took my phone, Googled Andie's name and showed it to Adam. "Lately, she's been solely focused on funding only women and minority businesses. Impressive, huh?"

"Yes. She's very impressive. You should see your face right now. You're all googly-eyed. Look at you. You've gone gooey on me, big bro." And then he pulled back like he always did, knowing I was trying to have a serious conversation. "She is gorgeous, I'll give you that. And apparently smart too. But she's got to have something wrong with her. I mean, she's almost as old as you and not married?"

"Like I've explained to you countless times before, our generation just gets married later." I huffed, satisfying my need to fidget by taking the remote control and pushing its buttons nonsensically.

I was up against a twenty-one-year old's values and opinions. What did he know? None of us knew what we wanted or who we were at that age. That's how my mom had explained Father's transgressions. She'd always said he had outgrown her when his business succeeded. She'd stayed at home, didn't mingle, and had been content with raising her child.

Never get too comfortable, Warren. Always question the status quo. Life never stops. Time never waits.

"Okay, well, I'm pretty sure she has issues."

"Actually, she comes from this seemingly perfect family. She's super close to her brother who is a doctor in Spain. Her mom and dad still hold hands after thirty-six years together. She talks about her dad as if he is the best guy in the world. Honest, hardworking. Even her breakup last year sounded uneventful. She's very driven, just like me. I can tell by the way she put this business plan together. I'm definitely the messed up one. She's extremely grounded."

"You still haven't explained to me your momentary lapse of reason." Adam yawned before stretching out on the other end of the sectional. "I might take a nap after this. I'm beat."

"I'm falling in love with her. I know this because I can't stop thinking about her. I've never been like this before."

"I've never seen you like this. Man, that"—he pointed at my face—"is the classic whipped look. You've become a simp. And you know what?" He settled his head between the pillows and closed his eyes. "I'm happy for you. Just don't use words like *love* and *marriage* unless you mean them. You've got commitment issues. Call Dr. Norman so he can help you fix them."

"Yeah okay, Mr. Know-It-All."

Adam burrowed his head under a pile of pillows at the edge of the sofa—a sign that he was going to shut down soon.

I stood to leave. He shot his head back up. "Can I tell Mom now? She cares about you, you know."

"I know she does." I bent to pick up a towel, a T-shirt, and a pair of jeans on the floor. He watched me run my hand across them in an effort to remove their creases before folding them and laying them on the floor next to him. That's when I found his recently smoked hash pipe. Adam was high again. I hated to see him like this. The problem was, I could never tell because he'd normalized it. I looked over at him, zonked out on my couch, chips and salsa and cookies surrounding him. It broke my heart.

So, instead I said, "And no. Don't you dare tell a soul."

"I love you," he said, his words emerging from deep inside the cushion.

"Me too."

— 35 —

She Wore Pink

I t was early Friday morning and I had made a promise. This was no ordinary promise—it was my word given to children and it couldn't be broken. But I also found myself right in the middle of a deal I'd struck with Andie—our grand moments tour—which had fast become the highlight of my week.

Today would be no different as I pulled up to her apartment. She was out in front of her building, waiting for me with coffee and breakfast. I looked forward to our Friday morning ritual.

We set out early and there was a bite in the air. I had a special treat planned for Andie in the afternoon, but I hoped she'd enjoy what I had planned for the morning even more. In my experience, there were two types of women—those who loved other people's kids and those who didn't. I'd soon find out which one Andie was.

We pulled up to the antiquated YMCA in Waimamalo. I'd been a big brother here for the past five years and I had plans to completely renovate the facilities, give these kids something to be proud of. What was exciting to me was that neither Maineialoha, the woman in charge of the youth program at the Y, nor any of the kids, knew about my plans. Construction would be a total surprise, but I had blueprints drawn up and contractors hired who would give these kids the coolest hangout on the islands. Most boys liked to dress up as Batman, but I always loved pretending to be Bruce Wayne.

"Waimamalo is where a lot of middle and lower middle-class Hawaiians live. There is actually a pretty big problem Native Hawaiians are facing. Simply put, their land is becoming too expensive for them to live on anymore. In fact, on the west side, near Makaha where I took you to run rocks, is a part of the island where Native Hawaiians are allowed to live as they once did— outside and in villages where there are no permanent structures. We aren't allowed to go there, otherwise I'd show you."

"What are we doing here?" Andie asked, looking at the overgrown building with its cracked tennis and basketball court.

"I'd like you to meet a few of my friends before I take you kayaking."

We were greeted by fifteen of the bravest kids in Hawaii, made brave by their difficult circumstances. They were family to me. In a family, the elders shared wisdom. That's what I tried to do with these kids because I knew what it was like not having someone showing you the ropes, trying to navigate the world without a father figure.

We played games like football and tag and Andie lit up. Her face was peaceful and full of kindness and joy. She looked at home with these kids and they took to her immediately. At one point, the kids stood in a circle around her, moving in and out while holding hands like the iris of a camera—opening wide the circle and then rushing toward her and closing the circle. All the while Andie just stood there, happy and calm as if there was no other place in the world she'd rather be. In this picture-perfect moment, I knew she was the one. I had no idea what she was thinking then, but when our eyes met, I felt things for her I'd never felt for anyone. I was shaken to my core.

We said our goodbyes to the young ones after the obligatory foot race and sped off to the taco hut. It didn't have an official name, was just a hut on the side of the road that served the best fish tacos I had ever eaten.

"This is the best fish taco I've ever eaten in my life," Andie agreed.

After lunch, we made our way out to the Mokulua Islands. A spot on the north island was private and protected from the winds. We dragged the kayaks to the water from a nearby rental surf shack and got ready to go into the water. In my case, that just meant I just had to whip off my shirt. Andie, on the other hand, had to undress.

She looked like Jacqueline Kennedy Onassis that day, when Jackie O used to pull off the relaxed fashion icon look in blue jeans and a white polo shirt—classy yet sporty. But when I watched Andie unbutton her shirt to reveal a pink bra underneath, I suddenly felt like I was seeing something I shouldn't. It was just her bikini top, but it felt like I was spying on a very private moment, which was nothing compared to what came next because she began to peel her jeans off and I saw the bottoms that matched the top. I was thunderstruck.

Andie was so beautiful I lost the ability to speak for a moment. She stood in front of me, wearing the sexiest pink bikini I'd ever seen. It was hard to describe why it was sexy—in terms of what it revealed, it was innocent and simple. Maybe because it was her—

not just any woman on a beach wearing a swimsuit—but this spectacular woman who was smart, funny, and good with children. There were so many sides of her I had yet to explore. And it made me look forward to the future.

Her body was lean and tan, her skin perfectly smooth, almost like butter, but tight. Her long legs rose into the little pink suit that hugged her body perfectly and set off the color of her skin just so. Her lower back, her stomach, her waist, and her ribs were all revealed—her natural beauty was displayed in the sunlight. I suddenly realized I was just standing there staring. I tripped over my kayak as I grabbed it and headed down toward the water.

"I can't wait to show you the islands. They are just as God made them, perfect." I quickly shut up because I wasn't talking about the islands.

I had never had an issue making moves on a woman. In fact, shamefully, I had always been someone who—either through a charm offensive or sheer animal attraction—had been able to win any heart I wanted. In other words, I was a dog and not proud of it. At one point, I'd felt like a living, breathing Classic View-Master. Those little red, plastic nickelodeons with the little white disks of photos they called reels. Click and spin. I was the viewfinder, women were the reels, and it made me sad after a while. I didn't want to be that guy anymore, but I was filled with shame that no good woman would ever want me, so I'd do it all again.

Until I met Andie.

She made me want to be a better man, made me feel clean and new again, like I'd felt at five years old in the sunshine with my father, joyfully laughing at my mother doing cartwheels on the grass. I'd had about five perfect years on this planet before the fighting and crying and worrying and loneliness began. Andie was a direct line to the feeling of those glorious, tender, happy years. She was like the sunrise.

When we came ashore on the north island, my lustful side was hungrier than it had been in a long time. All I wanted to do was devour Andie inch by inch. I wanted her so badly I shivered. I watched her lay on the shore, digging her feet into the sand, the sun making the beads of sweat shine on her body like stars. I wanted to kiss her, but this other force took hold of me. A completely new force, one that respected Andie and valued her virtue and knew waiting would ensure a lifetime reward, not a momentary one.

So we sat there in silence on the hot beach, with the cry of a seagull in the wind. Andie stretched out like a washed up mermaid, and me just staring at this perfect work of art.

36

Lucas and Jade

"**M**orning?" Jade shuffled into the kitchen, looking at me like I'd grown two heads, when all I was doing was eating off the serving plate of cheese and olives they had left out the night before. The 8 a.m. sun was still caught in the haze of the thinning clouds. Beyond the white French doors was a picture worth a thousand words. Right at the tip of the Wai'anae mountains, my friend, Lucas, and his wife, Jade, had found the perfect summer home.

"Is Lucas in?" I asked, turning and trying to make it to the coffeemaker.

Jade came up from behind me, separating me from the coffee filters. "Here, sit. Let me make it." She had her hair up in a bun, green eyes showing through the crimson strands of hair covering part of her face. "If he's not in his office, he probably went for a run. I slept in. Mia had a stomachache last night."

"He's not there. And sorry about Mia."

The sounds and smell of percolating coffee made me hungry. Because she was intuitive, Jade placed a piping hot tray in front of me—thick tortilla shells, browned to a crisp in the compression oven. I smiled like a kid on his birthday.

"Tostadas with tomatoes and chorizo."

"What did Luke do to deserve you?" I asked.

"Huh." She sneered. "Keep it up and I'll give you churros for dessert."

She placed the coffeepot on a tray, took out some cups, and walked out to the veranda. "Come, let's sit out here and wait for Lucas." She retied her white fluffy bathrobe and beckoned me to follow, while she set the trays on a round stone table adjacent to the infinity pool. We took a seat on the heavy, ornate metal chairs, she across from me, facing away from the water. I looked at her and saw what I always saw, the prettiest girl in the room.

Two kids later and she still looked like she'd just stepped off a high fashion photo shoot. I had always been a little jealous of Lucas, but would never be the guy waiting in the wings if they broke up. They were perfect together and stepping into someone else's shoes was not my speed. But I had always wanted someone like Jade. Someone to make me a better man. Only one woman rivaled Jade in style, natural beauty, class and—for the rarest of female qualities—grace. That woman ...? Andie.

"This view. Priceless." I looked past her and out into one of the oldest mountain ranges in Hawaii. These eroded remnants of an ancient volcano were the highest peaks on the island. Below the mountains were lush, green sugarcane fields, and white sand beaches. Beyond that, the sea.

"What brings you out here this morning? Is everything okay?" Jade asked, pouring me a cup of coffee. "I did order tons of the Island Coffee Company variety. You were right. It's delicious."

"Oh," I said, fishing into my pocket. "I brought this for

Frankie." I handed her a USB drive. "It's the download of codes for his game."

"You didn't come all the way to the North Shore for this, did you? You could've given it to Lucas downtown."

"You're right. I didn't come for that." And then a follow-up. "Although, I do love my godson."

"Did Luke tell you his new thing is to say he's going to live with Tio Warren?"

"Well, he's going to have to fight with Adam for the guesthouse," I said with a laugh. "Is he up?"

"Not yet. Which is good. We can talk. Tell me why you're here. You didn't drive here at eight in the morning for nothing."

"I mentioned Andie to my therapist yesterday."

"Andie, the girl Lucas told me about?"

I nodded. "It just made it more real. You know, I've never really mentioned a woman to her before."

"Why is that different? You have a reputation of loving and leaving."

I wolfed down the tostadas. They were out-of-this-world good. "Who told you that?"

"What do you mean? *The Honolulu Star.*" She giggled.

"They have nothing else to do," I said, irritated. "They make stuff up."

"So those pictures are made up? The ones of you with a different woman each time?"

"No, but—"

"There you go," she said, pleased with herself. "What did she say?"

"Nothing, really. I hate when she just listens to me blab. She sat there, expressionless. She asked me why I felt so connected to this woman."

"And?" she asked, prodding me to think. That was good because I hadn't been able to. I mean, really think about next steps. I lied to Andie. Someone told me that a lie of omission is still a lie. I hadn't told her anything yet.

"I was thinking of taking her on a helicopter tour tomorrow."

Jade leaned forward, her face turning serious, eyes on me. "Listen, Warren. A girl doesn't have to be impressed by what you do, what you own, to love you. You're enough. Just being you is enough."

"Well, that's the problem. She doesn't know what I have. She thinks I teach surfing. Or if she does know, she certainly doesn't act like it. Everything is so simple with her. I think she's trying to get away from complications. And my life is pretty complicated."

"She can't fix you." She poured me another cup of coffee. "Trust is the foundation of every relationship. You need to start it out the right way. Tell her your truth." She just hit the bull on the nose.

"I know."

"Hey, hey. Look who's here." Lucas walked out, making a beeline to Jade and kissing her on the forehead. He looked like some kind of Spanish actor, bearded, messy thick black hair, in a well-matched jogging outfit. "Hi, *mi amor*." And then he pulled out the chair next to her, sat, and took her hand. "How's Mia?"

"Better. She's fast asleep."

Lucas leaned over and kissed her. Again. It was refreshing to see them still crazy about each other, even though they had been married for almost ten years. At times, I'd try to recall when I stopped seeing this between my own parents. It had started with long hours at work and evolved into fights and accusations. And finally, the truth. He had a child with someone else, a whole other family. The child was four years old.

"You rest and I'll take the kids to the beach today," Lucas whispered in Jade's ear. Loud enough for me to hear, of course.

"He stopped by to see you," Jade said, getting up and grasping the coffeepot handle. "I'll get more coffee."

When Jade was out of earshot, Lucas said, "What's up, man? What's going on?"

"Nothing, I guess I just wanted to stop by to thank you for getting that done for me."

"The loan? First, let me tell you that Paul Ma was enamored with your girlfriend. Said she was so smart and well put together. Second, her home in Chicago was worth twice the loan with zero percent LTV. You've met your match, dude."

He slapped my shoulder in jest, changing his expression as soon as he saw mine.

"Man, I have to tell her. I have to let her know about my involvement in all this," I said, craning my neck upward and covering my face with my hands. "What a mess."

"What's happening with the two of you? Didn't you say she was leaving?"

"She is. Leaving. I have a few weeks to make an impression on her, to show her how I feel, and maybe be loved in return. No big deal."

We looked at each other for a moment, Lucas weighed and measured me and saw something new and different. Something precious that needed to be guarded and nurtured, protected and grown. He recognized in me what he had with Jade, true love.

"I've never wanted anything more in my life."

"I know that feeling, man. And as I look at you now, I see so much of myself in you. The confusion, the torment. The pain of losing your mom and all the resentment that is going along with that. But she can't fix you. You're going to have to figure this all out, lose that anger before you can give yourself to someone else, because if this is real, and I know you, man, I think it might be, you need to fight for this with your life. Be honest, burn all that old shit down to the ground and start fresh."

"Jade just said that."

"She knows. Of all people," Lucas said, leaning back on his chair and reaching for a tostada.

"What did you do? How did you know?"

"When you can have anything else in the world that you want, but you're holding out for that one brief moment when she looks at you, and it's better than the best sex you thought you ever had, that's when you know," he said with a huge grin.

"Believe me, I've been taking cold showers every single time we've spent the day together. I haven't even thought about taking all … this, out on anybody else. I'd wait forever for her."

"You got it bad, man," he said. "When I met Jade, she had all sorts of things going on. She'd lost her daughter, her husband, had things going on in her career. I knew from the first time I saw her that I wanted her in my life. But I couldn't force things. She had to come to terms with everything that had happened and then allow me to help her see a future that wouldn't be filled with regret. She also"—he laughed, before softening his voice and mumbling— "was obsessed with the fact that she was older than me."

We fist bumped each other like teenagers.

He continued, "Every day, I wake up in the morning and can't believe my good fortune. Having her and Frankie and Mia. And the funniest thing is, she gets prettier and prettier every day."

"I want that. What you have."

"And you will. You're still processing things."

"I know. But it's been five years since Mom and I'm slowly seeing the light at the end of the tunnel. Which includes my feelings about Father. Adam has taken away most of that resentment."

Lucas nodded. "What's going to happen to the apartment on the Champs? We could probably get that sold like this." He snapped.

"Not ready, yet. I might keep it, actually. I was thinking that one day I'd be able to show my kids their grandmother's place. It's filled with her artwork. I'd like to keep her memory alive."

Lucas stared at me, eyes wide in mocking surprise. "Kids."

"Oh man, look at me. I'm thinking about having kids. Insane."

We laughed.

I smelled them even before she walked outside carrying a tray of heaven. Freshly cooked churros, Spanish style, with little side cups of chocolate syrup and cinnamon sugar. Lucas was a lucky man. Jade had embraced his culture, not only the language and its customs, but she'd taken on some mad culinary skills as well. He once told me she channeled all the energy she'd had from her full-time career into their marriage and their children. At first, he had worried that something like that would be temporary. But eight years later, she seems to have taken well to it, made it a part of her life.

"I heard my name. Tell me or I'll hold on to these," she teased.

"Nothing you don't already know, babe," Lucas assured her.

Jade slid the tray in my direction. "Okay, fine. Eat up."

I was able to chow down two whole sticks before little footsteps came at me from behind.

"*Tio* Warren."

"Hey, hey, Frankie."

Lucas was doing the same thing—decimating the churros. Jade remained standing between us, hands on her hips. Mom mode. "Frankie, *has visto lo que tio Warren trajo para ti?*"

Frankie slid easily into my lap, holding the USB drive. "Thanks for this. Did your friend who works there give this to you or did you and Adam do this for me?"

"Adam did. He said to tell you that the joystick doesn't work unless you type the codes in."

"Okay, thank you." Frankie wrapped his arms around my neck. "*Tio*, are you staying for a while? Wanna go swimming with me and Mia?"

"Frankie, I don't think *Tio* can stay today. Maybe next time," Jade countered promptly.

I shook my head. "Are you kidding? I have all the time in the world for this guy. Go ahead and get your swim trunks on. I'll be here waiting."

37

Past and Present

I was breaking the rules that morning. We'd made a deal not to talk about our past, but today I wanted to show her something that was special to me.

They say the past is who you are and there is no way to separate from it. No matter what my past was, Andie was my present.

As I pulled up in my convertible, I saw Andie waiting outside for me. Always early. She hadn't made me wait for her once. I saw that as a huge show of respect, and I'd moved heaven and earth to be on time for her in return. It was those simple unspoken contracts that could make or break relationships. And there was that coffee. She made a perfect cup of coffee and the cinnamon roll wasn't bad, either. I'd come to really enjoy our Friday Moments Tours.

Since I'd told her to dress for a day of walking about, she looked beautiful in khakis and a white button-down shirt. Her hair was swept away from her perfect face by a headband. I hadn't seen anyone rock a headband like that in a while. She had incredible style and incredible grace.

"Good morning."

Her smile brightened up the morning, as always. "Good morning, Warren. Here's your Beans and Books."

"Thank you, Andie. So today we are going to a special place. It's called the Valley of the Temples, located at the base of a pretty spectacular mountain range. There is a temple I'd like you see, and some trails we can walk. Plus there is a burger shack on the side of the road that makes a burger you will never forget. Shall we?"

We drove through Honolulu on the H1 and took the highway up the east side, past Sandy's Beach, through Waimmanalo, and past the YMCA where the kids had been told I would not make it there today. We drove by the twin islands off Lanikai Beach, where I'd thought I would explode for wanting to kiss Andie so badly.

Seeing those twin islands brought Andie to my mind, laid out on the beach in her pink bikini, digging her feet in the sand. How my body had vibrated with desperation that afternoon. I'd just stared at her. It had taken all my resolve not to break all the rules and make her totally mine. Andie had taught me there was a sweetness in not giving yourself everything you want right when you want it. The more I ached for her, the more I valued her. This, while common practice for some, was totally foreign to me. I had never had this much patience or self-control before, but she made me want to be a better man.

We pulled into the entrance of the valley and slowly drove down the long, narrow road to a parking lot. We walked toward the temple, but I knew what I really wanted to show her. The Valley of the Temples was also a graveyard and my mother was buried there. I wanted them to meet.

"This temple is amazing."

"Yes. It's a working Buddhist temple, built in 1960 as an exact replica of the 11th century Japanese Phoenix Hall of the Byodo-in Buddhist in Uji, Japan. But there are also other religions represented here as well. This is actually a memorial park. People from all faiths and walks of life are buried here. And these mountains …"

I could watch her all day. Those puckered lips, her little telltale sign that she was curious or thinking. She'd make a lousy poker player, or a brilliant one.

"This is the Ko'olau Range, all that land is private. I know you asked about waterfalls. Well, there is a waterfall deep in those mountains that you can't get to on foot anymore, but it is something to behold."

"You really know your stuff, Warren. You make an excellent tour guide."

"This is my home. I'm just happy I have someone to share it with, someone who appreciates it as much as I do."

Then she did something totally unexpected—she grabbed my hand. And there we were walking together hand in hand. We saw the golden statue of Buddha inside, the koi ponds, and walked until we finally made our way to my mother's mausoleum.

It wasn't garish or gaudy, rather humble. Sure, it was a mausoleum, but it wasn't ornate. My mother wanted simple. Once she was buried, I'd realized how someone's headstone was the final comment on that person's life.

"I wanted you to see this, Andie. My mother's final resting place. I know we made an agreement not to talk about our past, but she's still very much a part of my present. I just wanted you to meet her."

"I'm honored that you would bring me here, Warren. What a beautiful place. Do you miss her?" She pressed her lips tight and gave a shake of her head. "Of course you do, I can't imagine losing one of my parents. I just can't imagine." She paused thoughtfully. "Don't want to imagine. What it would be like."

"I hope you get to hang on to yours until they're old and frail. It's like being homeless, or rudderless, lost. She was the one I called for advice, the one who listened. I've actually called her about five different times expecting her to pick up, totally forgetting. It's, ah …"

I wanted to tell her that it had shut me down and made me feel stuck, that her death had placed me in a different tribe than everybody I met, that I hadn't handled grief very well—avoided it entirely, in fact—and that she was the first person who made me feel like myself since my mom's death. I wanted to tell her all of this and more, but instead I took her hand and held on to it for dear life.

"Warren?" she asked, squeezing my hand and looking up at me. "You still have one parent. And you still have a family. Maybe it's time to give in to the love that they're offering you."

"Maybe." I sighed. "Maybe."

We stood at my mother's grave, surrounded by the beauty and wonder of the Hawaiian tropics.

We stood quietly, alone.

But alone together.

38

Chasing Sunsets

"Hi there."

"Hey," I said, pulling Andie into my arms. "Long time no see."

She smelled of citrus and mint, reminding me of my childhood.

"What have you been up to?" I grabbed her hand and together we walked across the parking lot and onto the helipad.

"Been at the farm, getting ready for the cherries to bloom, leasing equipment. You know, the usual." She laughed. "You?"

I kissed the top of her head. "Visited some friends, worked, and still doing the last of Adam's classes."

"And that work is?" she asked, tightening her grip on my hand. I liked it.

"For my dad." I slowed to a stop and sent a text message to the pilot.

"Ah yes, the big secret." She said that with a laugh, but I wanted to tell her right then and there who I worked with and what I did for a living and what I knew about the plantation, but the time was never right to blow up your life.

"Sorry, I'm a bit late. Took a lot longer than I expected at the bank, but papers are signed and funding is on its way."

"No, this is perfect," I answered, pressing SEND. "We have an hour to catch the sunset. That's plenty of time."

"Where are we going?"

"You'll see."

We ran across the landing pad to a waiting helicopter, my new Airbus Eurocopter standing by to meet us. We ducked as we got close to the fast, dark gray machine with its five roomy seats. I'd gotten it with my latest commission check.

"Andie," I said, as I helped her into the seat. "This is Geoff. He will be flying with us today."

"Hi, Geoff," she said before turning back to me. "Who owns this, Warren?"

My, "I do," must have gotten lost in the thunder of the spinning blades, the whine of the engine, and Geoff's greeting because she didn't respond to it.

"Hello," he shouted back as he climbed into the pilot's seat. "Mr. Yates, do you want to take the controls today?"

"No, thanks. I'd like to stay back here with my friend." I placed a pair of headphones on her and helped buckle her seatbelt. "I'm going to speak to you through this mic. Can you hear me?"

"Yes, I can hear you," she said, gently tapping me on my cheek. She had a tiny blemish below her right eye. A thin scar of some sort. I yearned to kiss that scar, brush my lips against her smooth cheeks right then, but the whir of the propellers killed the moment. Before we knew it, we were soaring up in the sky overlooking Oahu.

"Where are we going?" she asked again.

"I thought I'd take you on an aerial tour of the island. See all the interesting sights we've already seen, but this time from the air. Sort of like a CliffsNotes version of our Moments Tour. Plus one extra treat I know you'll love."

"Yes." She raised her hands in the air just as the copter tilted to the side and maneuvered between two hills. We rose higher until we reached the pilot's desired altitude. I pointed out Pearl Harbor, the Waikiki skyline, and the Diamond Head crater. Fort Rutger had been built inside the crater, housing canon mortars and a large telescope for targets. Secret tunnels had been built on the floor of the crater, but none had been put to use in World War II. Andie marveled at the sights below, often glancing at me with delight. There was the house I'd grown up in down below. You could see the azure pool in the courtyard and the banyan tree I used to play under.

"Those are corals?" she asked, when I explained the greenish blue spots protruding from the ocean at Kane'ohe Bay. I called her attention to a thousand-acre sunken beach on this side of Oahu that appeared and disappeared twice a day. Next was a small island called Chinaman's Hat, just north of the bay and six hundred and fourteen yards from the shore. Only swimmers could get to the island, which allowed you to hike to the Hat's peak.

On impulse, I asked Geoff to land on the top. The wind was too strong for us to hop off and explore, but the view of the Koolau Mountains, when the waves were calm and the sun was getting ready to retire, was picture-perfect.

"Mokolii Island is called Chinaman's Hat because of its cone shape. We climbed this once and it was pretty intense. Thick brush and lava edges."

She listened intently, eyes shifting their view between the flocks of birds around us and the coral reef below.

I motioned for her to look far in the distance. "There's the Mokapu Peninsula. Do you see it? It's shaped like a turtle."

"Wouldn't it be great to live on your own island? Build a house at the very top and have this amazing connection with nature and wildlife?" she said. Then she laughed. "Or maybe not. I guess it would be pretty lonely after a while."

That's when it dawned on me. *That was my life.*

We circled around for a few minutes, tipping downward to see the sailboats by the shore. We saw so much life down below. Andie held her headphones to her ears, listening to my every word through the microphone. Every so often, she would nod and smile, or grab my arm whenever we made a sharp turn or an unexpected dip.

"You've asked about waterfalls—there are only two in Oahu. I've showed you one of them. Let's go see the second one—that's the extra treat I mentioned," I said, tapping Geoff on the shoulder.

We rose higher and flew for ten minutes until we reached the thousand-foot cascade of Kaliuwa'a. Andie gasped at the sight of the most beautiful waterfall in Oahu. As we hovered in place for a few seconds, she pointed to the narrow stream of water wedged between two lush, green mountains.

"Too bad it's closed to the public."

We raced against time to catch the sunset. There we were, at exactly 6:45 p.m., gliding across the water in Makaha, racing the sun as it skated in a burst of flames before sinking into the Pacific.

When the dusk settled, we flew through the skies, past the

Waianae Mountains and landed on a different helipad.

"Where are we now?" She laughed. "Sorry, I am so out of my range."

"We're at the Four Seasons in Kapolei. Thought we could have some dinner before I take you home."

39

Who You Are

I afforded myself a few pleasures in life and my office bathroom was one of them. About every other day, I'd run to work, arrive an hour before anyone else, and take a sauna, steam, then a shower. The bathroom was private—no one but me had access to it or my office. I loved taking time to prepare for the day, and the storms it might bring.

This was one of those mornings. I couldn't sleep the night before and I had gone for a long run right before sunrise and straight to the office after. But today was different.

I stepped out of the bathroom with only a towel wrapped around my waist, believing I was alone. I went to grab an outfit from my duffle bag when I noticed my father. He sat on the couch adjacent to my desk, holding a cup of coffee, waiting for me.

I felt caught with my hand in the cookie jar. "Father." I took a slow, deep breath to calm the quiver in my stomach. I was never comfortable around him. He wasn't supposed to be here. This morning routine is my private moment. He was supposed to be at home with his three dogs and his wife, Marta, taking business calls over the breakfast table until 10 a.m., like he did every day.

"I'll never understand this business casual thing," he said, mocking my towel as I stood there dripping wet. "But this is taking it to a new level. It's the same with this street style thing. Adam looks like he's dressed for the gym, which completely boggles my mind given the price we pay for those clothes. Marta too. We have enough money to buy good clothes and yet she wears jeans with holes in them, or those tight workout pants. And she's fifty."

My father always seemed upset, or bothered. It was a strange sensation—even when he was happy, he seemed like he was about to explode at the slightest provocation. Everything I did felt like a provocation.

His eyes traveled around every corner of my office. It was unconventional—at least for him—the white leather couches with studded edges, navy blue accents and an oversized architecture desk, adjustable so I could stand up behind it. Abstract artwork covered the walls, mostly made by my mother in the year we'd spent abroad.

My gazed stopped at the picture that reminded me of her so much, a bed of lilies—ivory on white canvas sparsely accented with yellow pistils and green leaves. "*A symbol of fertility, of life, and also death. The cycle of life all contained in this one flower,*" she used to say. She still brought me calm in the face of my father.

Sometimes at night, I would sit here in the dark, the lights of Honolulu streaming through the wall-to-wall windows, feeling less alone than in any other place I'd been. I think I'd fooled myself into thinking that my accomplishments would get me through anything, fill up the empty holes left gaping by the loss of my parents. Fat chance. When Adam had come into my life, I'd learned the value of forgiveness. It still didn't give Fate a pass for throwing me a curveball.

"Warren, did you hear me?"

"No. Sorry, Father. Say that again?"

"I was saying how despite the unconventional décor of this office, including your all glass bathroom," he reiterated, "Marta did a great job, didn't she?"

"She did. I love the way she made it look so clean and streamlined."

"You should charge all this to the office, you know. They should be part of the fixed assets."

"No need. I wanted to pay for everything."

He nodded, took a sip of coffee and unleashed the reason he was there. "The Robinsons saw you at the Four Seasons last night."

"And?"

"Is that the woman you've been seeing? The new owner of Island Coffee Company?" He placed the mug on the table and crossed his arms. Classic Father move. When I had been in middle school and my grades weren't straight A's, I'd be called into his library and he'd do the same thing. Then continue to tell me nothing I did was good enough.

"She's not the owner. She's been helping the Floreses to revive the company."

He slammed his fist on the cocktail table. That was always the next move, by the way. Fist slamming, report card throwing. "The company I told you to work on acquiring. I heard she also got an equipment and capital loan from Lucas. Why would you do that? We had a plan to take this business over."

"Correction," I said, holding my thumb and pinky fingers in the air. "You. You wanted to take this business over. I have always been uncomfortable about it. I did go over there to speak to Ms. Flores, but she wasn't in town. Either way, I think I would have given her a chance to learn the business before completely taking it over."

"Oh, really?" he said, sarcasm cutting through the room. "With what authority?"

"I own forty percent of the shares of this company. Mom wouldn't sell them back to you because she knew. She knew that one day you would use your control over me in cruel ways."

"Cruel ways. Grow up. Do you know how much that plantation land is worth? You don't like money? You don't care about growing this business. Our business. Not even for me, or for you. What about Adam? For somebody who seems to hate money, this business has made you a lot of it. You should be grateful."

"Adam doesn't want this. Have you even listened to him? He's already out there doing what he loves. Why would you try to force him to work at something he has no passion for? And this business—don't get me started about this business. Your business has done nothing but taken you away from our family. It made you who you are—a selfish, self-centered man who left his wife and son twenty years ago. I don't want any part of it. You keep holding this over me, but I don't want it either. I worked hard for my share, gave you all the profits from getting back into the fold five years ago. I deserve to do what I want to do."

"And what is that? Running a plantation? I sent you into that shop to buy it, not to meet a girl. How is it that she likes the guy who wants to run her out of town? Does she know, Warren? Does she know who you work for? Does she know the helicopter you used when you wined and dined her around Oahu is yours? Does she know that you live in the most expensive home in Kailua? How much does she know about you? Because that … seems cruel. "

I looked at him. Why did he know to ask exactly that? It was as if my soft spots were on full display to him alone because he was the only one mean enough to press on them. With fists clenched and jaw tight, I stood there dripping wet with my towel draped around my waist. I shivered violently, but not because of cold.

Anger flushed through my body, reigniting the fire that had raged inside of me for twenty years. I was about to explode when suddenly, as if somebody pulled the plug out of the drain in a bathtub, all the anger drained out of me. It vanished. In its place was acceptance. Of the things I couldn't change and of the things I could have done better.

Most of all, he was right. The S.O.B. was right. As it turned out, she didn't know a thing about me. I needed to see Andie. Needed to tell her the truth. I knew she couldn't fix me, but maybe she would stick around until I fixed myself.

"I have to go," I said. I dropped my towel and put on my underwear, then my jeans and a shirt. My dad just sat sipping his coffee, not watching me but not leaving as if to say, "even though you call this your office, it's really my office, everything is because of me." As I laced my sneakers, I couldn't help but feel like I was nine years old again. He hadn't been present then either.

When I finished dressing, we stood facing each other in silence for a moment. I wanted to say something tender to him, I didn't know what, but for all of his bombast, I saw a man who tried hard to make the best world possible for the people he loved. Even the ones he hurt along the way. We are only human after all, and this human was my father, the only one I had. He looked smaller that day, older to me.

He looked at me with equal intensity, his pain evidenced by the tremble in his chin and the dullness in his eyes.

"Your mom forgave me before she died. Love is complicated, Warren. Love is really, very complicated."

She wasn't at the coffee shop. For some reason, it was closed for the day. My texts and messages went unanswered. I figured something was going on at the farm, so I decided to head out there.

While on my way to Waialua, I called Adam.

"Hey, it's me," I greeted.

"Hey, just so you know, I'm at your house."

"That's cool."

"Okay. What's up?" he asked, his tone tentative.

"Adam, listen. Did I ever tell you the only good thing that came from losing Mom is you?"

"Dude, are you okay?"

"Yes. I'm okay. I just wanted to make sure you knew that."

"No, you never said, but I figured as much. I mean, I think I was the only one who gets you to do things other than work."

I laughed. A hearty, healthy, full-on laugh. "So true. Anyway, that's all I wanted to say. I'll see you when I see you."

40

I'm In Love with You

T his woman. Everything she had touched during her short time on the island had changed.

All for the better.

I couldn't believe the transformation. It was like night and day. The moment I drove past the open gate and into the plantation's premises, the old place I knew was no longer there. Gone was the dilapidated tourist building, the gravel parking lot, and the front door hanging off its hinges. In their place was a modern-looking structure with a brand-new roof and a big, bold sign. The interior was spacious, well-lit and airy, and decorated with well-organized shelves that were stacked with souvenirs and premium-packed coffee. I couldn't wait to see Andie. To tell her just how much she's added value to this place. And to my life.

I grabbed a map from the visitor's lounge and followed the track over to the plantation, walking the narrow path that spanned half a mile. I knew it would open up as soon as the farm came into view. Sure enough, as the path widened, so did the vista of the mountains and the coffee trees.

Then I saw her, standing alone next to a large yellow tractor, wearing cutoff jean shorts and a tank top. She ran her hands along its helm, checking out every inch of the machinery.

"Hi." I stood a few feet away, wanting to feel her warmth against me but hesitating since we were at her place of work.

"Warren. What are you doing here?"

"I tried to call you and no one was at B&B. I knew I'd find you here."

She placed my palm on the tractor, guiding it slowly with her hand. "Check this out. We now have two of these. This is going to change the life of the farm. Look how large the picking tunnel is— it's got an air-conditioned cab, a pinwheel agitator that's got so much power; it can remove the sticks on the leaves, and its power train is low to the ground, providing so much stability. We now also have two dryers and one grinding machine."

"I don't know what you just said, but I'm happy if you're happy," I said, chuckling.

"I am, I am." She stood on her toes and wrapped her arms around my neck.

"Andie, can we talk for a second? There are some things I'd like to tell you," I said, not breaking our embrace.

She pulled away slightly, her face close enough for me to kiss her. "Of course. But first, they asked me to come here today for some reason, so let me see what this is all about. And then," she said coyly, fluttering her eyes, "I'm all ears."

Together, we walked farther toward the plantation until we saw a large crowd gathered around a row of houses bordered by the coffee trees. Not far from where we stood was an extremely long table that was covered with a thin, white cloth and laden with food. Andie ran toward them while I stayed behind, still partly hidden by the second tractor.

As she approached, the people began to clap, loud and thunderous, whistling, cheering, calling out her name. Andie stopped and looked around, in shock and in tears, holding up her hands, nodding as the crowd continued to cheer. An elderly gentleman with tears in his eyes stood at the front of the line, along with the women from the coffee shop.

In from nowhere came the whistle of the wind, first a light breeze and then a whipping force. It blew away the tablecloth, causing the leaves and ground markers and clotheslines to flap furiously. Tiny white blossoms began to float in the air, lightly at first and then exploding into a flurry as the gusts grew stronger and the trees began to sway.

"Kona snow is here," yelled one of the children.

Andie looked up, pure joy on her face, her long brown hair peppered with flowers, like she was an angel nestled among the clouds. She raised her hands toward the sky, eyes smiling, lips moving to a song I could not hear. And then she began to dance, shuffling her feet and circling in the direction of the wind.

It was a rain dance, a snow dance, a dance of hope, of happiness, of peace and love and accomplishment. I stood and watched her in all her glory, being honored by her friends. After all, it was she who had given the farm its life back.

She stopped dancing, turning her head, searching and finding me right where she left me. "Warren," she cried, running over to me.

"Andie," I said, taking her into my arms.

"Remember this moment, Andie. At this time and on this very day is when I knew for sure that I have completely and hopelessly fallen in

love with you."

Her eyes lit up. "What did you say? The people are too loud. I can't hear you."

My shoulders sagged an inch.

"Can you stay? Can you stay and have dinner with us?"

"No, no," I whispered, kissing her ear before releasing her back to the world. "You go ahead and celebrate with your family. I'll see you in the morning."

"Okay," she said, letting go of my hands. "We'll talk tomorrow, I promise."

— 41 —
The Truth

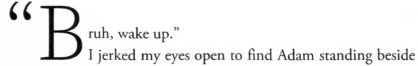

"**B**ruh, wake up."
I jerked my eyes open to find Adam standing beside my bed.

"Dude. You even move in your sleep? Your bed is all made up." He poked the top of my head.

I swatted his hand in response. "Stop it. What do you need?"

"Why are there so many workers here? What's happening?"

I grabbed my phone off the nightstand and swiped through my calendar. "Oh, shoot. Tonight's the annual benefit for St. Jude's Hospital. There'll be two hundred people over here. You'd better not be late."

"Well, it's too loud by the pool house and I need to go back to sleep."

"Adam, there are eight other bedrooms in this house. Go find one you can hibernate in. Just don't scare the cleaning lady."

He was about to say something smart when my phone rang. I walked to the dressing room to take the call.

"Hello?" It was an unfamiliar number.

"What the eff were you thinking, Warren?"

"Api, it wasn't supposed to end up like this," I said, walking to the middle of the dressing room and settling on one of the ottomans. I knew I had to sit for this.

She raised her voice, almost to a screech. "How was it supposed to end up? Huh? When she called me to tell me she was seeing someone, and then when I found out it was you? I, ugh, I just had to deal with her in person. Tell me what have you done with her? You …"

"You don't understand. I went to your store looking for you and there she was. She is so perfect. I'm in love with her."

"What? You?" That time she was screaming. "You? You've got the attention span of a fly. And a reputation for hurting the women who fall all over you. Fix this. You have to fix this. You have to leave her alone."

"Api, please calm down."

"Calm down? Calm down. Do you know that I haven't had the courage to see her? I arrived from Europe and went straight to James's place so I could call you. I've been on the ground less than two hours. I am so mad at you."

I stayed silent. Nothing could explain my intentions. She wasn't going to believe me; she knew the old me too well.

"Does she know you want to buy my farm and sell it to developers? And what about that loan she got for the machines at my father's farm, are those from you as well, did our friend Lucas help you out with those? When are you going to tell her? Is this a game? A ploy to get her to sell to you?"

"No," I exclaimed, exhaling loudly. She was exasperating. "I meant to tell her everything yesterday, but they were celebrating her at ICC. I'll tell her today. I have an engagement early tonight, but I'll leave and talk to her as soon as I can."

"Warren, do you know who she is? She's not someone you can fool like that. I'm surprised she didn't look you up."

"We made a deal." I felt hot shame wash over me, perhaps because deep down I knew what I was up to.

"Ugh. How could you? How could you take advantage of the fact that she was so busy, so confused, so alone on this island? She was probably so tired of being suspicious of everyone after what she went through. Warren, a deal? Who makes a deal?" She quieted for a few seconds before the screeching started all over again. "And this is what she gets for trusting you? Fix this, Warren. You have to figure this out."

"Okay. Stop yelling at me, please. I will tell her today. Just please, let me be the one to tell her. Please wait for me. It has to be me."

"Okay. I received an invitation to the benefit tonight at your house. I'm bringing her with me and you're going to explain everything to her. Do you understand? Do not see her today. I'm going to spend time with her now, I don't know how I'm not gonna say a word, but I will let you have this. And if James sees you tonight and decides to kick your ass, I'm not going to stop him."

"Understood."

Click. No goodbyes. I deserved that call and the ear-shattering silence she left behind.

Like any business-minded person, success is equal parts effort, knowledge, and intuition. With my day starting out with a phone call from Api, I knew in my gut that today was the beginning of the end. I called Andie to find a time to meet with her, but she said she was busy. I told her it was important, but she said she'd come a little early tonight and we could talk then. I didn't want to tip my hat, so I played it off super casually. As punishment, I spent the rest of the day in an uneasy state, trying desperately to calm my mind by catching the surf on The Wall off Queen's Beach. Though the swells were gentle and rolling that afternoon, a southern wind pulled the waves into perfect long rides. It would have been a great day if I weren't drowning in guilt.

When she arrived at the benefit, I was speaking to the mayor of Honolulu about the camping grounds we purchased for the city's underprivileged kids. I excused myself to meet her—the beautiful woman who was turning quite a few heads. Her red floor-length dress had a slit as high as her hips and her hair was pulled back, exposing her eyes, her lips, her long, slim neck. Five-inch heels made her look like she was almost as tall as I was. In more ways than one, I was grateful to Api and James for guarding her like hawks. They kept her in between them as they socialized, making sure she never left their sight.

"Hello, ladies," I said, giving Api a kiss on both cheeks and taking Andie's hand in mine. "You must be James. Congratulations on your engagement and it's a pleasure to meet you." I shook his hand.

Api regarded me with her cold, steely eyes. "Thanks. We're going to get a drink."

"In that case, would you mind if I speak to Andie for a while?"

"No," snapped Api, turning her attention to her friend. "Go ahead. But, Andie, text me if you need me, okay?"

I led her away quickly, walking back through the house and into the sitting room.

"Hey."

"Hi. Sorry about today, I was slammed with random work. I missed you." In a surprise move, she reached up and gave me a sweet kiss on the lips. I gently pushed her away and turned to shut the door. When I came back around she sank into me, leaning her cheek against my chest.

"We have to talk, Andie."

"I know. I've been wanting to since yesterday. This house is amazing." She looked around the room and spotted a framed photo of me and my mom in Paris. She walked over to the picture and took a good, long look. She leaned over and put her hands on her lower back. Then she stood to her full height and looked around the room again.

"I'm confused, Warren. Whose house is this? Is it yours?"

I drew a deep breath. "Yes, this is my house. And I'm hosting this event as board president for this charity."

"I don't understand. Api said this was the most expensive house in Kailua."

"Why does that matter?" I asked, walking over to her and taking both of her hands in mine.

"It matters because I thought you were some surfer dude guy

trying to find himself."

"I am," I barked, and immediately regretted my response.

When she looked at me with brows furrowed, I clarified.

"A surfer and a dude who's trying to find himself."

There was a soft knock on the door. Beth, my dad's secretary, stuck her head in, clipboard in hand, pen hinged in her ear.

"Sorry, Mr. Warren, your dad wants you. He's giving a speech and a toast."

I kissed her forehead before standing up to leave. "Sorry. I'll get this done quickly and be right back."

— 42 —

Exposed

The speech took longer than anticipated. As the major benefactor of the hospital's oncology unit, my father had quite a lot to say.

First, the history of Apex and how it began—in the garage of a two-bedroom home, pre-internet when client visits and in-person consults were still a thing. My father recalled packing me up in the back of their Volvo station wagon as he went house-to-house, offering people his financial services.

Next, there were people to thank, a whole network of teams he'd built to ensure the planning and construction of the new wing. There were suppliers who provided subsidies for the cost of medical equipment and experts who would consult on the latest technological advances. Everyone cheered.

At the very end of his talk, he called his family up to the stage.

"I'd like to thank my family," he began, holding a hand out to Marta, who pulled Adam, who in turn pulled me. "Marta, my wife, who has given me so many years of joy and inspiration. I continue to strive to become a better person, but with her perseverance and resilience, I know I am on the right track. And my sons—Warren, who is a better man than I could ever hope to be, and Adam, who keeps me young every single day." When the clapping ensued, he raised his hand to silence the crowd. "Five years ago, Warren lost his mother, Catherine, to cancer. She was a brave woman—kind, generous, and strong-willed. Life wasn't fair to her, but she never felt sorry for herself or let that stop her from loving fully and living a life pursuing her passions. She embodied grace. Her life was cut short, but in her wake, she has left a huge legacy. It is because of her that Warren has the strength and character and heart he has today. And it is because of me—"

He stopped abruptly, as if wanting to say something but not being able to, and all the while looking at me. The crowd rumbled, the cameras flashed. He cleared his throat before proceeding. "I am donating twenty-two million dollars to the Catherine L. Jones foundation for underrepresented families who need the utmost care."

One of the men in suits ran up to us with a giant check.

"Dad," I said, embracing my father for the first time since I'd come back five years ago. I was overwhelmed, and this time, it wasn't anger or disappointment or even indifference. The attachment I had to him, built by childhood memories, of a father who loved me as much as he knew how, felt real and complete.

My father invited Marta and Adam to join in, and the four of us closed in on each other, arms entangled. We made the picture of a perfect family. The family I could still have.

I thought about what Andie said to me as we stood next to my mother's gravesite.

"Maybe it's time to give in to the love that they're offering you."

Maybe it is.

I rushed back to the sitting room, expecting to find Andie alone. But instead, there they all were, scattered around the room—James and Api sitting closely on the sofa, Lucas and Jade leaning against the giant bay window, and Andie on the chaise by the tall, glass bookcase, staring at her hands.

I ran to her. "Andie."

She shot her head up, her eyes filled with tears.

"You're Apex?" she asked in barely a whisper, grimacing. "And these people"—she looked at Jade and Lucas—"are the ones who gave me my loan? You're all friends?"

"Andie, he was supposed to tell you," Api piped in.

She stood, straight and tall. Except suddenly, those five-inch heels didn't look so sturdy anymore. She wobbled as she went over to Api, who darted over to help hold her up.

"And you knew," she said, changing her mind and moving away from Api until her back was against the wall. "Can someone please help me? Help me wrap my head around all of this."

I dared not touch her. I knew she didn't want to have anything to do with me. But I couldn't help but wonder. If I'd had the chance to tell her while I held her, if no one else had been in that room, would there have been a better outcome?

The more things developed, I realized that it wouldn't have mattered.

"Andie, please let me explain. When I went to the coffee shop on Christmas Eve, I was intent on speaking to Api about my father's proposal to buy them out. Never in a million years did I ever expect to find you there. I couldn't help it. I was drawn to you, wanted to get to know you. And the deeper I fell, the harder it was for me to tell you."

"You had so many opportunities to just tell me, Warren. You knew everything I was doing in order to save this business. And to make matters worse, you stepped in and got your friends to cut me a deal." She choked on her words.

I had broken her heart and she was about to break mine.

"It wasn't like that," I explained. "I really wanted to help you. Sure, at first, I had to do what my father was asking me to do. But after I got to know you, I learned how passionate you are for the people at the farm. I wanted you to get what you worked so hard for."

"I didn't need your help," she snapped. "I needed the truth."

"Andie, please," Api pleaded, crying as James pulled her close to console her.

Andie walked over to Api, sat next to her, and held her friend's face in her hands. "I know, Api. I know you just found out the week before you came home. But why didn't you tell me when I told you his name?"

"I did. I told you I went to school with him. And I had no idea. No idea, Andie, that it was this serious. I thought it was a fling. He's the famous fun time guy, but I should have dug deeper. I knew I was coming home in a week and I wanted to deal with this face-to-face, but ... I'm sorry."

Andie nodded.

"What does it matter?" I asked. "What does it matter what I own, who I work for, or who I used to be? All that matters is, who I am when I'm with you is who I am. What I feel for you, what we have together is real. You know the best of me."

"How?" she cried, tears flowing now. "How do I know that, when this all started with a lie?" She composed herself as quickly as she broke down, wiped her face with the back of her hand, then straightened her dress and pushed her shoulders back. "I'd like to leave now. Api, can we go now, please?"

"Andie. Please don't go."

"Thank you, Warren. For teaching me how to live in the moment. I'll never forget you."

She started for the front door and I walked alongside her, pulling her elbow. "Please. If you just stop and listen for a second."

"Okay." She signaled for Api and James to walk ahead, then crossed her arms and faced me. "Two minutes."

"Five years ago, I went back to work for my father. I wanted to make peace, help build the business my mother left me, knowing it wasn't what I wanted to do forever. And yes, I made money. Lots of it. I had a huge deal for a resort island. I made enough to buy me this house in Kailua, pay for my mom's place in Paris. Heck, I could even buy Chinaman's Hat if you wanted to live there—but what. Does. It. Matter?"

She held up a finger, blinking as if she'd just thought of something. "That private beach, the night of the luau. That was here, in your house."

"Yes."

"Ugh." She huffed, walking away.

I pursued her as she ran down the driveway. "But you lied to me too. You never told me who you really were, what you had. It's the same thing. Didn't we make a deal?"

"By not going into detail about what I did for a living, I was able to forget for a while what had brought me here in the first place, Warren," she argued, shaking her head. "A nervous breakdown from working too hard. I'm sorry I wasn't specific about my job. But I was running away from something and I didn't want any part of it following me here."

"But that's just like me," I shot back. "We had a deal. No questions, no past, just the present."

"It doesn't erase the fact that you had a hand in the loan approval. That you walked into Beans and Books for an entirely different reason. I can't live with that. If I have to find myself, I need the things around me to be authentic—"

"You omitted some stuff too. But I don't care about that. Why can't you feel the same way? This." I clutched her hand and place it on my heart. "This is what matters. I'm in love with you."

She recoiled so adamantly, so strongly, that a slap on my face would have been better. At least that would have been a pain I could handle. "I can't," she said. "I'm going to mess this up, Warren. I always do."

"So, it's over? Just like that?"

"Be glad it never started." And with that, she walked away.

After we found out my mom didn't have much time, she'd insisted on talking about my future. She would make up scenarios about a wife and children, and we would talk about where I'd live, what my children would be like, if they would look like me or my wife.

On the night she died, I'd told her I was sorry she wouldn't be able to experience that part of my life with me. She'd said it didn't matter because she knew I would make a wonderful father and that anyone who captured my heart would be the luckiest woman alive. She told me never to forget that my father's actions had nothing to do with me. That he loved me just as much as she did. And it was his great loss to not have had the chance to know me.

"You will never be able to move on unless you forgive him, Warren. Promise me that you will."

When someone you love dies, a part of you dies too. There is such emptiness. Of knowing that you will never feel the touch of that person's skin or hear that person's voice again.

Losing Andie was different. It was the loss of hope and of what I thought my future could be. The pain of knowing she would one day move on without me. She would fall in love, have a life, live in moments and share them with someone else. It was a different pain. The pain of knowing that I'd once seen the future with her, but all we would ever have was the past.

Pain had always made me weaker. I had to find a way for it to make me stronger.

PART THREE:
There and Then
Andie

Small rooms warm quickly
From here to there in short strides
With you it is home

— 43 —

Hiding in Place

"So, you're leaving in a week?" Api asked me again, even though I already sent her my itinerary. "Because you know, the dresses are almost ready. You can try everything from Chicago when you arrive. I think they said there's a Vera Wang branch on Michigan Avenue."

"Will you please stop worrying? I take this maid of honor role very seriously."

Fall in Paris felt more like our Indian summers in Chicago. The leaves had just turned and the weather was pleasantly cool. I was sitting in a sidewalk café in the Les Marais district when she called, unwinding with a cup of coffee before meeting a colleague for dinner.

"Look at you. Every time I see you, you're all gussied up in your designer clothes, looking all glass ceiling breaker and all. Is it great to be back to your old life?" she asked, catching herself at the end. "What I mean is, aren't you going to miss it?"

"Not at all. I'm ready for the next chapter." If there was one thing I'd learned from my time in Hawaii, it was never to take my parents for granted. My dad was turning sixty-five soon and needed my help to run the free medical clinics he'd established in Florida and Chicago. I guessed I had Warren to thank for such a valuable lesson.

"Okay," she said. "Now it's time for my gossip for the week. He still calls me, you know. I know you told me not to talk about him, but he keeps sending you messages through me."

"Now that I know, I don't want to know."

"I'm sorry, Andie. I still feel so horrible about what happened. I regret not sharing my doubts with you right after you told me his name. I wanted it to be a different guy. I wanted you to be happy," she said, her high-pitched tone turning low and husky. "I miss you. You've been gone too long."

"And I miss you too. I needed this. But I'm ready to come home soon and get your wedding under way. How are Maele and Lani?"

"They're good. There are six of them now at Beans and Books, so the girls are adjusting to working less than twelve hours a day. Which reminds me, I need to get your thoughts on franchi—" Api stopped in mid-sentence, her attention stolen by the guy who took a seat next to me. "Ooh. Who's that?"

I laughed before handing my phone to my dark-haired, European friend. "This is my friend, Lucien. We work together. I'm handing my account over to him so I can go home."

"Is he the reason you won't come back?" she asked in a singsong voice. "Because I'll forgive you if he is."

Lucien must have thought it was cute because he laughed too. "Is it?" he taunted.

"Both of you, stop. I'm going to hang up now, Api. We have a few things to work on before I call it a day."

"Well, don't work on it too hard." There was the Api I knew and loved.

Didn't they know that the one keeping me here lives thousands of miles away, in one of the most expensive homes in Oahu?

They say time heals all wounds. I didn't know if six months was enough to say I'd healed completely. I mean, it had only been a four-month thing, and yet the loss of his friendship affected me deeply.

I had so many memories of the days that followed the incident at Warren's house. I'd packed up and left for Chicago two days later, but not without regret. Maybe I should have forgiven him for not telling me. Maybe my pride had gotten in the way, wounded for having realized he had a hand in saving the business. I should have looked him up, but I had been so fixated on running the coffee shop and keeping my part of the deal we made.

After I left, I found out that Warren Yates was a celebrity in his own right. How stupid of me to space out like that. All I'd had to do was Google him. A Google search which certainly made leaving easier.

That deal. A fresh start. Who makes a deal like that and follows it anyway?

I guess I did. It sounded nice.

And Maele? She'd known. She'd been there when Warren and Adam stopped by the coffee shop while Api was still in town. Maybe it's true that human nature has a way of blocking your sensibilities when you want to believe something. Maele had said she knew I wouldn't care who he was, some idealism about love conquering all. How could I blame her? Sometimes I thought I'd overreacted. Most of the time, I knew I would have always wondered what his true motives were.

No matter what, Warren had opened my eyes to what it felt like to want love. I wanted that again. Someday, I thought. I hoped.

By the time I'd shown back up at work, Nolan had been gone. He'd left six new business prospects with no one else to take them over. Despite my resignation, I'd promised Matt I would help recruit my replacement. I'd taken back my old team and divided the projects accordingly.

That's how I'd ended up here—in Paris—helping train a young, upcoming under thirty guy, who was a whiz kid at math, a top investment banker, and who looked like the most famous soccer player in the world. At first, the plan had been to live with my brother, Steven, but I decided I'd needed the time alone to get my bearings back. I did spend many long weekends flying to Barcelona on a local carrier, enjoying the time with Steven and his family.

I had a tiny apartment on Rue Saint-Antoine, directly above the most delicious pastry shop in the universe. With its cobblestone streets and magnificent architecture, Les Marais was the perfect hiding place, shrouded by quaint little shops and art galleries, narrow alleyways and hidden entrances.

Tonight, Lucien and I took a walk to our favorite spot for dinner. We cut through the Place des Vosges, and walked past old apartments and giant trees, leaves filtering the glow of streetlamps with soft yellow light. Bars and restaurants abounded on every street corner, full of jovial, happy people who seemed to come alive at all hours of the night. We settled on a rooftop restaurant in the museum of Contemporary Art. It held one of the most dazzling views of the Eiffel Tower at night. The place was dark and clubby, staffed with perfectly coiffed, intimidating servers dressed in all black.

But the truffle ravioli and tartare were to die for.

"No bachata at Bastille tonight?" Lucien asked.

I laughed. "No. I need to get back to my normal schedule. No more 10 p.m. dinners and midnight dance clubs." Case in point. The French sure knew how to blow off steam. "Did I ever tell you that dinner is at six o'clock in the Midwest?"

"Many times," he replied, smiling. He broke the raw egg on his steak tartare and took a sip of wine. "So, you've decided exactly when you're leaving?"

Lucien was smug about French wine. I couldn't say I disagreed. He'd often launch into diatribes about California wine, their density and darkness and alcohol levels. I hardly drank, so I'd nod along, though I really didn't understand a word.

"Yes, next week, if you're okay with everything I've turned over. I'm happy with the business plan that Miss Thibault has presented. All we need now is the funding and the sign off from Matt."

"Will you be coming back?"

"Not in this capacity. But for a visit? Most definitely. This is—" I paused, and course corrected. "Okay, well, this *was* my number one place in the world. It's still a close second."

He leaned forward, resting his chin on his hand. "What is the number one?"

"Hawaii, I think. If ever you get a chance to visit, you should. There is no place in the world more ethereal and spiritual than Hawaii. It's filled with legend and culture and the most stunning landscapes you've ever seen. Not just mountains, Lucien. Volcanoes—live ones."

"Is that where your heart is, Andie?"

"Ha." Then I inhaled and choked on a piece of pasta. After an awkward moment of coughing into my napkin and sipping water, I asked, "What do you mean?"

"Do you know why, despite the fact that we've worked together for four months, I never tried anything with you? Please. It's not because I'm a gentleman or that I don't want to—it's because you are always sad. Like you are waiting for someone. Who is this person? Who has stolen your heart, Andie? You've never talked about him. But yet you have this"—he waved a hand—"*je ne sais pas comment on dit*. You give this—"

"Vibe? Impression? Idea?" I laughed. "What?"

"Vibe, yes. Vibe. That your heart already belongs to someone else and yet, you've never mentioned him."

"It's complicated," I said, wrestling with a piece of ficelle that just wouldn't tear off. "Just like this piece of cheese baguette."

Lucien didn't appreciate my joke. "Then un-complicate it. Surely a woman as intelligent and sophisticated as you will know how to do that. What is his name?"

"Warren. His name is Warren Yates."

"Ah. There is a place in Normandy called *La Verenne*. This is where the name Warren comes from. It means protector."

"How apt," I remarked sadly. I looked at my lap and just stared. Had that been all he'd tried to do? Was it so wrong for us to want to protect each other from our pasts?

"I was in love once. And it was really good for a while. But then I started looking over at the other grass." He saw me blink.

"You know, the grass is always greener thing."

"Yes, I know what you mean. Don't worry."

He guzzled what was left of his wine, motioned for the gorgeous woman who looked like an actress on *Days of Our Lives* to bring us another bottle. And here I was, still nursing my first glass.

"I was on a business trip in Brazil and slept with someone else. A stranger. Gabrielle never forgave me. I lost her forever because of one night."

"I'm sorry," I muttered, my train of thought totally fractured.

There was a guy with his back to us, speaking to the hostess. Light wavy hair, tall, slim, muscular. I felt a flutter in my stomach. Could it be? I mean, he did have an apartment in this city.

I was thinking of excuses to leave our table, walk across the floor to get his attention. But when he turned around, I saw it wasn't him.

Lucien waved his hand in front of my face. "Yoohoo, Andie. Are you there?" He snapped his fingers, laughing. "That's it. That away very far look."

"Sorry," I said again. "I thought—" I rested my elbows on the table. "It's *faraway*, by the way. Please continue."

"What I said was that I never found that kind of love again. And it's not for lack of searching. Things like this happen only once. Don't ever let anyone tell you otherwise. The ones who follow are compromises. Do you love him?"

"Yes."

"My mother always said, '*On n'est point toujours une bête pour l'avoir été quelquefois.*' Being a fool sometimes does not make one a fool all the time. Stop being a fool, Andie. Go to Hawaii and get your love back. "

My phone buzzed repeatedly. I ignored it while we ordered a strawberry tarte for dessert. When it buzzed again, I fished it out of my purse. "Speaking of parents," I said to Lucien. "It's my dad. Hi, Daddy."

"Andie," he said between jagged breaths and loud footsteps. "It's Mom. We're at Northwestern. They think she's got cancer."

— 44 —

Best Laid Plans

Ow did the saying go? The one about us planning and God laughing?

I left Paris the very next day, met Steven at Heathrow in London, and arrived in Chicago twenty-four hours later. We didn't bother dropping our things off at home, rather rushed to see our mother, who had been confined the day Dad called. He said she'd had a low-grade fever for a week before they decided to take her in. Turned out, her white blood cell count had dipped to dangerously low levels and the only logical cause would be leukemia.

A bone marrow biopsy confirmed their concerns. It was stage one, acute but caught early and could be blasted with chemotherapy and radiation.

I had never seen my dad cry, never seen him crumble. And although I'd known it all along, I saw firsthand what she meant to him, how lost he would be without her.

He'd wandered around the apartment, looking like half a man, a lost boy without a compass. The experience had scarred him, brought him to such a vulnerable place, breaking him in so many ways. My rock, my defender, the unshakable healer, was now cracked and in dire need of being restored.

That had been three weeks ago.

Today, Mom was home resting, Dad doting over her, his relief evident. As a doctor, he knew that good results were fleeting and that every day going forward was his gift.

I was supposed to be in Hawaii by now for Api's wedding. Time had once again left me in its dust, carrying on like nothing had happened and I was desperate to hold it back.

That last night in Paris, I had been filled with the hope of seeing Warren again. Maybe this was for the best. Maybe he'd moved on, and time was saving me from a second broken heart.

There was no one on the Riverwalk today. The paths were empty under the bridge on Dearborn. I was a tad surprised, given it was a balmy forty-five degrees on Thanksgiving Day.

Steven and I were going all out, making a turkey and all the fixings. Mom was still in a hospital bed in the middle of the living room, but the dining room had been set and we hoped she'd feel strong enough to join us.

I ran down the stairs to the walkway and turned right on Wacker toward Michigan Avenue, past an underpass covered with murals and on to the docks by the lake. It was a five-mile loop south toward the Shedd Aquarium.

I took off along the sidewalk past the yachts and sailboats bobbing lazily in the water. The sun was bright, causing me to shield my eyes as I painstakingly dragged my feet along the lakefront. I was out of breath, out of energy, out of motivation. Pigeons strutted along, stopping to peck at some leftover crumb— their fearlessness forcing me to weave in and out of the walkway to avoid them. In more ways than one, Warren was still a part of my life. It was his playlist I was listening to. It was also his face I saw when the sky was blue and the water was bright.

I reached the aquarium and looped around in a figure eight, running around the break wall that separated the lake from the highway. The waves were higher than normal, lapping at the wall and spraying a fine mist that felt good on my face. I didn't slow down. After the curve, I ran back toward the apartment in the opposite direction.

There were people on benches and dogs on every single grassy surface area on my way back. The city was slowly coming to life. At mile marker four, I passed a jogging woman who looked up as I ran by. She wore a baseball cap, her red hair in a ponytail and her sunglasses shielding her eyes. From the corner of my eye, I noticed her slow down. I did the same.

"Andie?"

I turned around. She removed her sunglasses and walked toward me. "It's Jade Martinez."

"Oh, hey. Hi, Jade," I said. "How are you guys?"

"Lucas is here for a business meeting so we are home early. Whereabouts do you live? Are you in this area?"

"Yes, I'm on Dearborn and Ohio. Are you guys around here too?"

"Sort of. We're on Randolph and Clark," she said.

"Wow, that's close. I'm surprised I haven't seen you around here."

"Well, we're in Oahu most of the time when Frankie is off from school. It just so happened Lucas needed to be here so we're spending Thanksgiving with my parents. How have you been, Andie? It's been a while."

"I've been good, actually. Traveled for a few months and had a little scare with my mom, but she's okay now."

"Oh no," she said, cupping her face. "I'm glad to hear she's okay. Are you back here for good?"

"I think so. I'm supposed to be at Api's wedding next week, but my mom's still pretty weak from her chemo treatments."

Jade nodded, shifting her weight between her feet. "Andie, I hope you don't think I'm overstepping, but Warren's been working so hard on himself these past few months. He's made peace with his dad. Some days are still hard for him, but I always tell him that trauma like that takes years to heal."

"I'm so glad to hear he is good, Jade. Please send him my regards."

"It's been really tough for him. I just want to tell you one thing. I don't want you to think he closed the book on you when you left. He came to Chicago to find you, stayed at our place for a few days, but you were abroad. That should count for something, shouldn't it? He decided to work on himself before he tries again. He's in therapy and making great progress—he's been training for the Iron Man triathlon, and he started a nonprofit, but all he talks about is you."

It was my turn to nod and say nothing. I gently placed my hand on her shoulder. "Your words mean the world to me, Jade. Maybe this is what I needed to make sense of it all."

"Love isn't easy. If it were, it wouldn't be real. Nothing of substance comes without a price."

Beaten down with emotion, I couldn't think clearly.

She went in with the zinger when she saw I was lost for words. "I hate seeing him that way, but I know you both have to heal separately. If you still love him, tell him. Forgive him."

"Thank you," I said. This time, she saw my tears and I let her. I wanted her to know that the thought of him still brought me pain. Only love could do that. He'd been with me all this time. Through the days and the weeks and the months we'd been apart, he was trying to fix himself for me. "For letting me know. Maybe one day, after this is all over, we can be friends." I slowly turned around and slipped my earbuds back in, one at a time.

"Most definitely. Come see us if you ever make it back to the island. Take care."

I wasn't myself for the rest of the day. My mind burst with thoughts and my imagination ran wild. The *what-ifs* abounded.

He came here for me. And now I needed to go to him.

"Jim," I squealed, as soon as my former assistant picked up the phone. "Why didn't you tell me?"

"Tell you what?"

"Did someone come looking for me after I left for Paris?"

"Yeah. Matt said he would let you know. It was July 28th. I remember that day because he was sitting in the lobby with a bouquet of flowers. The receptionists on the floor were fanning themselves over how good-looking he was. He looked for you, asked when you'd be back and left."

"What are you smiling about over there, sis? Are you talking to the turkey rub?" Steven joked, handing me the electric knife.

We were so used to having big gatherings, that a twenty-nine pounder was staring us in the face. That was the only size I knew how to cook perfectly. Anything less would have burnt to a crisp, anything more would have been undercooked. To avoid being wasteful, Steven and I decided to take everything left to the food pantry on Wells the next day.

"He came here for me. I saw his friend Jade today on my run and she told me."

Steven rushed over to embrace me. "I knew it," he muttered in my hair. "I knew this wasn't over."

"How?"

"We don't give up on love just like that. It's a thing." And then he held me at arm's length and spoke to my eyes. "Now, it's your turn to try to find him."

"But Mom—"

He shook his head. "Talk to her after dinner. Go for Api's wedding. I'll stay until you get back."

We'd been in isolation, the four of us, nursing Mom to health by staying close together. Uncle Don would stop by from time to time, but that was it.

I looked around the dining room. Everything around me was a significant reminder of the past four years of my life. Pieces I'd collected like badges of honor. Each tied to every success. Oh, with this bonus, I'm going to get this. Oh, and with this one, I'm flying to Paris to get that.

But looking at the four of us right here and now—Dad pouring a glass of wine and joking about feeding an army, Steven making a plate for Mom, and Mom, too weak to laugh, smiling wanly with her eyes, sitting upright on the hospital bed—this is what makes a life. The ones who love you, the ones you love. If you focus on what's important, you'll see that everything else around you is fluff.

We stopped and said grace, like we did every year, holding hands and each saying what we were thankful for. It was usually a huge to-do, Steven and his wife, Emma, and their two kids, Mom, Dad, and about twenty other friends. We'd pick on the kids and the teenagers, embarrass them about having to speak out loud in public.

Tonight, it was solemn. Quite a bit of introspection had befallen our family. We were exhausted but hopeful.

Dad started and looked directly at my mom with tears in his eyes. "I am grateful for my family and for the grace God has given me through my wife, Lou. I am grateful for many more Thanksgiving dinners from tonight and the years to come."

Steven went next. "I am grateful for Emma and the kids and for Mom, who is and always will be a fighter."

Mom cleared her throat, her voice barely a whisper. "I am grateful for all of you here with me tonight. You make me want to be here for a very long time. Proud of you, Andie and Steven. And you are the love of my life, Doc."

I was lost in thought. Steven squeezed my hand. "Andie?"

"Oh, sorry. I have never been more grateful for the three of you here with me today. I am grateful for the most difficult year of my life. I am grateful for the love I have from you, and for all the things this past year has taught me. I would do it all over again, if I had to."

When Steven was done, I took the food from him and arranged a tray for my mom. She waited patiently as I settled next to her, dangling my legs off the hospital bed, and twisting around so I was facing her. She insisted on feeding herself.

"You should patent this stuffing recipe, *hija*," she said. "I know you didn't learn your cooking skills from me."

Dad and Steven were engaged in their own conversation—something about Dad wanting to invest in a unit at the Marina Towers. He'd always been so enamored by those historical landmarks, round in shape and called "corn cobs."

Mom took a sip of her ginger ale, then set it gently on the tray. "I saw you and Steven talking a while ago. Is everything okay?"

"He came here for me, Mom."

She knew right away who *he* was. "How do you feel about that?"

"Happy, of course. Maybe more validated, I guess. I spent all these months thinking that I'd misinterpreted his interest in me."

"I meant to talk to you about Api. Her wedding is coming up and you need to be there. She's been a good friend to you, all these years."

"All the years I wasted, I know."

She took my hand but said nothing. Steven and Dad had now stepped into the kitchen to prepare the cake we'd gotten for Mom. Her favorite—sans rival—a layered cashew cake filled with buttercream.

"I don't want to leave you, Mom. You're still the most important person in my life. I want to be here with you. I want you to know I'm here. I'll always be here."

"I know that," she said, touching the tip of my nose. "It's just for a few days. I'll be here waiting for you and by that time, I'll be strong enough to hit Michigan Avenue again."

We both laughed. "Yeah, the stores are missing you."

With wide eyes, she lifted her shoulders and tilted her head, waiting for me to respond.

"Okay. I'll play it by ear. I'll book a flight for the day before the wedding so I don't have to be gone longer than I need to."

"Deal," she said. "You don't have to worry about me. I've got my guy." She looked toward the direction of the kitchen.

I kissed her forehead before jumping off the bed and taking her tray. "I love you."

"Oh, and Andie." Her voice was suddenly stronger, louder— so much so that Dad and Steven stuck their heads out of the kitchen door. "While you're there, go get *your* guy. Bring him home to meet your family."

The Foghorn Sounds

I stayed through my mom's latest chemo session. It gave me one travel day before Api's wedding.

Anyone who's ever traveled with me, knows never to expect me until it's time to board. Colleagues complained about the stress I created by walking into the plane when the gates were about to close. It was no different today. I settled into my aisle seat just as the stewardess finished her final check. There was quite a bit of space between us, but I couldn't help noticing the woman sitting next to me.

She was me one year ago. Giving one-word answers to the stewardess, who offered us a choice of juice or water. One leg crossed over the other, back straight but wrenched sideways, shoulders hunched as she leaned over the armrest and stared out the window. On the shared side table was the book she'd brought, nonfiction about the future of advertising. How on earth was she going to stay awake with that kind of material? Or maybe that was the purpose.

I looked under the seat in front of me and smiled to myself. Maybe I'd convince her to read one of these swoony romance books I'd brought with me.

I'd never gotten her name—the happy, older woman I'd met on this plane one year ago.

Lillie. I'd named her Lillie.

Whenever she floated into my thoughts during the times I spent with Warren, the smell of lilies in bloom gave birth to the perfect name. She'd been with me in Paris too, an invisible guide whose words filled me with hope for a future rooted in love. I wished so much I could see her again.

To thank her, mostly, for opening me up to this blessing.

"You too, will be changed by these islands."

No matter what happens, Lillie, I am forever changed.

I fell into a deep sleep, besotted with dreams of Warren's lips on mine and his huge warm hands wrapped around my lower back, his thumbs on my hips and his fingertips dancing on my spine. I was upset when I was awakened by a tapping on my arm, attached to a fragrant smell. It took me a few seconds to realize—it was Lillie.

With the colors of the rainbow in her long, braided hair and her weathered eyes, she smiled at me. I jerked back in my seat and turned to her, grabbing her hand and holding it tight.

"Lillie." I gasped. "Oh, Lillie, you were right. I found it. I found love." There were tears in my eyes.

I love him. I am in love with him.

"What did I tell you about this magical place?" she said. I smiled. We spoke silently for a few seconds, hand in hand without any words. And then, as the seatbelt sign dinged and the captain prepared us for landing, she vanished.

We landed with no issues and the plane taxied along the

runway for a while. I saw the bus on the ground waiting to take the other passengers to other gates. As we got ready to disembark, I looked at the lady sitting next to me. She was shuffling through her purse, getting her things organized, checking her phone.

I stood to pull the latch on the overhead bin and, impulsively, leaned forward and addressed her quietly. "Listen, I know you don't know me. And I'm sorry if you think I'm being way too forward, but a year ago, I bet on the wrong things and lost everything. I gained it all back when I came here. I don't know why you're here or how long you'll be staying, but this place, it's extraordinary. Open up your heart and mind and soul to the enchantment all around you. The waves and the tides and the moon and the air itself, let it all knock you on your bottom. You will see it. Your life will be changed."

She relaxed her shoulders and leaned back, a big smile crossing her pretty face. I noticed her eyes were sad and swollen from crying. "Thank you. I needed that. You have no idea how much I needed that."

I drove like a madwoman, weaving through traffic on HI-92. I had a lot to accomplish in the next three days. In between Api's rehearsal dinner tonight and her wedding tomorrow, there was the farm and the coffee shop, and Warren. At first, the businesswoman in me kicked in, trying to prioritize my tasks. Who's on first and then who's next. By the time I was engulfed in the warm breeze and familiar fragrance of the island, I threw caution to the wind and let my heart lead the way.

It led me to Wai'alae beach, where Warren and I first went out on the water. The dolphins, the corals, the deal we made, together. I didn't know if he was still giving surf lessons, but it was the only place I knew where to start.

I was nervous, my heart beating wildly when I got out of the car and walked over to the hill that led to the water. I made a beeline for the shore where a group of kids were having a lesson. There seemed to be quite a few groups this time, different pockets of people scattered along the shore. I didn't know where to go but I was conscious of the time I had to make this move.

So I walked down the hill, steadying myself as my feet dug into the sand and holding on to drooping palm fronds to keep my balance.

And then I saw him.

It stopped me in my tracks. He had his back to me, hair a little lighter, his limbs a lot tanner. He had this unmistakable gait, this distinct way of shifting his weight from one leg to the other, pulling his shoulders back and running his hands through his hair. He had a board under one arm, so I knew what was going to happen next. I heard a voice yelling out to him as I ran down as fast as I could, tripping on a log, and then rolling all the way down until I hit the bottom of the hill.

I was quite the sight. My hair and face were covered in sand, my shirt was untucked and there were scratches on my arms. My bones weren't broken, but I was about to cry. I stayed on the ground, disheveled, disappointed, bereft with despair.

"Andie? Is that you?"

I looked up and saw a carbon copy of Warren, just a little younger and a little less refined. "Oh, Adam. Hi. I was just trying to catch Warren."

"Well, he—" Adam looked out toward the ocean.

"I know." I shook the sand out of my hair and off my face, all the while trying to hold the tears back. A solitary traitor rolled down my cheek. Adam stepped closer to me.

"I can sound the foghorn and call him back in."

I swiped my eyes and composed myself, shook out my hair and pulled it back in a knot. The wind caught the sand and blew it skyward. "No, no. It's okay. I have to go and get ready for Api's rehearsal dinner."

"Do you want him to call you? What can I tell him?"

I ran my schedule through my head. I had to be here for Api. There was no other time. "Would you please tell him to meet me here at four tomorrow?" Api's wedding is at one. I'll leave the reception right after my speech. This should give me enough time for the ceremony, the pictures, and all the bridesmaid duties I need to fulfill. Shouldn't she be on the way to her honeymoon by then?

"Of course, he'll be here. You don't know how happy I am to see you, Andie."

— 46 —

Maybe Tomorrow

They didn't call it the Flores estate for nothing. Api's home in Kailua had come to life, decked out in Christmas décor and lit up in every way imaginable. Tiny lights adorned each coconut nestled high up in the trees. The garden had been transformed to accommodate the wedding ceremony and the reception immediately following it. Two hundred white-clothed chairs lined the perimeter of a makeshift stage overlooking the ocean. Yellow hibiscus and white plumerias cascaded down every tree, covering their trunks in a veil of flowers. Dendrobiums in flutes created a dramatic effect in the middle of each table.

"You are the most gorgeous bride I have ever seen."

I entered the bride's room and found Api standing in front of the mirror, wearing a dress by a famous Hawaiian designer. One she hadn't been allowed to see or fit until a week before the wedding. It molded onto her like a glove, an off-the-shoulder gown with a scalloped hemline in all white Guipure lace. A double satin bow with a long train was set at the back of the gown. She was wearing a family heirloom—a tiara of teardrop diamonds passed on to her mom from her grandmother—and Maele's little blue diamond necklace. Her something blue.

She looked like a princess. Her father's princess.

"You look beautiful yourself," she said to me. I had to admit, I liked the dress she'd chosen. It was an ivory-colored creation in chiffon with a celadon green ribbon around my waist. It was fitted too, and the heels I wore made me look long and slim.

All morning long, I hadn't been able to contain my excitement. My friend was getting married.

And in a few hours, I'm going to see Warren. Should I run to him on the beach wearing this dress? Make it dramatic? Should I wear nothing underneath and when he peels off my dress he will find me naked on the beach and take me right there and then?

Time out. What if he's moved on and he's there to tell me that it's over?

I shook my head and drove those thoughts out for the moment. This was Api's day.

"This is it, Api. The moment we've all been waiting for. I am so happy for you and for James."

She bobbed her head. I helped straighten the tiara, loosened a pin in her hair and reinserted it.

"What's wrong? Are you nervous?"

She did the bobbing thing again.

"Let me go and ask Nana Juana to get us a shot of vodka. Kind of like in the old days. It should calm you down." I stuck my head back in the door. "And then I have a few maid of honor things to take care of but I'll be back."

After I found Nana Juana, I was sidetracked by a few things happening in the kitchen. Then I was in the garden, helping Auntie Mel put the finishing touches on the centerpieces. It took me thirty minutes to check all the seating cards and make sure the gardeners had laid out a solid path for Api to walk without tripping.

Nana Juana came out to get me. "Andie, Api is asking for you."

"Thirty minutes before showtime," I said to Auntie Mel before following Nana back.

Api told me to shut the door as soon as I entered.

"What's wrong?" I asked, walking over to her.

"Andie, my dad's not here."

I was confused at first. Of course, her dad wasn't there. And then it clicked. This is it. The time her mom had spoken about. And I would be there for her. I would.

Before I could react, she started to cry, removing her tiara and holding it in her hand. Her cries turned into sobs, her knees buckled and she was on the floor. I tried to hold her up but I got caught in the bubble of her train. We both fell to the ground and stayed there.

"He's supposed to be the one to walk me down the aisle. I miss him so much. Oh, Andie, I can't do this. I can't marry James. Please tell my mom. Let them know. I don't want to marry James."

"Shhh, Api. It's okay," I said. She'd sidled up to me in a fetal position. Hiding in my arms, wracked with sobs. Her body shook, all that sorrow escaping through her tears. "You don't mean that, do you? You love him."

"What if I just thought I loved him because I missed my dad? What if I was just escaping from this reality? My dad is gone. My heart is empty. Maybe I thought James would be able to fill it. But I was wrong. I would do anything to get my dad back. He was supposed to be here. Andie, I don't think I want to do this anymore. Please let my mom and James know. Tell them I'm sorry I'm such a disappointment."

"Shhh," I whispered, rubbing her back, kissing her head. She kept her face buried in my chest like she wanted to be invisible. "Let's just stay here for a while. It's okay, I'm here. I'll text your mom."

"Okay," she said, hiccupping between sobs.

We were now thirty minutes late. People were knocking. James was begging to come in. Her mother was sitting outside keeping everyone at bay. Api didn't want to see anyone. I didn't know what was happening outside, but I heard footsteps shuffling, men's voices, women's voices. My phone wouldn't stop ringing. James. His mom. Her cousin. Another cousin. Nothing from Auntie Mel but this one line:

Stay with her. Be with her. I will handle everything out here.

Two hours in, she was so tired that she fell asleep in my arms. I knew by then I wouldn't be seeing Warren. I had to give up my old phone, turn it back into the business. And for the life of me, I couldn't remember his phone number.

Three hours later, the wedding party had left. Api still sat huddled in my arms, her sobs having turned to heaves and deep breaths. We were a mess, mascara stains on the train of her dress, pins sticking out of her hair, my belt untied, my shoes somewhere on the floor. Her mother was still sitting on the ground, keeping guard on the other side of the door.

"Api?"

"Hmm?"

"When you were in Europe, how was that with James?"

"It was wonderful. People thought we would drive each other

crazy, being in a foreign place and him having all that pressure to do well in his fellowship."

"Did he take care of you? Make you laugh?"

She became wistful, smiling to herself. "He would walk across the street every morning and get me my favorite chocolate crescent roll. And on his way home from the university, he'd stop by the local market and bring me tulips." She followed this with a laugh. "And he's funny as hell. So snide and sarcastic. And guess what? A potty mouth worse than mine. And you should hear his mother." She let out a sob at this thought. Then deep laughter. "Worse than a sailor."

I shifted sideways before holding up her face. "Listen, Api. I know you're grieving. You lost your daddy, the most important person in your life, but this has nothing to do with your love for James. What he's done, what the two of you have, is rare. It's not something that was born out of your father's death—your daddy loved James. They knew each other—how special is that? He has memories of his own to share with your future babies. If anything, Api, hold on to the sweetness of grief as it will make you value what you have with James, and live your life to the fullest with him, keeping in the back of your mind that life is short and unpredictable."

She sat up. Patted her hair down and straightened. She stretched out her legs and leaned on the wall. "Ugh. I love him, I really do love him. What a mess. I made a mess, haven't I?"

"A really hot guy once told me, 'just because you've made a fool of yourself today, doesn't mean you're a fool every day.'"

She looked at me, brows furrowed, either mad I said that or not getting it. I opted for the latter choice. "Api, I know your dad would be very proud of you today."

"Will you call James? Tell him I want to get married?"

And so, at 5:30 in the evening on December 10th, there was a wedding. Instead of two hundred people, there were seven of us. James's parents, Api's mom, myself, the happy couple and of course, a priest. It was solemn and quiet, but there was enough love between the two of them to make up for a whole congregation.

"I'm going to leave," I told her, as the vows had been spoken and the ceremony came to an end.

"Fudge nuggets. You were supposed to meet Warren. Go. Go. Go."

So I went. I was two hours late, but I went.

I was smarter now, bunching up my dress, underwear still on, and walking carefully, slipping and sliding all the same, but keeping my heel on the sand and watching out for those evil random logs. In my head, I rehearsed everything I wanted to say to him, but I decided to cut the chase and just tell him what was in my heart.

I arrived at our meeting place, the place where he'd told me about sunsets and fresh starts. I waited and watched the sun retire for the night.

But he wasn't there. He was not there and like the horizon, my world became dark.

I was lost.

Truly lost.

In a matter of hours, all my hope had disappeared. Maybe he'd never tried to meet me. I guessed I would never know. There were things I still had to do—visit the coffee shop and see Duke and his family at the plantation. I considered scrapping it all and taking the first flight back to Chicago tomorrow. But I'd been running all this time and I was tired.

The coffee shop was closed by now, but the way to the back was open and free. I reclaimed my favorite place in the world, sat on the boulder and looked out into the ocean. While the coffee shop had changed, it felt like Maele and Lani had left this part for me.

The stars were out in full force, a contradiction to the way I felt. I was mad that they hadn't gotten the memo. Why were they lighting up the sky, when there was nothing here to celebrate? For a good while, I stared out in front of me, stubbornly refusing to lift my eyes, believing there was no longer anything out there for me to see. But then something called me to raise my gaze to the stars once again.

That familiar fragrance of flowers in bloom, of a field full of sweet, blossoming lilies. I heard her voice, loud and clear.

"Are you ready to forgive yourself?"

Hawaii would be that place for me. The place I'd found love, the place that had shown me who I was and the place that had given me my heart back. Tomorrow was another day. And maybe tomorrow would be different.

"Yes, Lillie. I'm ready," I whispered, breathing in her scent. A bouquet filled with hope and love and acceptance.

"Andie?"

I was terrified. I jumped to my feet and turned around, closing my eyes, afraid to face whatever his words were going to be. There he was, looking unsure at first, before taking huge steps toward me. My breath caught and my heart soared. He opened his arms and I floated into them.

"Oh, Warren. I thought you gave up on me. I'm sorry. Api had a—"

"I know. She called me. Told me her wedding was delayed and that you saved her marriage." He tipped my chin up, cupping my face in his hands. "How do you do that, Andrea Matthews? How do you bring light into everything you touch? You did that with me almost a year ago. And I haven't been the same since. And look at you"—he breathed, eyeing me from head to toe—"so exquisite, like an angel in that dress."

"I'm a mess," I said, looking down at my dingy, bare feet.

He led me to the boulder, took a seat, and set me on his lap. "I'm sorry to hear about your mom."

"She's better now. My dad, on the other hand …" I chuckled. "He is still a wreck."

"I don't blame him. She's the love of his life."

I didn't want to lose this chance to tell him exactly how I felt, so I went for it. "I heard what you said that night, you know," I began, looking directly into his eyes. "When I was dancing at the farm. I didn't want to believe it. But the truth is, I was in love with you even before then. It's a tie between rock running and the time I lay on the beach waiting for you to kiss me."

"Man," he said, a big grin on his face. "That pink bikini. I had to go home and take a cold shower that day. And many days since."

I laughed too. "You went to Chicago."

"Yes."

"I'm sorry I wasn't there."

"I was devastated. But in retrospect, I'm glad I got this time to figure things out. I worked on myself so I can love you with all my heart."

"And do you?" I asked.

"You've cut through every chain that's been holding me back." Gently, he pushed me off his lap and led me to the edge of the hill.

A comet streaked across the sky, like the one that had appeared on New Year's Eve when he'd first kissed me. I saw it clearly now—a ball of fire that shot a tail of light far out into the midnight sky.

"I've waited eight months for this moment. I'm not going to wait any longer. I love you, Andie. I love you when you're sitting the wrong way on a surfboard or saving a plantation or even a marriage. I want to live my life with you. Hawaii, New York, Paris, Chicago. I don't care. We'll figure everything out. As long as we're together, this life will be filled with amazing moments."

"I love you," I said, trying to find more words but there were none. "Thank you for finding me."

"I was meant to find you," he said, cradling my face. "I'm so glad I stopped at the coffee shop that night. I thank God for leading me to you."

As he planted a trail of kisses from my forehead to my eyelids to my nose, I was suddenly burning with the one question I'd had from our time together. Something I had always felt, but couldn't quite figure out.

"Ask him," said that small voice in my head. *"And you will know—it is destiny."*

"Warren?"

"Hmm," he said, lips brushing against my ear.

"What does L stand for?"

"What?"

"Your mom's middle name, L."

"Oh. Her middle name was Lilly. They used to call her Lilly Cat."

My reaction shocked him. He began caressing my shoulders, my arms, afraid he had upset me. I laid my hands on his chest and looked to the sky once more, eyes welling with tears.

"Thank you," I whispered before smiling ear to ear. I felt utterly connected and loved. Right there and then, everything that'd happened in the past year came full circle.

"Baby, what's wrong—"

I placed a finger on his lips right before tugging on his shirt, pulling him to me and holding on to him for dear life. "Nothing. Nothing's wrong. Everything's right." I laughed. "Kiss me first, and I'll tell you later."

As we kissed under the full moon and the bright stars, I closed my eyes and breathed in the fragrance that had been heavy in the air since I'd sat on this boulder one year ago. I thought of Lillie and her words and I knew that the Hawaiian Aloha spirit was here, surrounding us with ions and an ocean breeze and the sound of breaking waves. Life had knocked us off balance and we had fallen into love. I couldn't wait to tell him about my Lillie. Perhaps she was a friend of his mom's. Or maybe she was …

Maybe there are things we will never understand, things that we can't wrap our mortal, logical brains around. Extraordinary moments that feel like miracles, signs we are loved beyond our wildest imagination.

Either way, I got mine. On an island of myths and magic, born of molten rock and blessed by the gods of love and abundance, I got my happy ending.

Acknowledgements

Anna Gomez

It has been further confirmed – that I live a Never Say Never kind of life.

I write this with such heartfelt gratitude for this unbelievable project, one that literally came out of nowhere. I thought by now, I'd be cursing **Italia Gandolfo**, for convincing me to write another book. I swear, I was looking forward to using just one side of my brain for a while. She had this tenacity and belief in me, and a million reasons why it would be wrong for me to walk away from this industry. One more book, she said.

Instead of a swan song, it's the beginning of a five-book series.

Thank you with all my heart, to the following people:
Italia Gandolfo, my agent and friend, for being so relentless. To **LK Griffie** and the rest of the **Vesuvian Media Group** team, to **Rosewind Romance** and to our editors, **Holly Atkinson, Katie Harder-Schauer**, and **Karen Hrdlicka** for making this book the best it can ever be. **Mary Ting, Alexandrea Weis, Gareth Worthington,** you love me so genuinely, that is so rare in this book world!

Hang Le, for listening to our fifteen-minute rant and understanding exactly what we wanted. The cover is beautiful. **Meryl Moss Media** for helping us to get this book out in the world.

To my **Brae's Butterflies** for staying on and keeping the faith with me. There are too many of us to name now, but you have been in my life every single day for the past 7 years—including me and making me feel like a part of your world.

My family, who once again missed one spring and all of summer because they supported this crazy timeline. Thank you for your love. My babies, **Tim, Gigi, Marco and Izzy,** as you will always be. And my husband, **Bill,** whose patience and love have been my wings. Every single time, you ask me – "Why? You don't need this." And every single time, you close your eyes and jump in with me. I can't forget my sisters too, **Gerri, Tessa and Sandra** – my WHATSAPP buddies who protect me all the time.

And now I can even name my work friends, I mean, legit. **Jen Valentini, Katie Ogarek, Ellen McLoughlin, Joan Vivaldelli, Debbie Rudmin** – in the most politically incorrect way, I love you all so much. The Leo Burnett Company has made all my dreams come true.

Javier LaFianza, for taking a walk that day and instead of talking about yourself, you talked about me. You are one of the most selfless people I have ever met.

And last but not least, to my co-author, **Kristoffer Polaha.** When I think about how we came together, I'm finding so many holes in my story, I myself can't figure out how this really happened. It borders on uncanny, doesn't it? All I can think of is that there is a reason for this. Let's find that reason and use it to do good in the world. Thank you for taking me along on this journey with you. (If you can indulge me for a minute so I can fangirl)—you are big-time, KP! A gifted movie actor, writer, artist, creative. But most importantly, you are a kind, gracious and genuine human being. My words became your words, and together we wrote something so amazing. I can't wait for our families and friends to read it! You are a #Godwink and a blessing, and no matter what happens from here, you have given me the experience of a lifetime.

Writing a book, sharing your words with the world, is a scary, solitary process. Couple that with a pandemic that has isolated us, thwarted our plans, given us all the time in the world to think, to dwell, to relive our brokenness. Thank you, Kristoffer, for replacing the loneliness with so many laugh out loud moments. It's been a blast. And in more ways than one, writing this book during COVID 19 has been my saving grace.

And to all of you, **our readers**, we hope you love <u>Andie and Warren</u> as much as we do.

Choose Love. Always.

xo

Kristoffer Polaha

I grew up in Reno, Nevada and I remember once when my friend, **Graham LippSmith**, opened a book on his father's bookshelf and there, in a historical work on Boliva, was his father's name on the acknowledgments page. From that moment on, I always wanted to see my name on an acknowledgements page. It's thirty-five years later, and I suppose the only thing better than being thanked for helping to foster a book, is to be the one doing the thanking.

To that end, my deepest thanks to **Anna Gomez** who set up a totally random Zoom call during the Covid pandemic quarantine of 2020 and turned it into a partnership with ease and grace and trust that is, quite frankly, borderline supernatural. Anna, I have loved every moment of working on this book with you and I have experienced a creative pleasure writing it with you.

Whip smart and confident, I keep scratching my head at how easy you've made this partnership work. Thank you for your trust, endless generosity of spirit, sense of fun, and your boundless encouragement. Ours is a model collaboration. I quite literally couldn't have done this without you. Thank you for taking this leap of faith with me. I cannot wait to tell more stories with you.

My thanks to **Javier La Fianza** and his wonderful wife, **Anne Bowen La Fianza**. During quarantine, my boys and I would play football in an open green space next to our house and Javier and Anne, while walking their dog, would say hello, as people do. One day he asked if I'd like to set up a call with a friend of his, she was interested in turning some of her books into films, specifically for the Hallmark Channel. I had recently hung out my shingle as a producer, so I wanted to take the call. His friend, of course, is Anna Gomez and the rest is history.

My thanks go to **Italia Gandolfo** and **LK Griffie** who have dedicated hours upon hours on this book and have showed me the ropes of the book world. Italia for her encouragement and immediate support, instant enthusiasm, guidance, and wisdom and LK for jumping in to craft my website. In fact, I'd like to thank our cover designer **Hang Le**, our editors **Holly Atkinson**, **Katie Harder-Schauer**, **Karen Hrdlicka**, and everyone at **Vesuvian Media Group** and **Rosewind Romance** for taking a rather large gamble on me.

I'd also like to thank **Hamish Berry**, **Sally Ware**—little wins! **Paul Rosicker**, for always supporting me no matter what I do or where my adventures take me.

And to my family, **Erik Polaha**, **Jon Polaha**, **Mike Polaha**, **Blake & Mike Beck**, **Carol Tabor** and **Nila Vae Morris**, thank you for a lifetime of support.

To my old friend **Colin Trevorrow** for not only sharing his perspective on what cover Anna and I should choose, detailing why the boards evoke a personal memory, but for providing me an amazing place to write my chapters for this book. Written in room number 15 at The Langley in the UK while on quarantine to film Jurassic World 3 during a global pandemic, I had the time, solitude, and environment to simply create. All things considered, it was a perfect situation.

Thank you, brother.

My special thanks to **Scott M. Morris** and **Max F. Morris** who, for over the past 19 years, have put me in a writer's state of mind. Because of your influence and mastery of the written word I think I may have absorbed enough information to get by.

Since this is my first time thanking people who have encouraged me creatively on an acknowledgment page, it would be a travesty if I didn't thank my mom, **Esther Polaha**, and my dad, **Jerome Polaha**, who have supported and nurtured me throughout my entire life emotionally, financially, spiritually, and in every way great parents can and do. They told me to chase my dreams, which I did. First into acting, which has led directly into this venture, one they are thrilled about. Thank you, Mom and Dad.

And to my Nana, **Mae Smalley**, now you can say you've seen it all. I love you.

To my sons, **Caleb**, **Micah**, and **Jude** who have made me rise up from being just a dude to becoming a father. These young men are the reason I do what I do and the way that I do it. I've always wanted to be an example to you of the right kind of a father's love. Your motivation, the very simple act of the three of you being born, is why I am who I am, setting the table for the next generation. So, Poboys, thank you for the motivation.

And finally, my gratitude, my unending gratitude, goes to the love of my life, my wife, **Julianne Morris Polaha**, who has stood by my side whether I am flying high or getting my butt kicked by life. You have been my best friend, my advisor, my sounding board, my best girl, and you have shown me what a perfect kinda love looks and feels like. You have truly shown me what love is by the kind of wife and mother you are. Thank you for being on this ride with me. I hope to tell love stories both on the page and on the screen for years to come and Julianne, you are the inspiration for every love story I will ever tell. Thank you, babe.

And to you, the reader, thank you for reading this book. Enjoy.

About the Authors

Anna Gomez was born in the city of Makati, Philippines and educated abroad. She met and married her best friend who whisked her away to Chicago over twenty years ago. She is Chief Financial Officer for Leo Burnett Worldwide, a global advertising company founded in 1935. In her capacity, Anna serves on the board of several not-for-profit organizations, namely the Hugh O'Brien Leadership Organization and Girl Scouts of America. She is also the executive sponsor for a number of employee resource groups focused on Diversity and Inclusion.

Under the pen name Christine Brae, Anna has published six novels, has an established fan base, and a dedicated following. Her titles rank in the Top 100 months following their release. Her last three novels, *In This Life, Eight Goodbyes,* and *The Year I Left,* have won literary awards and were immediate bestsellers on Amazon, ranking #1 across multiple categories.

www.AnnaGomezBooks.com

Kristoffer Polaha is best-known for his long starring role in the critically acclaimed series *Life Unexpected* (The CW). Other TV series credits include *Get Shorty* with Ray Romano and Chris O'Dowd, the limited series *Condor* opposite William Hurt and Max Irons, The CW's *Ringer* (Sarah Michelle Gellar) and *Valentine*, as well as *North Shore* (FOX).

In addition to co-starring with Rainn Wilson in *Backstrom* (FOX), he had a multi-season role on the acclaimed series *Mad Men* (AMC) and *Castle* (ABC). Polaha is also well-known for starring in Hallmark Channel movies such as *Dater's Handbook* with Meghan Markle, and the *Mystery 101* franchise on Hallmark Movies & Mysteries.

Polaha first received attention for his portrayal of John F. Kennedy, Jr. in the TV movie, *America's Prince: The John F. Kennedy Jr. Story*, opposite Portia de Rossi. He has appeared in numerous independent features, including *Where Hope Grows, Devil's Knot* (Colin Firth, Reese Witherspoon), and the Tim Tebow film, *Run the Race.*

Polaha has a featured role opposite Gal Gadot in *Wonder Woman 1984* and the forthcoming *Jurassic World: Dominion.*

Polaha was born in Reno, Nevada, and he is married to actress Julianne Morris. They have three sons.

www.KrisPolaha.com